Praise for Novels by Brandilyn Collins

Gone to Ground

"What do you do with a truth that could shatter your world? That's the question at the heart of this rollercoaster suspense thriller. With memorable characters and intriguing plot twists, Collins leads her readers through a high-octane course as each woman confronts the price she would pay for justice."

—*CBA Retailers + Resources*

"Moves along briskly. The popular novelist's talent continues to flower . . . and sales will flourish."

—*Publishers Weekly*

"Collins does it again with her trademark suspense that will keep readers up late into the night."

—*RT Book Reviews*

"Well crafted. A page-turning suspense."

—*Examiner.com*

Over the Edge

"A taut, heartbreaking thriller . . . Collins is a fine writer who knows how to both horrify readers and keep them turning pages."

—*Publishers Weekly*

"Tense and dramatic . . . a dense and compact narrative that holds its tension while following the protagonist in a withering battle."

—*New York Journal of Books*

"A frightening and all-too-real scenario . . . very timely and meaningful book."

—*RT Book Reviews*

"Thrilling tale of vengeance . . . the pace is relentless, the suspense ramping up to greater levels as the pages fly by."

—*Mysterious Reviews*

Deceit

". . . good storytelling and notable mystery . . . an enticing read [that poses] tough questions about truth and lies, power and control, faith and forgiveness."

—*Publishers Weekly*

"Solidly constructed . . . a strong and immediately likable protagonist. One of the Top 10 Inspirational Novels of 2010."

—*Booklist*

"Filled with excitement and intrigue, Collins' latest will keep the reader quickly turning pages . . . This tightly plotted mystery, filled with quirky characters, will appeal to suspense lovers everywhere."

—*RT Book Reviews*

". . . pulse-accelerating, winding, twisting storyline [that will] keep your attention riveted to the action until the very end."

—*Christian Retailing*

Exposure

". . . a hefty dose of action and suspense with a superb conclusion."

—*RT Book Reviews*

"Brandilyn Collins, the queen of Seatbelt Suspense®, certainly lives up to her well-deserved reputation. *Exposure* has more twists and turns than a Coney Island roller coaster . . . Intertwining storylines collide in this action-packed drama of suspense and intrigue. Highly recommended."

—*CBA Retailers + Resources*

"Captivating . . . the alternating plot lines and compelling characters in *Exposure* will capture the reader's attention, but the twist of events at the end is most rewarding."

—*Christian Retailing*

"Mesmerizing mystery . . . a fast-paced, twisting tale of desperate choices."

—*TitleTrakk.com*

"[Collins is] a master of her craft . . . intensity, tension, high-caliber suspense, and engaging mystery."

—*The Christian Manifesto*

Dark Pursuit

"Lean style and absorbing plot . . . Brandilyn Collins is a master of suspense."

—*CBA Retailers + Resources*

"Intense . . . engaging . . . whiplash-inducing plot twists . . . the concepts of forgiveness, restoration, selflessness, and sacrifice made this book not only enjoyable, but a worthwhile read."

—*Thrill Writer*

"Moves from fast to fierce."

—TitleTrakk.com

"Thrilling . . . characters practically leap off the page with their quirks and inclinations."

—Tennessee Christian Reader

Amber Morn

". . . a harrowing hostage drama . . . essential reading."

—Library Journal

"The queen of Seatbelt Suspense® delivers as promised. Her short sentences and strong word choices create a 'here and now' reading experience like no other."

—TitleTrakk.com

"Heart-pounding . . . the satisfying and meaningful ending comes as a relief after the breakneck pace of the story."

—RT Book Reviews

"High octane suspense . . . a powerful ensemble performance."

—BookshelfReview.com

Crimson Eve

"One of the Best Books of 2007 . . . Top Christian suspense of the year."

—Library Journal, starred review

"The excitement starts on page one and doesn't stop until the shocking end . . . [Crimson Eve] is fast-paced and thrilling."

—Romantic Times

"The action starts with a bang . . . and the pace doesn't let up until this fabulous racehorse of a story crosses the finish line.

—*Christian Retailing*

"An unparalleled cat-and-mouse game wrought with mystery and surprise."

—*TitleTrakk.com*

Coral Moon

"A chilling mystery. Not one to be read alone at night."

—*RT BOOKclub*

"Thrilling . . . one of those rare books you hurry through, almost breathlessly, to find out what happens."

—*Spokane Living*

". . . a fascinating tale laced with supernatural chills and gut-wrenching suspense.

—*Christian Library Journal*

Violet Dawn

". . . fast-paced . . . interesting details of police procedure and crime scene investigation . . . beautifully developed [characters] . . ."

—*Publishers Weekly*

"A sympathetic heroine . . . effective flashbacks . . . Collins knows how to weave faith into a rich tale."

—*Library Journal*

"Collins expertly melds flashbacks with present-day events to provide a smooth yet deliciously intense flow . . . quirky townsfolk will help drive the next books in the series."

—*RT BOOKclub*

"Skillfully written . . . Imaginative style and exquisite suspense."

—1340mag.com

Web of Lies

"A master storyteller . . . Collins deftly finesses the accelerator on this knuckle-chomping ride."

—RT BOOKclub

"Fast-paced . . . mentally challenging and genuinely entertaining."

—Christian Book Previews

Dead of Night

"Collins' polished plotting sparkles . . . unique word twists on the psychotic serial killer mentality. Lock your doors, pull your shades—and read this book at noon."

—RT BOOKclub, Top Pick

". . . this one is up there in the stratosphere . . . Collins has it in her to give an author like Patricia Cornwell a run for her money."

—FaithfulReader.com

". . . spine-tingling, hair-raising, edge-of-the-seat suspense."

—Wordsmith Review

"A page-turner I couldn't put down, except to check the locks on my doors."

—Author's Choice Reviews

Stain of Guilt

"Collins keeps the reader gasping and guessing . . . artistic prose paints vivid pictures . . . High marks for original plotting and superb pacing."

—RT BOOKclub

". . . a sinister, tense story with twists and turns that will keep you on the edge of your seat."

—*Wordsmith Shoppe*

Brink of Death

". . . an abundance of real-life faith as well as real-life fear, betrayal and evil. This one kept me gripped from beginning to end."
—*Contemporary Christian Music magazine*

"Collins' deft hand for suspense brings on the shivers."

—*RT BOOKclub*

"Gripping . . . thrills from page one."

—*Christian Book Previews*

Dread Champion

"Compelling . . . plenty of intrigue and false trails."

—*Publishers Weekly*

"Finely-crafted . . . vivid . . . another masterpiece that keeps the reader utterly engrossed."

—*RT BOOKclub*

". . . riveting mystery and courtroom drama."

—*Library Journal*

Eyes of Elisha

"Chilling . . . a confusing, twisting trail that keeps pages turning."

—*Publishers Weekly*

"A thriller that keeps the reader guessing until the end."
—*Library Journal*

"Unique and intriguing . . . filled with more turns than a winding mountain highway."

—*RT BOOKclub*

"One of the top ten Christian novels of 2001."

—*Christianbook.com*

DOUBLE
BLIND

BRANDILYN
COLLINS

DOUBLE
BLIND

A NOVEL

B&H
PUBLISHING GROUP

NASHVILLE, TENNESSEE

Other Novels by Brandilyn Collins

Stand-Alone Suspense

Gone to Ground
Over the Edge
Deceit
Exposure
Dark Pursuit

Rayne Tour YA Series

(cowritten with Amberly Collins)
Always Watching
Last Breath
Final Touch

Kanner Lake Series

Violet Dawn
Coral Moon
Crimson Eve

Hidden Faces Series

Brink of Death
Stain of Guilt
Dead of Night
Web of Lies

Chelsea Adams Series

Eyes of Elisha
Dread Champion

Bradleyville Series

Cast a Road Before Me
Color the Sidewalk for Me
Capture the Wind for Me

978-1-4336-7164-7

Published by B&H Publishing Group
Nashville, Tennessee

Dewey Decimal Classification: F
Subject Heading: GRIEF—FICTION \ DEPRESSION
(PSYCHOLOGY)—FICTION \ SURGERY—FICTION

Author represented by the literary agency of Alive
Communications, Inc., 7680 Goddard Street, Suite 200, Colorado
Springs, Colorado, 80920, www.alivecommunications.com.

Scripture quotations are taken from the New King James Version,
copyright © 1979, 1980, 1982, Thomas Nelson, Inc., Publishers.

1 2 3 4 5 6 7 8 • 16 15 14 13 12

Where can I go from Your Spirit? Or where can I flee from Your presence? If I ascend into heaven, You are there; If I make my bed in hell, behold, You are there. If I take the wings of the morning, And dwell in the uttermost parts of the sea, Even there Your hand shall lead me, And Your right hand shall hold me. If I say, "Surely the darkness shall fall on me," Even the night shall be light about me; Indeed, the darkness shall not hide from You, But the night shines as the day; The darkness and the light are both alike to You.

Psalm 139:7–12 (NKJV)

SATURDAY, MARCH 3

Chapter 1

DESPERATE PEOPLE MAKE DESPERATE CHOICES.

In my kitchen I took one look at the envelope in the stack of mail and dropped it like burning metal. It landed askew on the counter, the gold Cognoscenti logo pulsing up at me.

If I had known, I would have trashed it right then and there.

Nine months before The Letter arrived, my husband had been killed in a car accident. Ryan, with his lanky body and loving touch, that dimple in his right cheek. His quirky smile and teasing way. He'd been only thirty-five—six years older than I. Four months after his funeral a robber attacked me in a mall parking lot and nearly choked me to death before a security guard happened by. My attacker got away. He's still out there somewhere, walking the streets. And during the two years before Ryan's death? I'd had three miscarriages.

Five traumatic events in a row. I was bent, near broken. A wind-battered sapling. Abandoned by God.

Have you ever battled depression? That black, biting maw that devours you whole and turns your world to darkness? Your life becomes unlivable. You become . . . nothing. One day you're a speck in the universe, blown here and there. Trod underfoot. The next you're weighted and shackled, the chains too heavy to lift.

The envelope looked thin, maybe one sheet of paper inside. A single piece of paper that could alter the very core of me.

One last hope.

My fumbling hands picked up the envelope. I slid a finger under the flap and edged it open. Pulled out the answer on which I'd hung my future.

Dear Lisa Newberry,

It is my pleasure to inform you that you have been accepted into the medical trial for Cognoscenti's new Empowerment Chip. Please call our research director at your earliest convenience to set up an appointment so we may proceed. The number is below.

Dr. William Hilderbrand, President and CEO

Oh. *Oh.*

Weakness rushed me. I leaned against the tile, relief exploding in my chest. Heat blew through my limbs. This was *it*. I was in. I could be whole. My mind could hardly contain the thought.

Not until that moment had I realized the true depth of my despair. If this had been a *No*, who knows what I would have done.

My next thought was of Ryan. *I know you would want this for me.*

And then—it all blitzed away. The euphoria melted as quickly as it had come. In its place, the inevitable pessimism of depression. No way could I be so fortunate. Surely I'd read the letter wrong.

I read it again. A third time, daring the answer to change, knowing it would. But no. The word *accepted* burned from the page.

Excitement rose again, propelling my hand to the phone, sitting next to me on the counter. I picked it up and called Sherry Grubacker, my one friend in the Bay Area. The news trembled on my tongue, ready to jump as soon as she said hello.

Her canned voice mail kicked on. No Sherry.

Well, of course. With such incredible news as this, how could I expect to find someone to share it with?

I hung up.

Next thing I knew I was punching in my mother's number—a reckless choice in the passion of the moment. My mother had known nothing of my many screening interviews with Cognoscenti, the physical and mental workups. She'd only nagged me for my weakness in the past few months. Wasn't it time I pulled myself together? She'd had her own difficulties in her lifetime, she reminded me. Losing her husband when I was only two. But she'd managed to throw back her shoulders and move on. Raise me alone.

True. And she'd criticized me the entire time.

What was I *doing*? My finger slowed, then hovered over the last digit. My mother would never condone this decision.

I dropped the receiver back in its cradle. Then slumped over the counter, hands to my temples, adrift. The familiar ennui settled in, dragging along its chilling companion—fear.

Reality clunked in my chest, and I tried to breathe around its weight. The gleaming promise of the letter dulled before my eyes. Cognoscenti's prize had seemed so miraculous while I pursued it. But now that it was within my reach—what was I doing?

No way could I go through with this.

I wandered into the living room of my corner apartment. Gazed through the front window at the sun-strewn afternoon. Early March in Redwood City, California, and the daffodils were up, the magnolia trees in pink bloom. Spring was coming. Renewal time.

For nature, maybe. Not for me.

I pressed cold hands against my cheeks. Brain surgery. *Brain surgery, Lisa.* How could I even think of putting myself through that?

But the procedure was simple, they said. Cognoscenti's advancements in brain chip implants went far beyond any other company's research. If I got the real implant I would instantly escape my whirlpool of defeat. A short stay in the hospital, and I could be a new person. Imagine . . . nurturing all the memories of Ryan without the deadening grief. Imagine recalling my attack with head knowledge only, not the sucking, terror-drenched memory from my gut.

Who wouldn't want to turn off their pain?

But it wasn't quite that simple.

In what they called the "gold standard" of research—double-blind, placebo-controlled—I could end up with the placebo. The blank chip. The surgery done—for nothing. Amazing they would put people through such turmoil. But that's the way medical research worked.

Still, it was a chance. One little Empowerment Chip, and I could have the strength to rebuild my life. I could *feel* again. Breathe again. If I didn't try it, what future did I have?

I dropped my head in my hands. I wanted this. How very much I needed the hope. Without it I didn't know how to go on.

But what if something went wrong?

TUESDAY, MARCH 6

Chapter 2

I PULLED INTO THE COGNOSCENTI PARKING LOT, A BRICK IN my stomach. Last night I'd hardly slept. This was the first time I'd been to these offices in Palo Alto, twenty minutes from my apartment. Previous interviews with company psychologists and doctors had been held at their medical clinic.

All I needed was just enough strength to go through with this. But that was so very much to ask of myself.

The acceptance letter was folded in my purse. My ticket to a possible new life. I'd been told to bring it—and two pieces of identification.

As I turned off the Camry's engine my cell phone rang. I jumped. How tense my muscles were. I steadied myself, then picked up the cell. Sherry's name filled the display. "Hi."

"Hey, you! Wanna come over for dinner? Jay's got a meeting, so it's just me and the kids."

Kids. Such an easy word to slip from your mouth when you had them. My funny friend Sherry had a girl and a boy, ages seven and two. Rebecca and J.T. I loved them dearly, though I hadn't seen them in months. I'd lacked the energy.

"Oh, and I'm making my finest-this-side-of-Italy spaghetti."

Memories hit. Eating Sherry's spaghetti at her house. Ryan next to me, laughing with her husband, Jay. I winced and closed my eyes. "Wish I could. But I just got to my appointment. At Cognoscenti."

"Oh."

The silence vibrated.

"I haven't said yes, you know. This is my meeting to decide."

"Yeah. Okay."

A hesitant tone. For some reason I resented it, which wasn't fair. Sherry was a great friend, had been ever since we met at an office party for the investment company where Jay and I worked. After Ryan's death, then the attack, she'd often carried me. Goodness knows I'd been a dead weight.

"Lisa, I hear those cogs in your head. Stop it."

"Okay."

"I'm just afraid for you."

"I know."

So much was at stake. The operation could go badly. I could get the placebo. Even if everything went perfectly I'd still need to build my future without Ryan. "That'll still be hard," Sherry had warned me. "It's not like this operation will erase all your troubles."

Yes. But what if I didn't do this? Even Sherry had no idea what my life had been like. No one could possibly know.

"So, okay." Sherry's voice lightened. "Miss the best spaghetti on the planet. Just let me know what happens. And whatever you decide, you know I'm with you."

"Yeah. Thanks."

A man stepped out of the building, heading for the parking lot. Even in daylight I pressed back in my seat and checked the door locks. Was he an employee? A trial participant? I watched him approach a blue sedan some distance away and open the door. My body relaxed a little, but my heart pinched. Ryan's car had been that color.

"Lisa. Promise you'll call me."

"Promise."

I clicked off the line and dropped the phone in my purse.

The building loomed before me. The air seemed suddenly heavy. Was that an omen?

I glanced around and saw no one. The frail promise of safety in a parking lot. Purse in hand, I slid from the car.

The building's glass-plated door was huge. I forced it back and edged inside to a white-walled lobby with shiny tile floor. Across from me sat an imposing U-shaped desk and behind it—a security guard. He looked in his fifties. Thick gray hair, a jowly face. His name badge read *Richard Mair.*

He allowed a half smile. "Can I help you?"

"I'm Lisa Newberry, with a 5:30 appointment to see Jerry Sterne."

My eyes landed on a row of monitors to the security guard's right. Six in all. One for each floor? They displayed fish-eyed views of elevators and hallways, skewed forms moving across black and white screens. On one monitor—me, looking small and vacant.

I glanced up at the ceiling. There sat a tiny camera, mounted against the corner.

"May I see two pieces of identification?"

Security cameras in a company like this made sense, but they unsettled me, all the same.

I pulled out my driver's license and credit card. Why did they even need to see them? Surely they had a picture of me in my file. But that must be upstairs with Sterne.

Mair checked them over, then gazed at me. He handed the items back. "Thank you."

I put them away.

"Here's your visitor's pass, Ms. Newberry." Mair printed my name and the date on a white square and slid it into a clear-covered badge with a long loop. He also asked me to sign my name and the time into a logbook. "Hang this badge around your neck. Return it when you leave. You can have a seat over there." He nodded toward two plush sofas facing each other, a magazine-laden table between them. "I'll let Mr. Sterne know you're here."

On weak legs I crossed to a couch and sat. Gazed at the magazines of all colors and sizes. So much life promised on their covers. Did such a world still exist?

Oh, Ryan. He'd be so disappointed in my desperation. He'd worked so hard to fill me up emotionally, especially after my miscarriages. My failures. His faith in me was a steady pour. I'd been a leaky pan.

"Ms. Newberry?"

I jerked up to see a man on my right. "Hi. Sorry, I was. . ." I stood.

He held out his hand. "Jerry Sterne, research director for the Empowerment Chip trials."

Midforties, maybe? A friendly face and chocolate brown eyes. Receding dark hair. He was built like Ryan, tall and slim.

The familiar pain needled my gut.

I shook his hand. "Nice to meet you."

"This way, please." Mr. Sterne gestured toward the elevator.

We stopped at floor three. In his office, a sitting area held four armchairs, in one of them a severe-looking woman with gray hair slicked into a bun. Not a wrinkle on her skin, and her ice-blue business suit matched her eyes. She stood as we entered. Her lips curved, but the smile didn't reach the rest of her face.

"Ms. Newberry."

She held out her hand, and I took it. As expected, it was cold.

"I'm Clair Saxton, second research director for the trials. Jerry and I are teaming this one. So nice to meet you." Her voice had a polished edge. Like steel.

"Nice to meet you. Please call me Lisa."

"And we're Jerry and Clair." Jerry Sterne indicated a chair. "Would you like tea or coffee?"

"No, thank you."

He settled next to Ice Queen, the two of them facing me. On a table near Jerry sat a folder with my name on it, two pens, and a small wooden box. I crossed my ankles, hoping they wouldn't tremble.

Jerry spread his hands. "Welcome, and congratulations on being accepted into the trial. We wanted to meet with you today to go over any questions you might have. I know you've had numerous explanations before, but this is your chance to tie up any loose ends in your mind. Also, due to the proprietary nature of our trial, our people who interviewed you could not be as forthcoming about all aspects up to this point."

"I know."

Jerry rose to pick up two business cards from his desk and handed them to me. "Keep these and call either of us anytime if you need to."

I slipped them into my purse. "Thank you."

He resettled in the chair. "So, first—do you have questions for us?"

Only a million. "I want to hear more about how this works. And what the side effects could be."

"Sure, common questions. As you know this is a double-blind, placebo-controlled trial. Until it's completed you won't know whether you've been given a viable chip or the placebo, and neither will we. That way neither you nor we are subconsciously biased as to the results we observe."

"I *can't* get the placebo. I need this too much."

"I understand it's hard. But we can't guarantee that. People undergo trials like this to test new products in the hope they'll get the real thing—which is likely to benefit them. In our case, this is our third round of trials, and we've seen some wonderful results. At the same time, the power of suggestion is a strong force. In trials like this, a fair percentage of people claim improvements even from the placebo. That's taken into account when results are reviewed. The tested item—here, a chip rather than medication—must prove positive results above those from the placebo."

"You're telling me I could feel better just for having the procedure?"

"It's possible."

I studied my lap. If the power of suggestion was that strong, why couldn't I overcome this depression on my own? Why was I dying a slow death, when I wanted to *live*?

"How does it work, then? The real chip."

Clair jumped in, her chilly eyes gleaming. "A little background might help. Cognoscenti isn't the first to research brain implants. But we're definitely the best. For example, some patients with depression or Parkinson's have been successfully treated with implants. Also Darpa, a science unit of the U.S. military, has been part of a project funded a few years ago that involves numerous universities, including Stanford. They've been concerned about the number of soldiers coming home from Iraq and Afghanistan with brain injuries. They're working on repairing those injuries through a new technique called *optogenetics*, which involves emitting light pulses to trigger precise neural activity in a certain area of the brain." She waved a hand. "We surpassed them long ago by developing a tiny chip made of electrodes that send out similar pulses. Our chip's energy is renewed through motion of the patient, much like a no-wind quartz watch. So there's no replacement of batteries needed. And we place our chip on a different part of the brain—amazingly close to the surface, not deep inside. These two points of our technology alone are far advanced over anyone else. In fact, many researchers told us neither one of them could be done. Yet we've done them both—and on the same chip. As a result of our placement technique, our procedure is as minimally invasive as it can possibly be."

I nodded, trying to take it all in.

"Regarding our focus, it's not been on physical brain injuries, like Darpa is doing, but on emotional issues such as depression and Post Traumatic Stress Disorder. How to stop the trauma without erasing actual memories. The result is a person who knows his past and can learn from it but is no longer tortured by it. With the Empowerment Chip, we've seen this happen immediately."

Immediately. My life—changed. Energy renewed. The terror gone. My fingers curled into my palms. It was too much to hope for. Like wanting to steal a piece of the sun. Could this amazing thing happen to *me*?

Jerry held up a finger. "Of course we need to remind you that the chip isn't a cure-all. It does help people deal with past trauma and grief, but beyond that, the emotional strength you use in dealing with life comes from *you*."

"Yes. I understand that." One of the screening people I'd seen previously described depression as trying to run with a broken foot. Healed bones wouldn't make that person a bionic runner. It would simply return him to his own normal ability.

I took a breath. "What about side effects?"

"Well, of course there are the chances taken with any surgery." He went down the list.

"But can the chip itself hurt me?"

"Not that we've seen. You might experience some tingling in your hands. We're not sure why that occurs. A small percentage in the first trial reported memory loss."

My head drew back. "I thought it wasn't supposed to harm your memory."

"It isn't. And it usually doesn't. The reported cases had to do with insignificant recollections, not major ones."

I focused out the window. I didn't want to *forget* Ryan. My incredible husband. He didn't deserve that.

Jerry shifted in his seat.

"Why me?" The question popped out of my mouth. "Why am I a good candidate?"

Surely I'd shown severe signs of depression and grief. Paranoia and fear. Was that why? Because I needed the chip so badly?

"You're physically healthy, for one," Jerry said. "You've shown a strong desire to proceed, and we think you're someone who could possibly benefit very highly."

In other words, yes, I desperately needed it.

"But, Lisa, you don't have to continue. It's your choice."

I looked from Jerry to Ice Queen. "How long do I have to decide?"

She raised her thin eyebrows. "A day."

"One *day*?"

She nodded. "Jerry and I are meeting with candidates until nine o'clock tonight. Tomorrow we start another thirteen-hour day. Many people are excited about this opportunity, and many more qualify than we can accommodate. If you decide not to go forward, someone will quickly fill your place."

I focused on the floor. One day—for such a decision? That was impossible. I could spend an entire day just trying to get out of bed.

This was beyond me. I couldn't do it. Why had I even come here?

Why had God let Ryan die? Why did He do this to me?

Jerry tapped the arm of his chair. "Before you decide, we'd like to go over the actual procedure with you."

And the babies I lost—why did *they* have to die? And why was I attacked?

"Lisa?"

Years ago in Sunday school I'd memorized verses from Psalm 139: *"Where can I flee from Your presence? If I ascend into heaven, You are there. If I make my bed in hell, behold, You are there . . ."* God had once been a sustaining part of my life. He was always there for me, a comfort and a strength. But I hadn't felt His presence in a long time. That absence was like falling into a deep well. I'd lost everything. And now even God didn't care.

"Ms. Newberry?"

I blinked. "Sorry. I'm listening."

For the next ten minutes Jerry went over the rest of the important information. The procedure would take place at Hillsdale Hospital in Palo Alto—at the full expense of Cognoscenti. The doctors would drill a small hole in my skull and attach the chip to the cerebral cortex—the outer sheet of neural tissue covering the cerebrum. A two-inch patch of hair would need to be shaved on the top left side of my head. The procedure would take place on Friday morning. I'd stay in the hospital two nights.

Two nights? After that I'd have to go home. Alone. Then . . . what? Would I be renewed? Or implanted with a placebo and worse off than ever?

"If I get the real chip, you say I'll start to feel better right away?"

Ice Queen nodded. "The light pulses work immediately. If the chip proves beneficial to you, yes, you should feel the difference quickly."

My chest fluttered. The very thought of that . . . I *had* to have it. It had to come true.

I folded my arms, chilled, and stared at the table.

Jerry paused. "Any other questions?"

I nearly laughed. I had questions that could keep us in that office all night—most of which no human being could answer. So many unknowns crowded my mind that I couldn't articulate a single one.

My gaze landed on the box. I gestured toward it with my chin. "What's in there?"

"Ah, thought you'd never ask." Jerry leaned forward. "Want to see what the chip looks like?"

Oh! "Is one in there?"

With an almost reverent air, Jerry opened the box and handed it to me. "This is a replica of the EC."

Gingerly I took the box and held it close to my face. There, against a white fabric bottom, rested a dark chip. *This* could be my salvation? I didn't want to breathe on it for fear I'd whisk it away. "It's so small."

"Yes."

"Can I pick it up?"

"Sure."

I lowered my forefinger into the box until it touched on the chip. Then turned the box upside down and lifted it away. The EC sat on the tip of my finger.

I gaped at it. How tiny it was. This little thing could alter an entire life? *My* life?

This had to be the most important invention on earth. Computers, the Internet, cell phones—all the latest technology amounted to nothing compared to what this chip could do. Just think how many emotionally crippled people it might cure. They would go on to lead productive lives. Not to mention the millions of dollars saved from their medical bills.

This chip could change the world.

I gazed at it a minute longer, not wanting to part with it, even though I knew it was only a replica. Finally I replaced the chip in its box with care. Set it on the table. "Thank you." The words were a mere whisper.

I stood, unable to say anything more.

Jerry and Clair rose also. Jerry held out his hand. "Thanks for coming in, Lisa. Remember, we need to hear from you by 5:30 tomorrow. Should you decide to proceed, we'll need you back here to sign the necessary papers."

"Okay."

"Hope to see you again." Ice Queen tried to smile.

I picked up my purse, mind still spinning. "No need to see me out. I know the way."

Numbly, I walked out of the office. I reached the elevator and stared at the down button. My finger wouldn't rise to push it.

Out of nowhere my mother's voice rose from childhood. My haunting, oldest failure: *"A picture for me? Here's how you can make it better . . ."*

Would the Empowerment Chip save me from the painful memories of my mother too?

I tried again to lift my hand—and couldn't. I could only stare at the gray elevator door, thinking of the shaft behind it. Empty, like my life.

Once I got home I knew what would happen. The fear would descend, and I'd be paralyzed. My twenty-four-hour deadline would seep away. The promise of that chip I'd held in my hand would be gone to me forever. A lifelong regret. Then what would my future look like? Tomorrow, next week, next year? I was drowning here.

The Empowerment Chip was a thrown lifeline.

But what if I got the placebo? My last dare to hope—dashed.

My thoughts fisted. I heard myself breathe. For a long, quivering moment I hung there.

Something beyond me turned my feet from the elevator. The next thing I knew, I was standing at Jerry's closed office door. Voices drifted from inside. My hand knocked on it, and the conversation stilled. Footsteps . . . and the door to a possible incredible new life opened.

Even as my voice trembled, I looked Jerry in the eye. "Where are the papers I need to sign?"

FRIDAY, MARCH 9—
SATURDAY, MARCH 10

Chapter 3

THE NEXT THREE DAYS PASSED LIKE EONS. WE'D SET MY surgery for Friday. In those three days I came close to cancelling a hundred times. Somehow the morning of the procedure managed to arrive. I was due at the hospital at 8:00 a.m. The first two hours would be prepping, then into the operation. I couldn't drive myself, since I'd need someone to bring me home in two days. Sherry said she'd pick me up, but she couldn't take me. She was busy getting her daughter to school. I'd scheduled a cab.

"Where to?" the taxi driver asked.

I carried a small overnight bag, my purse inside. No makeup, no jewelry. I'd put my wedding rings in a dresser drawer.

"Hillsdale Hospital in Palo Alto."

His dark eyes flicked me a look in the rearview mirror. "You sick?"

"No."

"Visiting someone?"

"No."

He left me alone.

Sherry and I had talked at length on the phone last night. "I still can't believe you're doing this," she said.

"Me either."

"It's just so . . . drastic."

"I need something drastic. And they insist it's a pretty simple procedure."

"It's your *brain*."

"It's my life."

Silence.

"Are you scared?"

"Petrified."

She grunted. "Me too."

The cab pulled up in front of the hospital. My nerves jittered. I walked inside and headed to the second floor, as I'd been directed. With each step my legs grew heavier. What was I doing? This was the last chance to change my mind. I didn't even like hospitals.

In the clinic area a young nurse with chic brown hair met me, all smiles. Pretty face. Such graciousness and calm. *Deb Smith*, read her name tag.

Such a common name. Was it fake?

I frowned at myself. Why in the world would I think that?

"This is for you." She handed me a multicolored cotton gown. "All your jewelry's off already?" She looked me over. "That's good. You can put your clothes in the rubber bin over there." She pointed behind me.

"Where's the surgeon?" I hadn't even met him. Or was it a her?

"He'll be along shortly."

"Where's the brain chip?"

"He's got it." Deb Smith patted my hand. "Don't worry. This is a straightforward procedure, really. I've seen many a person before you sail right through it."

But what about afterward? Would my life be changed? "Tell them not to give me a fake one. *Please*."

"Well, that's out of my jurisdiction, I'm afraid."

"I don't want a broken one either."

The nurse gave me a mild look. "There's a sealed and sterile envelope with your name on it. The chip inside is meant only for you. And it's been checked and rechecked. No way it's broken. Now just get dressed in your gown, and we'll be back for you soon."

She pulled the curtain closed with a *swoosh*.

I changed into the gown. My body shook. I'd never been through surgery before. Not even for tonsils. What if I was allergic to anesthesia?

Hugging myself, I sat on the gurney and waited. It was cold. A wave of aloneness rushed me. If Ryan were still alive, this wouldn't be happening. Even if I'd been attacked, I could have made it, with Ryan.

Soft footsteps sounded. They stopped outside the curtain. "Ms. Newberry? May I come in?"

"Yes."

The curtain drew back.

My doctor looked in his sixties. Thick gray hair, a round face. "Hi, I'm Dr. Rayner. I'll be doing your procedure, along with Dr. Frank. Do you have any questions?"

So many. My lungs clogged at the sheer weight of them. "Are you . . . do you work for Cognoscenti?"

"Yes. Dr. Frank and I have done many of these procedures. You're in good hands, if I do say so myself."

I nodded.

"Anything else?"

My head shook. I simply could not talk.

He spoke with me until Deb Smith returned, clearly trying to reassure me. "Okay." The doctor smiled. "I'll go prep, and we'll see you soon."

"So. Looks like you're set." The nurse's eyes drifted to the bin behind me, containing my clothes. "Whoa, cool bra. Bright blue."

What? I blinked.

"Where'd you get it?"

I looked at the bra, bewildered. Was it bright? I hadn't noticed. "Victoria's Secret."

She raised a shoulder. "Of course. Where else?"

How surreal, discussing underwear at a time like this.

Another nurse appeared. I needed to lie down so they could prep my head. I obeyed, a rag doll. Sections of my hair were parted. A shaver whirred.

Fear crammed my throat. I was really doing this.

Next thing I knew, they were wheeling me into surgery. I watched the ceiling go by, my thoughts hazed. What was I doing here? Had I lost my mind?

I still had time to pull out of this.

The operating room felt even chillier. "Why's it so cold in here?" I asked one of the masked docs. Which one was he?

"The lower temperature keeps the germs down."

Oh.

"All right," somebody said. "Ready to go."

My eyes squeezed shut.

"It's okay, Lisa, you can relax."

My heart cantered.

A plastic-feeling mask descended over my nose and mouth. "Okay now, just breathe normally."

Panic spun through me. I gasped in air. *Let me out of here. Out, out, out!*

Was someone above me telling me everything was okay? It wasn't. Not at all. I sucked more oxygen.

Dense fog carpeted my veins. So . . . heavy . . . Desperately I tried to move my mouth. Yell *Stop!*

Nothing happened.

Another breath, and the fog thickened.

No, please. I don't . . .

A third breath. It sucked me down, down, to the depths of the ocean. I struggled to swim up.

But my feet . . .

Got . . .

Tangled.

Chapter 4

A SECOND LATER I WOKE UP.

Sensations and thoughts chugged in my head. This ceiling—not the one in the operating room. A different blanket on me. My body felt like lead. An IV needle was taped into a vein in my arm.

How did this happen? I'd just gone under.

I blinked hard, *feeling* my mind. Nothing seemed different.

Maybe they didn't do the procedure. Maybe something went wrong

Or did I get the placebo? The thought leadened me. I couldn't even hold it in my head. Couldn't bear to think it.

Ryan. Were memories of him still with me? I visualized his face. His smirk when he used to tease me. I could hear his voice. His off-key singing.

Yes, he was there! I wanted to cry but didn't have the energy.

Footsteps. The curtain around me edged back. Carefully I rolled my head to the left. I sensed bandages on that side of my skull but felt no pain.

"Lisa?" A quiet voice spoke. Deb . . . somebody. Smith?

"Huh?"

"Ah." She stepped inside. "You're awake. How do you feel?"

"Uh-huh."

Deb smiled. "That good? Well, all right."

I swallowed. My throat felt like a desert. "Did they do it? Put in the chip?"

"Sure did. Everything went like clockwork."

"But I passed out only a second ago."

She was checking the IV. "It just feels like that. Anesthesia puts you so deep under, you don't have a sense of time like when you're asleep. A total time warp, isn't it?"

Way beyond a time warp. Downright eerie. "You sure? 'Cause it doesn't feel . . ."

She patted my arm. "Trust me."

I closed my eyes, trying to absorb it all. I'd done it. Really gone through with it. Should I laugh—or cry? "What . . . happens now?"

"We'll take you to your room. A private one."

Good. I didn't want to talk to anyone. Just wanted to sort things out.

"I feel . . . heavy."

"You're drugged."

"What happens when I'm undrugged?"

"You won't feel heavy anymore." She threw me a smile, as if to apologize for her lightheartedness. "Your head may hurt some. We can give you more pain meds."

"I don't like pain meds. Can't function on 'em."

"Okay, your choice. But we'll send you home with some, just in case."

Decoration for my medicine cabinet. "Where are my clothes?"

"You'll find them in your room. Like magic."

My other questions evaporated. I just wanted to sleep.

"You ready to get out of here?" Deb asked.

"Uh-huh."

"All right. I'll get another nurse, and we'll take you up."

I drifted into unconsciousness.

Sometime later I found myself in a private room, propped up on pillows in the bed. Questions stormed me all over again. Did I get a real chip? What did I feel? What was my life going to look like?

Deb got me comfortable and made sure I had water. She showed me how to put the bed up and down, and where the nurse call button was located. "You just give us a ring if you need anything, all right?"

I nodded . . . and once again floated into sleep.

Dreams of Ryan came, vague and rambling. Then he stood before me so clearly. I held a baby in one arm. I could see my husband, touch him, smell him. I reached out, ran my fingers through his hair—

And woke up.

My bleary eyes saw a hospital room. But Ryan's face still pulsed in my mind. The dream had been so real. I'd had them like this before and always woke up sobbing.

Not this time.

I held my breath. Could that be *true*?

Any minute now it would hit. I braced for the familiar pain . . .

It didn't come.

Had this really worked? *Please, please, please.*

I waited longer—and still nothing.

After a few minutes I made myself picture Ryan again. I went over the dream in detail. Seeing Ryan's face. Touching him. Even with that, my heart lay still.

This was beyond amazing. I could feel my husband, remember him with warmth and love. I could even smile at the image of the baby we never had. But that deadening grief was *gone*.

I'd gotten the real chip. It was working!

Lightness surged through my body. Had I ever felt such joy in my life? I wanted to jump up and run through the hallway. I wanted to shout and sing. Tell the world it had happened! To *me*. This promise, this unbelievable gift—

But I could do none of those things. Drugged and weak, I could only lay there, tears running down my temples. Smiling until my cheek muscles burned. Eventually the tears ran out. My throat was thick and my nose clogged. I didn't care. I just smiled on.

At that moment I didn't think I would ever stop.

Chapter 5

SOMETIME LATER I WOKE UP AGAIN.

How had I ever gone back to sleep? With all the elation knocking around inside me?

I bunched the covers up to my neck and closed my eyes. What if my head wasn't quiet anymore? Maybe I'd dreamed the whole thing . . .

At first I was too scared to test it. Then I focused on more memories of Ryan. Our wedding and honeymoon. The first time we'd kissed.

And still my head was quiet.

New wonder surged through me. I wanted to tell the world! I longed to phone Sherry, but trial participants weren't allowed calls. Cognoscenti didn't want me talking to anyone who might influence my thinking.

My hand fumbled around for the call button and pushed it. In a few minutes a middle-aged nurse with large brown eyes appeared.

"Hi, hon, how we doing?"

"I'm healed! My brain is healed!"

She smiled. "Well, that's great."

"No, you don't understand. My depression is gone! I can remember my husband and everything—but I don't feel the grief in my heart. I can think. I can even be *happy*."

The nurse beamed at me. "That's really wonderful, hon."

She had no clue.

"You need to go to the bathroom while I'm here? I'll help you up."

She really didn't get it. How could she not just fall over?

"Uh, yeah. Okay."

Sherry would understand. Tomorrow I could tell her.

The nurse fussed over me, taking the IV out of my arm.

When I got up my legs were sluggish, but not as bad as I'd expected. More good news. Just think—in a few days I'd get my physical energy back, too. That would be so awesome. The things I could *do*.

When I was done in the bathroom, the nurse helped settle me back into bed. "You need any more pain pills?"

"No way. I just want to feel . . . everything."

She raised her eyebrows. "You've got quite a high pain tolerance there."

I'd hardly noticed the pain. It didn't matter.

The rest of that day I dozed on and off. Every time I woke I felt stronger. Over the hours my excitement settled into the most wonderful sense of peace. How had I managed to live through the past nine months? The time since Ryan's death now seemed like a black hole. I could never, ever go back to that.

I passed the time soaking in my new sensations. I remembered funny moments with Ryan and laughed. *Laughed.* I pictured the three times I'd miscarried and knew the pain. Understood it. But it wasn't that smothering darkness that had threatened to kill me.

By late afternoon more incredible things had happened. I dared myself to even relive the attack—and didn't *feel* it. I visualized my car as I walked toward it in the dark. Remembered my hand rummaging inside my purse for the keys. Heard the pounding steps behind me. I felt the sudden hit of an arm clinched around my neck, a force pulling me backward. *Scream, scream,* my brain wailed, but no sound would come. I could smell the man's sweat, almost taste it.

I saw myself at the San Mateo Police Station, wrapped in a blanket, shivering, shivering. The smell of old coffee and despair. A detective taking my statement.

Then I thought of the months after that. The sleepless nights and shuddering days. The clotting depression. I saw myself unable to think, finally quitting my admin job at the investment company. Collecting the two hundred thousand from Ryan's life insurance and putting it in the bank with no care to spend a dime.

And I thought of my mother. How I'd failed her so often. I hadn't been the cheerleader type, as she'd been. Or athletic. Hadn't excelled in anything. Was an average student. Hadn't given her grandchildren. I could hear her voice from childhood. *"Lisa, you can do better than that, and you know it. Do you try to disappoint me?"*

Those memories hurt. But not like before. Their trappings of guilt and shame were gone.

I'd never guessed that was possible.

During my depression, no one could really help me. Not even Sherry. And they couldn't possibly know what I was going through. I'd felt lost, utterly alone, and without the energy to *do anything about it.*

Now it was like someone had flipped a switch in my brain.

That day I cried a lot. Happy tears. It was almost more than my heart could contain.

By dinner time the drugs had worn off completely. Then I could feel more than ever that the old weight in my chest was gone. Thought came more easily. Clearer.

I missed Sherry.

After eating I got up and shuffled around the room. Ventured a few steps into the hall. A nurse I hadn't seen before asked how I was doing.

"Fabulous!" I spread my arms. "You wouldn't *believe* how the chip has worked."

Friday night I slept soundly for the first time in months.

Saturday morning I felt even better. I told every nurse that came in how my life had changed. What the Empowerment Chip had done for me. They couldn't shut me up. That afternoon Jerry and Clair came by.

Ice Queen carried a notebook and pen. "How do you feel?"

Couldn't they see, just by looking at me? "I'm healed." The words bounced off my tongue.

Jerry's eyebrows rose. "How so?"

I told them, my words tripping over themselves. Ice Queen took notes. She seemed to record not only what I said, but my gestures and tone. Her chilled poker face remained in place, but she couldn't keep the gleam from her eyes. It was the same excitement I'd seen when she talked about the chip a few days ago.

A lifetime ago.

Now I fully understood why she felt so passionate about the Empowerment Chip.

"I know I got a real one," I declared. "You can tell me now."

Jerry shrugged. "We don't know. We *won't* know until the trial is over and we report our findings."

Didn't matter. I *knew*. "Who do you report to?"

"Richard Price, V.P. of Research. And he reports directly to Dr. Hilderbrand himself, who developed the chip."

"Tell them they did it." My voice caught. "Tell Dr. Hilderbrand thank you. For my life."

Jerry smiled. "They'll be glad to hear you're better."

They set a meeting for me to see them at the Cognoscenti offices the following Friday. Jerry wrote the time on the back of his card and left it on the tray near my bed. Next Friday. Just think of all the things I could accomplish by then.

I shifted my top pillow. My head hurt only a little. I'd taken a couple over-the-counter pain relievers. "I can't wait to get out of here tomorrow. I'll be able to *do* things now. The future is a promise, not a threat."

"That's great." Clair smiled and managed to look half warm. "But don't make decisions too quickly, all right? Just let yourself continue to heal from the surgery this week."

"Okay." Although I couldn't imagine just sitting around for a week. I wanted to *move*.

"Once you get home someone will call you about setting up your post-op appointments," Jerry said. As part of the trial I'd continue to report how I was doing to a Cognoscenti interviewer once a week for six months.

"Yeah. Good."

After they left, the room was silent. But far from empty. I stared at the blank TV screen, just *being*.

Were there other Cognoscenti patients in this hospital recovering from the procedure? Imagine some of them getting the placebo. I couldn't have stood that. I'd be devastated.

Thank You, God, so very, very much. My first prayer in a long time rose as natural as breathing.

You're welcome, child.

My mouth fell open. Did I really just feel that?

I knew I had. It had come just like that. So . . . real. So complete. God *was* here. In this room with me.

Tears sprang to my eyes. This was the final thing I needed. This was *everything*. God had come back. He wanted to be with me. *Me.* The warmth of that knowledge spread through my whole body.

How had I ever made it all those months without Him? I pulled the covers around me, sealing Him to my heart.

Don't quit talking to me now, please, God. I need You so much.

I thanked Him again for the surgery. For Cognoscenti and the chip. And Sherry. For the new life I could live. But the more I talked to Him, the more something nagged at me. At first it wasn't clear. Then it materialized.

Surely God hadn't come back just because of a brain chip. He was way bigger than that.

I dwelt on that for awhile.

If He hadn't just come back . . . then what? Was He never really gone?

The thought punched me in the stomach.

When I felt like He'd abandoned me—could that have just been *me*?

The answer spilled over me like warm perfume, soaking the covers. Soaking me. God had never really left me. I just hadn't been able to feel Him.

He *hadn't* betrayed me. I could trust Him. I really could.

The shift in my understanding was so immense I hardly knew how to handle it. Sherry had told me again and again that God was there for me. But I didn't listen.

I couldn't wait to tell her this!

Dinner came, but I had trouble eating. I was just too overwhelmed. My lightness had become near weightlessness, the peace within me so very profound. I was healed, and God was here.

True—I still didn't have Ryan. Or kids. My relationship with my mother was still broken. But I was whole. I could deal with these things. And God would help me through.

Time passed, and sleepiness finally stole over me. When I turned out the light, I brimmed with anticipation for the morning.

Mere hours later my nightmare began.

Chapter 6

 THE VISION CAME AS I WAS FALLING ASLEEP.

I was standing in a richly furnished living room. Large, overstuffed couch and matching love seat. Beige walls, a large impressionist painting of a seascape. Hardwood floors with a Chinese rug. Glass-topped coffee table. White marble fireplace.

A petite woman stalked in, dressed in jeans and a blue silk top. A dark-haired beauty. "Why can't you stop cheating on me? You're nothing but a liar!"

What?

"Shut up!" a male voice shouted. But it came from me.

"I'll tell them all what you really are." She jabbed a forefinger at me. "I'll make you pay!"

I glanced down at myself—my big hands and long legs, clad in khaki pants. Brown loafer shoes.

I was a man.

The woman kept yelling. "I'll leave you, how will you like that? You can't kick me around like some dog!"

My hands—the man's hands—shook with anger.

I/he strode across the room. Through his eyes I saw the woman getting closer, saw fear cross her face. She cringed.

He wrapped his hands around her neck. Tightened his grip.

She choked. Grabbed at his fingers, clawing, trying to pull them away. He watched her face turn red, then white. She gurgled. Her eyes rolled back. Her legs gave way.

He let her fall.

For a moment I/he stood over her, panting. He wiped an arm across his mouth. Steadied his breathing.

She moved.

He cursed and grabbed her feet. Roughly dragged her out of the room, into a big kitchen with lots of stainless steel, more hardwood flooring. Beyond a glass door lay a deck and large backyard. She tried to kick him. He cursed again and let her go. Lunged toward the butcher block on the counter. He grabbed a knife. She wailed. He collapsed to his knees beside her. Arched the weapon high. The knife sliced down toward her chest—

My eyes popped open, my heart kicking the walls of my ribs. I lay there, shaking, sucking oxygen.

No kitchen. No knife, no man. Just my hospital room, dark.

Sweat itched my forehead. I raised a hand to wipe it away. The fingers looked like my own. Not a man's. *Mine.*

My lungs relaxed a little. *Deep breaths, Lisa.*

I licked my lips. Reached for my glass to drink some water.

It was a dream. Just a dream.

But I hadn't been asleep yet. Had I?

Whatever it was, the memory of my attack must have spawned it. But something . . .

Long minutes passed. I stared at the ceiling. Sleep stole out of the room. Fresh fear swept over me, weighting me to the bed. My mouth went dry again. Why was I so terrified?

Had I gotten the placebo chip after all?

No, that couldn't be. I wouldn't be able to handle that. Besides, I still felt different. Stronger than before. This . . . *thing* was something else. Something new.

Lisa, it was just a nightmare.

Really? When had I ever had a dream about being a *man*? His actions—I'd witnessed them from *inside* his head. I could still see those fingers around the woman's neck. The cold promise of the knife in his hand. Could see it arcing down toward her heart.

She couldn't have survived a stabbing like that. He'd killed her.

Lisa. It was just a dream.

No it wasn't.

I drank some more water. Carefully turned on my right side. An hour passed. Two. Squalling drowsiness threatened to overtake me, but I fought it. I didn't want to relive that scene again.

Just before finally drifting off, I remembered the anesthesia and pain pills. All those drugs. Of course they were the cause. That scene was just a hallucination. I'd be better tomorrow, when everything was out of my system.

When I could go home and start my new life . . .

SUNDAY, MARCH 11

Chapter 7

SUNDAY MORNING DAWNED.

I lay in bed trying to figure out what I was feeling. Brittle relief, maybe? I'd had no more bad dreams during the night. And today I got to go home. Most of all, the Empowerment Chip was still working. But that awful murder scene pulsed in my head. It didn't seem like a dream or hallucination at all. It seemed real.

Which, of course, was ridiculous.

I got up and managed to shower. Just had to be careful not to get my bandage wet. The warm water washed the dream away. A little.

After breakfast a nurse brought in a phone, and I used it for my one allowed call to make sure Sherry was coming at noon.

"Lisa! How *are* you?"

"Healed, Sherry." I loved that word. "The chip worked. I'm not depressed anymore. It's absolutely incredible!"

She gasped. "Oh, Lisa." Her voice cracked. For a moment she couldn't say anything.

I babbled on about all the wonderful things I'd experienced. How I was able to remember events without feeling the pain. I'd planned to tell her about the horrible dream, too. But suddenly I couldn't. She was so happy that I was well. I didn't want to spoil that. Besides, talking to Sherry dampened the memory of the nightmare even more.

"I can't wait to see the kids," I said. "It's been so long."

"And they'll love to see you."

By the time I hung up I had tears in my eyes.

Dr. Rayner arrived to check on me, performing all the typical doctorly tasks. He didn't ask if I felt better emotionally. That was Jerry and Clair's job. Instead he read the nurse's computerized chart for my vitals. Made me follow his moving finger with my eyes. Then he removed the bandage from my head and peered at the stitches. "Yes." His fingers were gentle. "Looks good." He replaced the bandage and stood back, hands in the pocket of his white coat.

I just wanted him to pronounce I was allowed to leave. "Do I have to come back to get the stitches out?"

"In about ten days."

I winced. "Won't I look terrific in the meantime."

Wow. I was thinking about how I *looked*. How many months since I'd worried about that?

My lips spread in a lopsided smile. See, I was fine. Better than fine. That nightmare had been a rattling bump in the road. Now my path was clear.

"You don't need to be going out anyway," the doc said. "Remember all the instructions you were given before surgery? Take it easy this week. Even with a procedure that goes smoothly, anesthesia is hard on the body. How are you feeling now?"

"Good."

"Been up and around?"

"Yes."

"All right." He nodded. "Looks like you're ready to go home."

Yes! "I can't wait." I shifted against the pillows. "Did you hear how well the chip's working? It's cured my depression."

He smiled. "That's terrific. I'm so glad for you. And for Cognoscenti."

"Yeah. I haven't felt like this—"

The knife raised up in the man's right hand.

I froze. My vision glazed over.

On his fourth finger sat a huge ring. A gold dragon's head, with emeralds for eyes.

"Ms. Newberry?"

No, not again. What was happening? My fingers dug into the bedcovers. These were new details from that dream. But I was fully awake. How could I see this now, when I was *awake*?

"Lisa? You feeling dizzy?" The doctor's voice sounded far away.

"N-no."

He eyed me. "Are you sure? We can keep you another day."

"*No.*" I gripped the bed sheet harder. It had to be the hospital, this room. Get me home, and I'd be fine. I wanted to see Sherry *today.* "It was nothing. I really want to get out of here."

He gazed at me, then finally nodded. "You have someone coming to get you?"

"Yes, at noon." I swallowed, trying to lighten my voice. "Really, I'm fine. The chip has made such a difference—"

The knife rose up. The dragon ring glinted in the light.

No, *stop!* I cringed. That ring. It was so ugly. And scary.

Dr. Rayner studied me.

The knife disappeared. I forced my breathing to return to normal.

No more pictures came.

Somehow I managed a smile for the doctor. Any more of this weirdness, and he'd make me stay another night. "Thanks for checking on me. And thanks for doing such a great job on the surgery. I can't believe how easy it was."

"You're welcome."

He looked me over one final time, then made a few more notes in the computer and left.

A long breath whooshed out of me. I stared across the room. Why had I seen those things now? I couldn't have any more drugs in me. But that knife and ring. They were clear as daylight.

I tossed back the covers and slid from bed. Lying there was no good. I needed to be moving, occupying my mind. Sherry would be here in an hour.

So I concentrated on getting ready. When thoughts of the man and knife tried to return, I pushed them away and imagined greeting Sherry. She'd be tongue-tied when she saw what the chip had done for me. Next I thought of Ryan. I pictured our first date, our wedding. Moving to California for his new bank manager job. The memories made me smile. Made me feel Ryan, almost as if I could touch him.

I stopped in the middle of the room and hugged myself, eyes closed.

My legs got tired, and I sat in a chair. I checked my watch. Earlier that morning a nurse had reminded me to move it forward one hour for daylight savings time. It was now eleven thirty. Only a half hour until Sherry came. What would I do first when I saw her? Hug her? Burst into tears?

Time passed slowly.

I wandered into the bathroom, checking my reflection in the mirror. The bandage on my head looked strange. Even when that came off and the stitches were out, it would take awhile for my hair to grow back. My face still looked thin. I'd lost twenty pounds since Ryan's funeral. But my *eyes*. In the past nine months their milk chocolate color had muddied. Now they shone with new hope. And my mouth no longer turned down.

Footsteps sounded in the hall—that bouncy walk that could only belong to Sherry. She stopped at the threshold of the room and stuck her tousled blonde head inside. "Hi!"

"Hey!" I hurried out of the bathroom as fast as I could. Sherry looked wonderful in jeans and a long-sleeved cotton top, with her Sunday-go-to-church makeup. And look how blue her eyes were. I'd forgotten that.

She hustled over to me. I hugged her hard, unable to let go. Finally I pulled back, tears in my eyes.

She gaped at me. "Wow. I just . . . You really look different."

"So do you."

"But you're . . ."

"I *am* different. From the inside out. I have energy even though I'm recovering from surgery."

Her eyes glistened. "It's so amazing what I see in your face."

It's called life.

Love for her simmered in me. What a terrific friend she'd been, especially all those months I'd had nothing to give back. Somehow I'd make it up to her. "I don't know how to say this, Sherry. It sounds so crazy, but . . . I can feel you again. I've been so disconnected. It's like you were in the dark, and now someone's turned a spotlight on you."

She laid her hands against her cheeks. "I just can't believe this. It's more than I hoped for."

Me too. Way more. I smiled. "Let's get out of here." I walked to the nurse call button and leaned down to push it. "Silly nurses insist on taking me out in a wheelchair—"

The woman lay on the kitchen floor, eyes fixed open. Blood bubbled from her mouth. Her blouse was stained red.

I halted, stunned. My hand hung in the air.

"Lisa?" Sherry's voice sounded muffled.

The woman's face filled my head. *No, please. Go away.* But still— there she was. Those eyes. The blood . . .

Somehow I shook off the horrible sight. Pushed the call button. "Yeah."

Sherry moved closer. "What just happened? For a second you looked petrified."

That woman. So very *dead.* "I-I'm fine. Really. Sometimes I just . . . get dizzy."

Sherry folded her arms. "So much for those silly nurses."

"Yeah, sure." Those dead eyes still vibrated in my head. "You're right."

I sat down hard on the bed. We waited for the nurse, Sherry watching me with concern. Twice I opened my mouth to tell her what was wrong. But I just couldn't. She was so glad to see me well. I didn't want to trample on that.

Besides, these . . . whatever they were would go away.

Sherry cocked her head at me. "You're starting to look tired."

"Yeah. Guess my mind has more energy than my body. I just need to rest a few days, the doctor said."

"Well, you have just had brain surgery."

The nurse finally appeared with the wheelchair. I rode out of the hospital like a good patient. Sherry got her car and brought it up to the entrance. The nurse helped me inside. I nodded at my friend. "Home, James."

She grinned and started driving. "Listen, once I get you back I'll see what food you need and go to the store for you."

How well she knew me. Before the operation I'd been too worn to think about stocking the kitchen. "That would be great. I take it Jay's on kid duty."

"For the whole blessed afternoon. Maybe we oughtta make a run for the border. We could be in Mexico before he even knows I'm gone."

"Uh-huh. You wouldn't last a night without your kids. Or your husband."

I winced at my own words. But it wasn't like before. *Nothing* was like before.

Surprisingly we were quiet the rest of the way home. I was busy just taking it all in. The blood in my veins now coursed instead of clogged. And I would have sworn the world looked brighter. The trees and grass were greener, the flowers more vibrant. Best of all, the thought of being in my apartment alone no longer terrified me.

Know what—I should start exercising again. Go running. Do Pilates. Maybe I'd buy some new furniture and clothes.

The hand raised the knife, dragon ring glinting.

No, no. *No.*

I stared straight ahead, willing the scene to dim. It only grew brighter. My breathing turned shaky. I fought to keep it quiet enough that Sherry wouldn't notice.

Where were these pictures coming from? Had I seen the ring in some movie? Maybe the whole thing was from an old film.

But if that's all this was, why did the scenes shake me to the core?

Sherry parked on the street in front of my apartment building. She carried my suitcase to the second floor for me. My legs wobbled, but I made it up the stairs.

In my apartment, I did a slow pan of the living room, flowing into the kitchen. A long counter served as a separator between the two areas. I'd lived here for almost three years. Now it felt like I was seeing the apartment for the first time. The couch and chairs were brown and beige, with a plain wooden coffee table. Basic colors Ryan had liked. How dull it seemed now. Wouldn't the place look better with more blue? Maybe some snappy yellow pillows for contrast. And new lamps.

"Remember all my plants, Sherry? I had flowers everywhere." It had been my one hobby, and I was forever buying more. I'd loved every one of those plants. I had tulips in the spring. A Christmas cactus. Incredible orchids and bromeliads. Gardenias, and hydrangea, and calla lilies. I'd potted, and fertilized, and nurtured them. But after Ryan was gone, I didn't care anymore.

"Sure do. I miss them."

"Yeah. They all died."

"Watering helps."

I elbowed her in the ribs.

She raised her eyebrows. "So you gonna get some new ones now?"

"Lots. I'm going to put them all over the place."

Sherry's eyes glistened. "Lisa. *That* will be fabulous."

We smiled at each other.

She and I walked down the hall to my room. Sherry placed the suitcase on my bed. "There you go."

I stood in the bedroom, seeing its decor with new eyes. Same blah colors. Everything needed brightening. And plants should be in here, too, of course. When I looked in the second bedroom—the one that would have been a nursery—it needed work as well. So did the bathroom.

"Know what I'm going to do, besides getting plants? I'm going to redecorate this place. It looks really boring."

"Think so?"

"Absolutely."

She dipped her chin. "Me too. Go for it."

Maybe once I was working again, I'd buy a house, like Ryan and I had dreamed of doing. If I could ever manage that by myself in the Bay Area. Prices here were astronomical. But I so longed for my own place, where I could plant flowers and pretty bushes in the ground. In the front yard and in back. All around the house. I wanted to get down on my knees and work in the soil and make things grow. I wanted to enjoy the colors and the beauty.

The thought made me cry.

Sherri watched me in wonder. "More happy tears, right? I never thought I'd see that."

My throat tightened. She held out her arms and we hugged each other. I pressed my fingers into her shirt. "I just can't tell you what it feels like to have the pain gone."

She patted my back. "Yeah, baby. No pain, whoa, gain."

The man's hand raised the knife.

I clamped down my jaw. *Stop!* My arms tightened around Sherry so hard she grunted.

"S-sorry." I pulled out of the hug and turned away, busying myself with the suitcase. Not wanting her to see my face.

Why did these pictures keep coming back?

By tomorrow they'd be gone. I just needed to rest.

Sherry touched my arm. "You all right?"

"Yeah."

She hesitated, as if wondering whether to believe me. "Let's go check out your kitchen."

"Okay."

We looked in my refrigerator and small pantry. Not much food there. Sherry made a list and headed for the store. I stretched out on the couch and tried to relax, but the visions rose up, fast and hard. I broke into a sweat. By the time Sherry came back I was exhausted. What *was* this in my head?

God, please turn it off.

I started to lug myself up to help put groceries away. Sherry took one look at me and ordered me to stay down. I obeyed. She banged around the kitchen. I trembled on the couch.

"All right, Miss Bionic Woman." Sherry stood over me, hands on her hips. "Anything else I can do for you?"

"No. You've done plenty."

Her head tilted. "You're looking so pale. I think I'll stick around and make sure you're all right."

The thought of her watching me as I fought to hide my panic . . . "All I'm going to do is sleep."

"You sure?"

"Uh-huh."

"What happens when you wake up? Maybe I should be here to wait on you. Like your own private nurse."

I managed a wan smile. "I'll be fine. You saw me walk up the stairs."

"You've just had brain surgery."

"I've just gotten a new life." I smiled again, wider this time.

She pushed her lips out. "Okay. Well then, guess I'll have to drag myself back to those noisy kids of mine."

My thoughts swam. Another minute of her hanging around, and I'd break down and tell her what was happening. Then she'd get all worried and call the doctor. And they'd make me go back to the hospital . . .

"Kiss them both for me, Sherry. Tell them I'll visit them soon."

"I will. And listen, you—call if you need me, and I'll come back over. At the very least, check in with me tonight. If you don't, I'm calling you. And you'd better answer, or I'm breaking your door down."

"Okay, Mom."

Sherry made a face. She did not like my mother one bit, not after the scene at Ryan's funeral. She gave me a final once-over. "Don't make me sorry I left you alone, now."

"I won't."

Sherry leaned down to kiss my cheek and left.

I got up to bolt the door behind her. Turned around to head toward my inviting bed—

A large black suitcase sat before me. Waiting.

I stopped. Threw wild glances around the living room. A suitcase? *Here?* Where'd it come from? It looked so real. So . . . evil.

That suitcase meant death.

What?

The man's hand—my hand—reached for the handle of the suitcase . . .

My feet backed me up against the wall. I pressed against it, shivering. *Run away from it,* my mind cried. But where? Why? I was alone in the apartment, locked in. No one could hurt me here.

He picked it up. It lifted from the floor with a soft whoosh.

A muted scream gurgled out of me. I pressed against the wall, hands before my face. The sound was *here.*

I shook harder.

No, this wasn't really happening. I just needed to calm—

The woman lay dead on the floor, blood trailing from her sagging mouth. Eyes wide and fixed.

I slid to the carpet and hugged my knees. What was *happening* to me?

The living room swelled, suddenly too big, too dangerous. I crawled to a corner and huddled there.

No, not enough! I needed to hide.

From what?

I lurched to my feet and stumbled into my bedroom. I'd jump into the closet—

What if someone was already in there? Waiting for me . . .

I stared at the closet door.

No one's in there, Lisa. Get a grip.

A long moment passed. Slowly my terror began to ebb.

I scraped up bits of courage and flung open the closet door. Pushed aside clothes.

No one hiding. No suitcase.

I sank to the floor, relieved. Spent. My breathing was ragged.

When I could get up, I locked the door to the room and fell on my bed. That gripping paranoia I'd felt—that was like the fear from my old life.

Was I regressing? Had the chip stopped working?

No way.

Sleep, that's what I needed. If I could just sleep . . .

I crawled under the covers and curled into a fetal position. Squeezed my eyes shut.

A big, black suitcase. Lying on a wooden floor. I saw myself zip it open with my right hand—the man's hand. On his fourth finger sat the dragon's head ring. The metallic whir of the zipper rang in my ears. He pulled the cover back. The bag gaped wide, ready to be filled . . .

My eyes opened, but the picture still shrieked. My body flushed with heat, then chilled. Every limb locked tight.

God, make it stop!

But the daymare wore on.

An hour passed, and still I huddled there. The visions intensified. A second hour went by. More scenes. The clock ticked slowly. Four o'clock came. The woman died again and again, choked and stabbed. Ten, twenty times the man's hand with the ring opened the suitcase. Five o'clock came. I never slept. I only saw the murder. Over and over and over. Relived every detail through the man's eyes.

My eyes.

"Why can't you stop cheating on me? You're nothing but a liar!"

"Shut up!"

Every time I saw the scenes, they cut deeper into my gut. I was awake. These weren't dreams. My mind wasn't making them up. I could practically feel these people. Taste the woman's fear, smell the death. Even so I tried and tried to convince myself it was just my imagination run wild. But I knew that wasn't true. These events weren't stories.

They were real.

But that couldn't be right. It wasn't even possible.

Then how do you explain this, Lisa?

I'd just had surgery, with anesthesia and drugs, that's how. Maybe the combination had caused my mind to make up a terrible story. Now it was obsessed. These were more hallucinations, that was all. They would pass.

They didn't.

Six o'clock. The pictures screamed at me.

Seven.

By 8:00 my muscles were so cramped I could barely move. The killing wouldn't stop. And I was going flat-out insane. Every bit of energy had drained away. Blaming the drugs no longer worked. This was Sunday night. I hadn't taken any meds since Friday morning. They were long out of my system. This wasn't medication or anesthesia. And it wasn't my old fears rising up.

It wasn't *me* at all.

"You'll be okay, you will, you will," I chanted to myself through clenched teeth. But I wasn't okay. Because if these visions weren't from me, they were from something else. And that could be only one thing: the Empowerment Chip.

My fingers fisted. I pressed them against my face. No. Not something wrong with the chip. Not some foreign, awful *thing* in my own head. The chip was *good*. It had *helped* me.

How could a few electrical circuits even do this?

"I don't want a broken one."

Why had I said that to the nurse? Was it a premonition?

But Deb Smith had insisted the chips were fine. So had Jerry and Ice Queen.

It couldn't be the chip. These visions *weren't* coming from there.

At 8:30 Sherry called. I almost didn't answer—until I remembered her promise to break down my door if I didn't. I picked up the bedroom phone.

"Hi." My voice croaked.

She gasped. "You sound *terrible*."

"Thanks."

"What's wrong? Are you okay?"

"Fine."

"You don't sound fine."

"I was sleeping."

"Oh, sorry. When you didn't call I got so worried."

The man's hands clinched around the woman's neck. I heard her gurgling, choking.

I closed my eyes. Smacked a palm against my temple.

"Lisa?"

My throat convulsed. I really wanted to tell Sherry. I needed her right now. But then what? She'd fly over here—and . . . ? She couldn't help me. Couldn't make the visions go away. How would I even explain what was happening? I'd turned into some man who kept killing the same woman? Sherry would panic and rush me to a psych ward.

"I need to go back to sleep now."

"Have you eaten?"

"No."

"You need to get some nutrition in you."

"Yes, Mom."

I heard her breathe frustration over the line. "Do I need to come over and make you eat?"

"No. I just want to sleep."

Sherry paused for a long moment. I could practically hear her calculating a reason to come anyway.

"Really, Sherry. There's nothing you can do. I just need to rest some more."

"Okay." She still sounded reluctant. "But I'm not happy about this."

"It's the right thing."

She sighed again. "Call me tomorrow, okay?"

"I will."

"You *sure* you're all right?"

The words rushed to my tongue—*No, help me. Please. I'm going crazy.* But I had no energy to say them. "Yeah. I'm going now." I ended the call.

The woman's fingers loosened from his arm. She dropped to the ground . . .

I crumpled into a ball on my bed. The visions kept coming, fierce and hard. They sliced to the very heart of me, so vivid. They were *real*. I knew it. Deep inside, I knew. They were memories. From that man. That killer. Memories on the chip inside my head.

Lisa, no.

Then where else had they come from? They'd started the very day of my surgery.

I thrashed on my bed, begging God to make them stop. And still the scenes seized me.

By 10:00 I'd run out of denials. The scenes *were* from the chip. I didn't know how or why. The Empowerment Chip had healed my grief and pain. I'd felt that—still felt it. I was different. But the procedure had left me with something new. Something even worse. An unknown terror that would crush me.

I couldn't keep living these visions. They would drive me totally mad.

Panic shook me then, until I fought to breathe. And I knew there was only one thing to do.

I had to get that chip out of my brain.

MONDAY, MARCH 12

Chapter 8

WHEN I WOKE MONDAY MORNING, COTTON STUFFED MY throat. I couldn't have slept more than a few hours. Even when I had, the woman's murder filled my dreams. I saw the killing again and again. The man. The choking. The knife arcing down. His hands opening the suitcase. By morning the scenes had become as much a part of me as the memory of my own attack.

No way could I live through another day like this.

I showered, trembling, praying for strength. Got dressed and forced down some cereal. I could barely swallow.

As soon as the clock read 8 a.m. I pulled Jerry Sterne's business card from my purse and called his direct line. My stomach quivered as I listened to his phone ring. *Please, please answer.*

The rings cut off. "Jerry Sterne."

"H-Hi. It's Lisa Newberry."

"Lisa. Everything all right?"

No, nothing was right. I was dying here. "I need to see you. Now." My voice pinched. "I'm . . . seeing things. This picture of a murder plays over and over in my head. It's coming from the chip, I *know* it."

He hesitated. "A *murder?*"

"Yes."

"Have you ever had anything like this before?"

He knew the answer already. Cognoscenti had interviewed me up, down and sideways before letting me into the trial. "No. This is so awful, I can't stand it!"

"Why do you think it's coming from the chip?"

"It started in the hospital. At first I thought it was just from the drugs, but it's not. This is real." I let out a half-sob. "I'm so scared. You have to help me."

"All right. Let's talk about this."

"Now. I have to come see you *now.*"

"I have a meeting—"

"I don't care!" My fingers gripped the receiver. "You have to do something!"

"Perhaps this afternoon."

I'd be dead by then. "I'm coming to see you *right now!*"

"Ms. Newberry, calm down. I don't want you driving—"

"I'll take a cab." I'd walk if I had to. "I'll be there in half an hour."

I punched off the line before he could protest.

Immediately I called a taxi.

Ten minutes later the cab showed up. I climbed in, hazy and feverish. The black suitcase throbbed in my head.

At Cognoscenti I demanded to see Jerry Sterne right away. Evidently he'd left word at the security desk that I was coming. Richard Mair phoned to tell him I'd arrived, and an assistant materialized to escort me upstairs.

I practically stumbled into Jerry's office. Right away my gaze landed on a Cognoscenti envelope lying faceup on his desk. No address, just my name written on it.

What was that?

"Please have a seat." Jerry pointed to the same chair I'd used before.

Ice Queen hustled in behind me. Today her business suit was jet black. Same slicked hair in a bun. She took her same place, her face set.

Jerry closed his office door. "Can I get you something to drink, Lisa?"

"No."

He sat down, paper and pen in hand. "We understand you have some concerns about the procedure. Tell us what you're feeling."

Some concerns. Yeah, right. "You have to take the chip out of me."

Ice Queen's eyebrows shot up.

"Okay." Jerry held up a hand. "Let's start at the beginning. We need to know exactly what's happening."

I took a deep breath and told them, my fingers gripping the arms of my chair. Told them how the first scene had come in the hospital when I was almost asleep, then continued the next day when I was awake. I didn't give them every detail. But I did say the visions had come all day yesterday, getting worse. And last night.

"It's always the same woman. Same man. Same knife and suitcase. I don't know who the man is. But I do know it's all real. It truly happened."

The words bounced off the walls. Just saying them aloud made me shiver.

Jerry was scribbling notes. "Why do you think that?"

"I just know. It's like I lived it. I'm in the man's head, watching it all happen."

Jerry wrote some more, then lowered his pen. "Anything else?"

How could he be so *calm*? His expression never changed. Neither did Ice Queen's. Couldn't they understand how this terrified me? "Isn't that enough?"

He surveyed me.

"I want the chip taken out."

Jerry shifted in his chair. "Lisa, remember our discussions of how the Empowerment Chip emits electronic impulses that 'turn off' the trauma in your brain? You were sure the chip had done this for you."

"It did. It really made me better. Then *this* happened."

"Okay. But you have to understand the chip only emits signals. It has no data on it. It can't place some picture in your brain."

"I can't tell you how it's doing this. I only know it is."

Jerry put his paper and pen on the table between us. "What you're describing is impossible. The chip has no capability for such a thing."

"But it's *doing* it."

He spread his hands.

"Okay, maybe the visions aren't real." I didn't believe that, but anything to make them listen. "Maybe the impulses the chip is firing are causing me to see them. They just seem real because my own brain is making them up. Like a dream seems real when you're having it. Either way the chip's still doing this to me."

"Perhaps." Jerry spoke the word slowly. He wasn't buying it.

"So it has to come out."

He studied me.

Ice Queen spoke up. "You really are telling us you want a second surgery to remove the chip."

"Yes!"

"Have you thought this through? All the good that chip is doing by holding back your grief and fear—that would go away. The minute the chip is gone, the signals are gone. You'd be like before. And you were desperate to change that."

Her words slugged me in the stomach. I pressed back in my chair. Why hadn't I thought of this? I'd been so obsessed with the visions . . .

I *couldn't* return to that life-sucking depression.

But at least it was something I understood. These visions were evil nightmares come true. They were making me way more crazy than depression.

"Then give me a new chip. One that isn't tainted."

They looked at me like I was crazy. New fear flung itself through me. If they didn't help me . . . "Listen, both of you. I. Can't. Handle this."

Jerry considered me. "I can set you up with one of our psychiatrists. Maybe a few sessions—"

"I'm not crazy."

"I didn't say you're crazy. I just think—"

"I want the chip taken out."

"Lisa. We can't do that."

"Why?"

"It's in the papers you signed. Remember? We had to put the language in there to cover those receiving the placebo. The chip stays, either way."

"Mine isn't a placebo."

"The same rules apply."

"But it's hurting me!"

"It's not, Lisa. It is not. Your brain is hurting you. This isn't coming from the chip."

"It has to be. The thing is cursed!"

Jerry leaned back with a sigh. Placed a fist beneath his chin.

Great. They thought I was insane.

I inhaled a ragged breath. "Please. Whether you think the chip is doing this or not, I want it out."

Ice Queen's expression hardened. "There is no provision in this trial for that."

"There has to be."

"I'm afraid not."

I glared at her.

"Look, Ms. Newberry." She spoke as if talking to a child. "Do you have any idea the cost of that procedure? There is no way Cognoscenti could provide a second surgery to everyone in this trial. It was never promised."

"I'm not everyone. I'm just me."

"It wasn't promised to you."

My muscles tightened. Much more of this and I'd punch her out. Jerry too. "I'm telling you I want this chip *out* of me."

"If you want it out that badly, you're free to do so," Jerry said. "But it would be at your own expense. And you'd be talking a great deal of money."

My arms folded. "You said a second surgery wasn't promised to anyone in the trial."

"Right."

"So I *quit* the trial. I'm done. And I want this fixed."

"You can stop the trial if you want." Jerry's voice remained so infuriatingly calm. "But I'd think twice about that. As part of it you have access to a psychiatrist's help. If you pull out, you're on your own."

"Looks to me like I'm on my own anyway."

Frustration flicked across Jerry's face. His mouth opened, then shut.

"Please, Ms. Newberry." Ice Queen again. "Let us help you."

"You *can* help. By taking out the chip!"

"We can't authorize that."

"Then get somebody higher up! Let me talk to your boss."

"The answer will be the same."

My feet pressed into the floor. "Fine then. Maybe I should just go to the police."

She blinked "About what?"

Why had that popped out of me? *Yeah, Lisa, about what?* "The vision. The murder. Like I said, I think it really happened."

"It's not a real murder. It's all in your head."

"If it's all in my head, the chip put it there!"

"But it didn't."

We were going around in circles. "Then where's all this coming from?"

"Your own brain." Jerry emphasized his words. "What you're describing are panic attacks. Lots of people have them. And they don't have implanted chips. Our brains are intricate, complex pieces of machinery. We have not begun to understand the depths of them. But take a hard look at this 'vision' you're having. Notice how it involves a man strangling a woman? That's right out of your own experience."

"Really? What about the knife and the house I've never seen before? And the suitcase?"

He shook his head.

My jaw twitched. "Maybe I should talk to a newspaper or something. Tell them what's going on with this company."

More stupid threats. I'd never do that.

Ice Queen's head tilted. "I'll tell you what's going on—you're seeing things. Any reporter you talk to would come to us next for our side of the story. We'd have to tell him the truth."

"And what would that be?"

"That you're a depressed, traumatized woman who voluntarily entered our trial. That when things didn't go your way, you pulled out—after the expensive surgery, I might add—and made threats."

Tears filled my eyes, and that only made me madder. "I'll tell them what you've done to me."

"Ms. Newberry, please," Jerry said. "For your own sake, don't do that."

My own sake? "Is that some kind of threat?"

He smacked both hands on his legs. "Just . . . *Can* you stay a part of this trial and let us help you?"

"You're not helping me unless you take out the chip!"

"Then we'll have no choice but to terminate your participation."

I threw my hands in the air. "Who cares? What difference does it make now anyway? You've messed up my life—and you *won't fix it*!"

Jerry let out a long breath.

Ice Queen's jaw flexed. "I will *not* sit by and let you undermine this project."

Jerry waved his hand at her. "Clair—"

"No, Jerry, she needs to hear this." Ice Queen faced me square on. "Do you have any idea how important this trial is? And how well it's been going?"

Oh, it was important, all right. Important enough to make Cognoscenti millions of dollars. "I'll bet you own stock in the company."

Ice Queen's cheeks flushed. "I'm talking about the good the Empowerment Chip can do, Ms. Newberry. Imagine people like yourself, so traumatized. Imagine all the vets coming back from Iraq and Afghanistan with PTSD. Or people so depressed they want to commit suicide. This chip will save people's *lives*."

I'd thought the same thing.

"Do you really want to go out there"—Clair pointed toward the window—"and tell people this chip is bad? You really want to place the welfare of other people at risk because *you* are having panic attacks?"

Oh, so now *I* was the bad guy? "I'm having *panic attacks,*

Ms. Saxton, because of *your* chip. If it's going to do this to other people, you can *bet* I'm going to tell the world about it."

Ice Queen lasered me with her eyes. No point in punching her now—I'd break my hand on her jaw.

"Fine then." She rose and plucked the envelope with my name on it off Jerry's desk. It was sealed. She sat down again, holding it in both hands. "You want out of this trial?" Her voice was dead quiet. Condemnation oozed out her pores. They had offered me life through the Empowerment Chip—the new invention that would change the world—and I had the audacity to drag it through the mud.

"Yes."

"You got it." She opened the envelope and pulled out two pieces of paper. Her eyes lingered on the first. For a split second her poker face twitched with . . . surprise? Vindication? She held out the paper for Jerry to see. He read it, blinked, and nodded.

Ice Queen leaned forward to hand me the second sheet of paper. "This is the form you need to sign, saying you're pulling out of the trial."

Jerry held out his pen.

I snatched the paper from her hands and started reading. The second paragraph stopped me cold. "This says I don't hold you accountable for anything. But I do."

"If you want out of the trial, Ms. Newberry"—Ice Queen's tone chilled—"you need to sign it."

"I do—and I won't." I tossed the paper on the table.

"All right, then." She picked up the document. "We'll have to sign for you on the next line, did you see it? That for reasons of refusing to participate, we are withdrawing you from the trial."

"Go right ahead. And I'm just letting you know, when I get home, I'm calling the *San Jose Mercury*. And probably a TV station or two. Not to mention I'll sue Cognoscenti for everything it owns." All bluff. But I was desperate.

Disappointment crossed Jerry's face. "You won't want to do that, Ms. Newberry."

"Oh, really?"

He exchanged a look with Ice Queen. She placed the first piece of paper in his hand. He folded it in half. Unfolded it again. "Now that you're withdrawn from the trial, you're entitled to know about the chip you were given." Jerry's voice was grim. "The vice president in charge of the trial placed the information in this envelope in case things didn't go well in this meeting. Clearly, they haven't. We had not known the content until opening it."

What did it matter now? My gaze flicked to Ice Queen. She eyed me, mouth firm. So I'd sounded that wacked on the phone, had I. Crazy enough that they'd talked to their boss. Before I ever walked in here, they'd planned for this. I was making too much noise, and Cognoscenti just wanted me out. Didn't want to admit their miracle Empowerment Chip had some major flaw.

Well, good riddance to both of them.

I lifted a shoulder. "So what does it say?"

Jerry held the paper out to me. "You received a placebo."

Chapter 9

THE CAB RIDE HOME WAS A BLUR. JERRY STERNE'S STUN-
ning words circled in my head along with scenes of the
murder.

A placebo. A blank chip.

Could my brain really be making all this up? Could it be just
coincidence that these "panic attacks" started right after the chip
was implanted?

No way.

And by the way, if the chip was a placebo, why had my depression lifted? The huge difference in my emotions couldn't be merely
from the power of suggestion. I *knew* what I felt. I'd been better.
Really better. Then—this.

When I walked into my apartment the phone was ringing. I
checked the ID. Sherry. Guilt washed through me. I'd never called
her. I picked up the receiver.

"Hi, Sherry."

"Where have you *been*? I've been calling you for the past hour."

I could hear J.T.'s kiddy music playing in the background. "I'm so sorry. I should have called you before I left."

"Left? You felt like going somewhere?"

My throat hurt. I tried to answer but couldn't.

"Lisa?"

"Hmm?" My voice wavered.

"What's wrong?"

Tears spilled from my eyes. "Everything."

She inhaled a sharp breath. "Did the chip stop working?"

A hysterical laugh choked me. "More like it's working overtime."

"What do you mean?"

I fought back the tears. I didn't want to lose it, not now. Then a thought hit me. I was actually handling this. As scary as the visions were, I'd been able to face Jerry and Ice Queen, demand they do something. I never would've had that kind of strength during my depression. If I'd been given a placebo *and* now had to deal with these visions—I'd be a total basket case.

I stared across the living room, the realization filling me up. That chip was no placebo.

Had Jerry and Ice Queen lied to me? Or had their boss lied to them?

"Lisa!"

I jumped. "Sorry. I'm here."

"Talk to me."

The phone.

I pulled the receiver away from my ear and stared at it. How long had I been gone from the house—ninety minutes? By the time I got to Cognoscenti, they already suspected I'd be a threat. They'd prepared that false placebo document. What if they'd sent someone to bug my apartment?

Okay, that *was* paranoid. Still . . .

"Lisa, please." Sherry's voice drifted up to me.

I pulled the receiver to my ear. "Sherry, I have to go right now. I promise I'll call you back."

"But—"

I punched off the line.

Sadness speared me. This was no way to treat my best friend. But I pushed it away for the moment, staring at the receiver in my hand. Could I take it apart? Would I even know what to look for?

My fingers tightened. This wild way of thinking—it was a bad sign. Very bad. Maybe the chip *was* a placebo. A tainted one.

Whatever it was, I had the right to be paranoid.

But really, Lisa, a tapped phone?

I set the receiver down and slumped over the counter. One thing I did know—the visions came from the chip. But how to prove it? No one at Cognoscenti would listen to me now.

My stomach growled, but I couldn't think about eating. I shuffled to the couch and sat down. Bent over, elbows on my knees.

Two choices rose up. First: do nothing. Just work through the terror, hoping the visions would eventually fade, even though it felt like they'd really happened. But even if that were true, the murder was done, no changing it. What was I supposed to do about it now? If I did try to do something, I could end up in a lot of danger. Of all people, I was the last one to place myself in the sights of a man who would choke a woman.

Second choice: do something. Somehow get help for myself, and stop the Empowerment Chip from going on the market. But how? I was one person against a corporation funded by millions of dollars. And Ice Queen had made it clear if I said anything to anyone, they'd label me a crazy, vindictive woman. Plus they'd have the paper to prove my chip was nothing but blank.

I pictured Ice Queen's face as she first read the placebo document. And Jerry's expression. Their reactions had seemed genuine. If that was true, and if my chip wasn't a placebo, then their boss,

Mr. Vice President, had lied to them—and me. Maybe some investor had forced him to. Any investor would have a lot of money at stake.

If the company had lied to me, what about others in the trial? Maybe I wasn't the only one in trouble. What if the chip was severely flawed, and they needed to silence anyone who complained? Someone in the company who believed in the chip enough, who wanted to make millions, could convince himself it was the patients' fault.

Imagine the product in my brain released into the general market. The thought made me want to throw up.

I fell back against the couch and stared at the ceiling. If only Ryan were here. He'd know what to do. I'd sit on his lap and hug him, as I had so many times after my miscarriages. And he'd wrap his arms around me, pressing his love into my skin, my heart, until I was able to think again. Until we could talk things out.

From the end table I picked up a framed picture of my husband. He was standing on the Golden Gate Bridge, feet apart, wind ruffling his hair. His arms were crossed, a satisfied grin on his face. It had been our first sightseeing trip after moving to the Bay Area.

My heart panged. If Ryan were here, I wouldn't be in this situation in the first place.

I put the picture back down.

Cognoscenti against Lisa Newberry. An elephant against a gnat.

The phone rang. I barely heard it, too busy staring at the carpet.

If the murder was real, who was the woman?

A second ring.

There'd be news about the homicide—with her picture. I could search online. If I found her picture, I'd *know* I was right.

But what if the crime didn't happen here? That house could be anywhere. And the murder could have been long ago.

A third ring.

I closed my eyes, focusing on the scenes. Seeking any clues about the time or the place. The kitchen in those visions had looked modern. But nothing more than that came to mind.

The fourth ring cut off. The phone's auto answer clicked on.

"Lisa!" My mother's commanding voice filled the apartment. My head jerked up.

"What is going on? Get back to me right away. Some company in your area called about you. Name starts with a *C* or *K*. The man did not sound nice, and that's an understatement. He told me to give you this message:

"'*Don't* do it.'"

Chapter 10

 I JUMPED UP AND HURRIED TO THE COUNTER TO SNATCH up the phone. "Mom?"

Silence.

"Mom?"

She'd hung up.

I lowered the receiver and stood there, hearing myself breathe. A company name starting with *C* or *K*. Cognoscenti. Sending a threatening message.

Why had they called my mother instead of me?

Of course they knew about her. Cognoscenti knew everything about me after my screening interviews. I'd told them of her charm and beauty, how she always looked so perfectly put together. How she'd tried to make me just as perfect. I told them about the drawing I'd given my mother when I was five, only to be lectured on how I could improve it. They knew about her coldness—a mom who rarely hugged or said "I love you."

Cognoscenti also knew how much Ryan had helped me deal with my mother. He'd believed in me, loved me for who I was.

When *I* didn't even know who I was. I'd come a far way from being under my mother's thumb. Still, things were hardly great between us. To this day I tried to tell myself I didn't care what she thought of me. But I did.

My hand hovered over the receiver. I pulled it back.

I'd never given Cognoscenti my mother's number. Only her name and where she lived. For the required emergency number I'd listed Sherry. Yet Cognoscenti hadn't bothered her. They'd called my mother. They'd taken the time to track her down. But why? To intimidate me?

Mom had said *he*. Jerry? One of my original interviewers?

I picked up the phone and punched in Mom's number. The second ring cut off.

"Lisa!"

"Hi."

"What's going on? Who is this company?"

Now what was I supposed to say? "Someone I interviewed for a job with." The lie slipped out so easily. My conscience twinged.

"Why are they calling *me*?"

"I don't know. Probably got your number mixed up with mine in their file."

"No, he meant to call me. He addressed me by name."

He did? Maybe it was Jerry Sterne, and Ice Queen was in on it. Maybe they were better actors than I thought.

"This isn't about a job interview, Lisa, and I know it. He sounded far too menacing. Are you in some kind of trouble?"

If she only knew. "No."

"What does 'don't do it' mean?"

"I don't know."

"I think you do."

"Mom." My fingers tightened around the phone. "Forget it."

She sighed. "I'm terribly worried about you. So far away. Why don't you move back home? There's nothing to keep you there."

Except for distance from her—

The black suitcase lay on the floor. The man unzipped it hurriedly. I saw his right hand, the dragon ring on his finger. He threw back the cover.

I swayed. Held on to the counter for support.

"Lisa, are you listening to me?"

Where was my tongue? "Look, Mom, I need to go. Sorry they bothered you. I'll tell them not to call you anymore."

I hung up.

Through the man's gaze I saw the dead woman, lying on his kitchen floor. Her eyes were open and fixed. Blood stained her silk blouse. The knife was not in sight.

He dragged the suitcase next to her. Bent down and thrust an arm behind her neck. Raised her torso. He forced his other arm under her knees and lifted. Her ragdoll body folded in his grasp. The man dropped her into the suitcase with a heavy thump.

I gasped and whirled around. That sound—it was right here.

The woman's shoulders fell out of the suitcase on one end, her feet out the other. The man used both hands to turn her on her side. He forced her knees up toward her face. Pushed her body down until her head rested inside the bag.

He stood back and studied her. Then he closed the cover over the suitcase and zipped it.

The *whir* of the zipper vibrated right through me. I sagged against the counter and hung on for life. Gritting my teeth, I fought to get hold of myself. He'd put her in the *suitcase*. How awful. How heartless.

Would he bury her next? Would I have to see that, too?

Come on, Lisa. Pull it together.

For a long time I shivered over the counter. The fear heated, then melted like running wax. I was left to cool. Then harden.

My unsteady gaze landed on Jerry Sterne's business card. Maybe I couldn't stop the visions, but I didn't have to put up with threats from Cognoscenti. Before I lost my courage I jabbed in the digits. His voice mail picked up. I barely waited for the beep after his message.

"It's Lisa Newberry. *Don't* you call my mother anymore with threats, you hear? And if you didn't do it, some other man there did. You can send this message up your chain of command: *Leave my mother out of this.* Clearly you thought you could intimidate me by using her. Guess what—all you've done is made me madder."

I clacked the receiver hard into its base. A moment passed as I glared across the apartment, wondering what to do next.

My stomach groaned with hunger, and tiredness hit. But I couldn't eat or rest now. Anger still coursed through me, and I needed to channel it. I had to do something.

That poor woman—dumped in a suitcase. And she'd fit so easily. She'd really have to be petite. Shorter than I thought.

A realization surfaced. I raised my chin. These were details I could use. Black suitcase + woman + murder. Maybe I'd find something online . . .

I headed into the second bedroom to fire up my computer.

Chapter 11

THE COMPUTER TOOK FOREVER TO BOOT UP. I RESTED MY forehead against my hand, trying to gather all the details of the murder in my mind. Then I pulled out a pad of paper. I needed to write down everything I knew so far. What the furniture in the room looked like, and the kitchen. The woman's description and her clothes. The suitcase. Had I seen a brand name on it? I closed my eyes, trying to remember.

Nothing.

My Google home page came up on my monitor. I kept writing—everything I'd seen, and in the order the details had come. I looked over my notes, filling in blanks until I couldn't think of a single thing I'd missed. Finally I turned to the computer.

I typed in my search: black suitcase + woman + murder. Hit *Enter*.

Over 4.5 million results.

I gawked at the screen. How could I possibly look through all these cases?

My eyes fell on the top one: *"Former air steward arrested over murder of woman found in suitcase at Heathrow."* It was a murder in Britain in

2010. I clicked on the link. The victim was blonde. Not the woman in my visions. I returned to the search page.

"*Woman's body found in Sydney park, teen charged with murder, sexual assault.*"

This case was from March 2011. Could the man's hands that I'd seen belong to a nineteen-year-old? I doubted it. The murder was in Australia. No picture of the victim, but I'd seen nothing about sexual assault in my visions.

"*A woman suspect in the Sandra Cantu murder case.*" This victim was only eight. Such a beautiful child. And a *female* did this? I clicked out of the link as fast as I could, sickened.

"*Police looking for murderer of woman stuffed in suitcase.*" The victim was twenty-eight, no picture. The suitcase was found in Harlem. Had the dark-haired woman I'd seen been that young? I didn't think so. Probably more in her later thirties. Besides, the victim in this case had been strangled to death—nothing about a stab in the chest.

On down the list I went. Many of the other results covered the same crimes. For over an hour I read about murder and gore and bloody suitcases, but nothing fit the pictures in my head. Finally I couldn't take any more. Nausea rose in my stomach. I hurried to the bathroom and slammed back the toilet lid to throw up. There wasn't much in my stomach to part with. Afterward, weak and shaking, I curled up on my bed and hugged myself. The left side of my head around the stitches throbbed.

Now what was I supposed to do? The murder I kept seeing apparently didn't exist.

Maybe the visions weren't real at all. Maybe Jerry Sterne was right—they were panic attacks, my brain conjuring them up.

But it wasn't just what I felt in my brain. In my gut I knew those scenes had happened. They were just too real.

Fine, Lisa. Prove it.

I rolled on my back and stared at the ceiling.

Maybe the woman's body hadn't been found yet. Maybe the man had buried it somewhere, and now her family was going crazy, wondering what happened to her. If that was true, I *had* to find her. For their sake.

But where to look?

I should change my online search for articles about a missing woman. But I didn't know where she lived, or when. The hits would be astronomical.

Wait. The dragon ring.

I pushed myself off the bed. For the first few seconds I swayed. I still needed to eat. But later. First I dragged myself back to the computer. In Google Chrome I typed in "dragon ring." Four hundred twenty-seven thousand results came up.

My shoulders sagged.

The ring I'd seen on the killer's hand was big and ugly. Gold, with glittering emeralds for eyes. Looked like it was worth a lot of money. But the first links I followed showed rings made of pewter and silver. And they were cheap. Others included gems, but they didn't look the same at all.

Many of the links mentioned a fantasy story or some game associated with the rings. Could the man in my visions be part of that world? His house was big and expensive, so was the furniture. Didn't fit with someone who sat around and played computer games. Maybe he owned a company that made them?

I sat back in my chair and sighed. This wasn't working.

If I only knew who the woman was. I could picture her face so well. But how to look for one face in a world of people?

And the biggest question of all: If these visions really were memories from that killer, *how* did they get on my chip? Someone would have to transfer them over from his brain. Which was crazy. And probably impossible.

Or was it?

I could search that, too.

My fingers typed in "brain chip" and hit *Enter*. I'd done this one before, out of curiosity when I first began interviewing for the Empowerment Chip trial. The same articles came up. Ones about chips that allowed people to move a robotic arm just by thought. Or enabled a monkey to reach for a banana via a mechanical arm merely by thinking about it. The computer chip maker Intel reportedly wanted to design a brain-sensing chip that its customers could use to operate a computer without a keyboard or mouse, using thoughts alone. (Undergo brain surgery, just for *that*?) There were chips the size of a grain of rice that could be implanted to track people. Or function as a smart code to allow them access into secure sites. And the chips I'd read about to treat Parkinson's.

I refined the search: "brain chip" + "memory transfer." I didn't expect much. But over 34,000 hits popped up.

A vision surged into my head. The dead woman, folded into the suitcase. The man's hand closing it. I could almost hear the bite of its zipper.

No, go away! I shook it off and forced myself to concentrate on the search.

The first page of hits were all about one research project, posted in June 2011: "Scientists successfully implant chip that controls the brain: allowing thoughts, memory and behavior to be transferred from one brain to another."

My nerves tingled. I clicked on one of the links.

"Scientists working at the University of Southern California, home of the Department of Homeland Security's National Center for Risk and Economic Analysis of Terrorism Events, have created an artificial memory system . . ."

The research had been done on rats that learned to press one of two levers for water. Future plans called for research in monkeys. Human trials were far into the future. Dr. Theodore Berger and his team had worked with scientists from Wake Forest University, focusing on the brain's hippocampus area, which converts short-term memory into long-term memory during the learning process . . .

My brain swam. I dropped my head in my hands. This science was beyond me. All I knew was if this technology *was* possible, Cognoscenti had taken it to greater heights—and into humans.

Into me.

But it still sounded crazy.

And even if they had, what could I do about it? Who was I to fight against them?

I forced myself to click on another link. It talked about research similar to Dr. Berger's, but more along the lines of knowledge transfer. In the future, the article said, it could be possible to download information from one person onto a chip and implant it into another person's brain, allowing the recipient to have "instant knowledge" from the chip. Say someone wanted to learn French. No more needing to study for hours. Just pay for a chip loaded with the data of how to speak the language.

This stuff sounded like science fiction.

I read on. The research was based on the understanding that knowledge is actually memory, the article said. The cerebral cortex appeared to act as the major repository for long-term memory. And memories are formed through changes in the synapses between nerve cells. Once a data-loaded chip was implanted into a brain, the data would begin to release, fanning out over nerves and across synapses to re-create the memories in the recipient's brain. The major hurdle to creating such a chip was learning how to translate brain waves into encodable data, sort of like the binary system of zeroes and ones for computers but far more complicated—

The phone rang. I jerked toward the sound. My mother again?

A second ring. And third. Sighing, I made my way to the kitchen counter. Why did I still use this landline, anyway? Ryan was the one who'd insisted on it. I could cancel it now, just use my cell phone.

Not a bad idea.

Look at me. Even fighting these horrible visions, I was thinking about my future. Planning things on my own terms. I couldn't do that if I was still depressed.

That chip was no placebo.

I picked up the phone and checked the ID. My eyes widened.

Clair Saxton.

Chapter 12

I STARED AT THE RECEIVER, STEELING MYSELF. WHATEVER this woman wanted, it couldn't be good. And that ID showing up—was she calling from her cell?

Just before my auto answer could click on, I picked up the phone. "Hello." I didn't even try to hide the suspicion in my tone.

"Lisa? This is Clair Saxton."

I headed toward the couch. "Hi."

"A little while ago I heard the message you left on Jerry Sterne's line. When he got it he called me into his office to ask if I knew anything about you getting a phone call. I didn't."

I reached the sofa and sank into it.

"I checked with Richard Price, our V.P. He knew nothing of the call either."

How convenient. "So you're denying it happened?"

She hesitated. "What exactly did the caller say?"

"The caller was a man. He left a message with my mother for me. Three words. 'Don't do it.'"

"'Don't do it?'" She sounded shocked.

"Tell me something, Clair. Do you have my mother's phone number in your file on me?"

"I don't know."

"Well, I can tell you, you don't. Because I never gave it to anyone. Which means someone at Cognoscenti had to go looking for it. When he could have just called me directly. Why do you suppose someone would do that?"

"This is . . . I really can't think why that would happen."

"Well, it did. And it sounds like quite a threat, wouldn't you say?"

"Lisa, hear me. I don't know who would do that. No one here has any knowledge of this."

Uh-huh. "Why are *you* calling me? Why not Jerry?"

"He's tied up in meetings. He asked me to look into this."

"And so you have. Now what are you going to do about it?"

"I don't know what else I can do about it." Her voice chilled. "Because that call did not originate from us. If it really happened at all, someone else placed it."

If it really happened at all? My jaw worked. "So now I'm making this up? Just like I made up the visions I've seen of a murder. Which I'm still seeing, by the way."

"We offered you help for that. You declined."

I pressed back against the couch. "What do you want from me?"

"I called you to get to the bottom of this. You left no explanation in your message."

"I didn't think I had to—seeing as how the threat came from your company."

"We are *not* threatening you, Ms. Newberry. We have not and never *will* threaten you."

"Then who called my mother? All the way in Denver."

"I have no idea. I can only tell you it wasn't anyone at Cognoscenti."

"Right. Just like the chip you implanted in me was a placebo."

A disgusted sigh blew over the line. "Clearly you are nursing some sort of vendetta against Cognoscenti. I am very sorry for that. I called to set your mind at ease, but since you show no sign of listening, it's time to end this conversation."

"Ever seen a dragon's head ring?" It was a detail I hadn't told her and Jerry.

"What?"

"Big gold thing with emeralds for eyes."

"Why are you asking me this?"

"The man in the visions I'm seeing wears it. The murderer."

A beat passed. Her animosity pulsed over the line. "Ms. Newberry, you need help."

Tell me about it.

Anger pushed me to my feet. "That chip you put in me is doing this. I *have* to get it taken out. And I'm going to find out how this terrible defect happened in the first place. And why. I can't stand by and let you do this to other people."

"And I won't stand by and let you attempt to ruin the technology I know can save people's lives!"

I thrust a hand into my hair. Thing was—I agreed with her. The Empowerment Chip *could* help people. It had changed me. "I know it can." The edge in my tone smoothed a little. "It's just that something happened to mine. Something you all couldn't have foreseen. A bug, a defect that needs to be fixed. If you'd just listen to me. We could work together, try to figure out—"

"Do you know why I believe in the Empowerment Chip so strongly, Ms. Newberry? I'll tell you why." Ice Queen's tone intensified. "I've seen it work in people who were emotionally crippled. In PTSD patients who couldn't even hold a job. In men who'd come back from Iraq, utterly broken. My own father returned from the Korean War like that. My mother, brother, and I—we longed for my father's return, only to see he'd never be the same again. Three years after coming back to us, he took his own life. If only he'd had the Empowerment Chip. His death, his funeral is burned into my memory. Our chip can keep that from happening. Can keep other fathers—and mothers—from giving up hope. No other child should have to go through what I did."

The words bit into me. So this was the reason behind Clair Saxton's cold armor. As surely as my childhood had molded me, Ice Queen's had molded her. In a strange way that united us. And we'd both lost our fathers at an early age. But childhood experiences ran deep. Because of her past, she could no more change her belief in the chip than I could deny the lingering effects of my mother. No matter what, Clair Saxton would cling to her narrow focus of protecting Cognoscenti, blind to any truth that its hot new product could be seriously defective.

And that made her my enemy.

My spine stiffened. "I'm very sorry for what you went through." And I was. "Just don't let it color your judgment."

Before she could reply, I hung up.

I crossed to the counter to put down the phone—

The man's hand reached for the zipper. Pulled it shut around the suit-case. For a moment the hand paused, dragon ring shining in the light.

He took hold of a handle at the left side of the bag. Raised it upright until the suitcase rested on its wheels. I heard the woman's body shift toward the bottom.

The man pulled out the suitcase's long black handle. Rolled it toward a door, painted off-white. I saw his feet in brown shoes, his legs as he drew back the door and propped it open with a stopper. He pulled the suitcase through the door into a garage.

The scene faded.

Every inch of me shook. Even with the scene gone, I could still hear the sound of that woman's body shifting in the suitcase. He was going to take her somewhere. Dump her like trash.

My right hand still held the phone. I dropped it into its base with a clatter. I hovered over the counter, afraid to move, afraid that more scenes would come.

Nothing.

Slowly my lungs filled with air. Dizziness washed over me. I really needed to eat. If I didn't, I'd surely fall over. I made my way to the refrigerator and pulled out a yogurt, some ham slices and cheese. Slumped in a chair at the table, I forced the food down, barely tasting.

I *had* to get this chip out of my brain. Now. I couldn't stand another day of this. Without Cognoscenti, I'd have to find another doctor to do it. Fortunately I had the money, thanks to Ryan's life insurance.

Except—then what? My depression would surge back. The thought nearly drove me to the floor. I couldn't bear that either.

What was I going to do?

Somehow I'd fight the depression. Somehow. At least I knew that enemy. These visions—every time I saw more details of the murder, I understood them less. If they weren't real, how could my brain just keep making them up on its own? And yet—how *could* they be real?

The food had disappeared. I drank a glass of water.

The black suitcase roared back into my mind. At first I tried to shove it away, but the rational side of me snagged on the new clues. The man had pulled that bag into a garage. He'd probably put it in a car and driven it somewhere. Would I see him doing that in some future vision? If I could just see the car's make and license plate . . .

I glanced at the clock on the kitchen wall. After 3:00 already. I needed to start looking for a new doctor. But how does someone find a brain surgeon? It's not like they're in the phone book. Wouldn't I need some kind of referral just to get an appointment?

Exhaustion hit me, just like that. I didn't have the strength for this search, not now. Instead I went to the couch and lay down. Sleep pulled at me, but I was afraid to drift off. What if someone broke into the apartment? What if the murderer in my visions came here, for me?

More paranoia, Lisa. And completely illogical. Even if the man was real, he couldn't know that I knew what he'd done. That alone kept me safe.

But if I tried to stop Cognoscenti from putting the Empowerment Chip on the market, and the media got hold of the story—the man may very well find out. What would he do with that knowledge?

From somewhere in my mind, three words surfaced: *Knowledge is memory.*

I stilled. Those words—they were important.

Where had I heard them? Or had I been reading it on the computer before Clair Saxton's call?

Knowledge is memory . . .

Shaking off my tiredness I rose from the couch and headed for the computer. The screen saver was on, rolling random photos. Ryan smiled at me, squinting, on a pristine beach in the Bahamas. A honeymoon picture.

My heart crimped.

A push of the mouse, and my husband's face blitzed off. The monitor filled with the article I'd been reading about the instant knowledge chip. My eyes flicked down the paragraphs. There. *"Knowledge is memory . . . Data releases from a chip to create the same memories in the recipient . . ."*

Wait . . . what? I read the paragraph again. Then backed up and read it a third time in context. And a fourth. Somewhere along the way its meaning sank in.

It was too late to find a doctor.

I sat back in my chair and stared glassy-eyed at the monitor. No. *No.*

A fifth time I read the passage, begging to find another interpretation. But my fate was there in black and white. Even if I was right, if the chip in my brain did contain data from someone else, removing it wouldn't matter. The knowledge had flowed from that chip across my nerve synapses, becoming an integral part of me. Of my own brain.

The murderer's memories were now *my* memories.

Forever.

Chapter 13

THE REMAINING HOURS OF THAT AFTERNOON MELTED into each other. One minute I hugged myself on the couch. In the next I paced the floor. Twice I found myself back in bed, curled into a fetal position. The new reality sank into me like steel sinking in the ocean. When it hit bottom it dug in deep.

I would never be rid of the terrible memories.

Memories and experiences—that's who we *are*. I thought of Jason Bourne in *The Bourne Identity*. He had no memories, and was utterly lost. Imagine if his brain had been filled with false memories. He'd have become someone entirely different. Yes, that was only fiction. But what I'd read online proved the science was real.

Here I was, remembering details of a murder. No matter what I did, they would haunt me for the rest of my life. How could I carry these horrible pictures in my head *for the rest of my life?*

That evening I tried to eat some soup. Mostly I just cried into the bowl. My head throbbed, and my body shook with chills. Wild thoughts of fleeing halfway across the world ran through my mind. Anything to make myself forget.

But how do you run away from your own brain?

In the evening Sherry called. The minute I saw her ID, guilt washed over me. I'd never phoned her back.

"Okay, Lisa." Her voice was firm. "The kids are in bed, and I can talk without being interrupted. And I *have* to know what's going on with you."

Of course she did. She was my best friend. Must have been worried sick all day. "I'm so sorry I didn't call. I just . . . so much has happened, and I didn't know how to deal with it. I want to tell you. I *need* you to help me. I just don't know what to *do*."

"What's going on? Is the chip working or not?

"Yes. But I keep seeing a murder."

"What?"

"A murder. Some man kills a woman. Strangles, then stabs her. He zips her body in a suitcase and takes it out to his garage. So far that's all I know. But I'm willing to bet more will come."

Silence splayed out, my best friend's shock simmering over the line. I could only let her stew in it.

"I'm coming over. Be there in ten minutes." Sherry hung up.

I set the phone down and dropped my head in my hands. "God, please help me." I poured out prayers, knowing God heard them. And He needed to do something. Just when I thought I was getting a new life—

The suitcase wheeled across the garage floor.

I jerked up, then went still, waiting.

The man rolled it toward the back of a black SUV. It had gold rims on the tires.

My eyes closed. The car!

He halted to open the hatchback. The door swung wide on perfectly oiled hinges—

A loud knock sounded at my door.

The scene scampered away.

No, no, come back. For once, details rather than fear crowded my head. Had I seen the make of the car?

A second knock. Had I been praying that long? Sherry had gotten here fast.

Sweat popped out on my skin. I swiped at my forehead and pushed up from the chair. Somehow I had to find the energy to explain all this to her.

My legs felt like lead as I approached the door. A third knock came, harder. "All right, all right." Hand on the knob, I checked through the peephole.

And saw my mother.

Chapter 14

I PULLED OPEN THE DOOR AND STARED AT MY MOTHER. SHE looked back in horror, her gaze drifting from my face to the bandage on my head. Before I could stop it my hand lifted to the stitches.

"Lisa, what happened to you?"

She was dressed in tan slacks, a gold knit top, and brown jacket. Looking so put together and perfect. A chic purse hung from one shoulder, a leather laptop case from the other. Next to her sat a black suitcase. I cringed at the sight of it.

"What are you doing here?"

She eyed me a moment longer, then reached for the handle of her suitcase. "Is that any way to greet your mother?" With a flick of her hand she motioned me to move back. Robot-like, I obeyed. She wheeled her bag into the apartment. I closed the door.

We looked at each other some more. Any remaining energy I'd had drained out my feet.

She straightened her back. "I came to take care of you. And clearly you need it."

Not from you.

At my telling silence Mom's mouth opened, then closed. She glanced past the living room. "As I remember, you have an extra bedroom."

She'd stayed with me when she came for Ryan's funeral. "Yes. The computer's in there."

She gave me a look.

"And a bed, too, I mean."

A corner of her mouth lifted. "Good. I'll just put my things in there. First on the right?"

I nodded.

I watched her go. When she returned I still stood there.

She put her hands on her hips. "Looks to me like you should get off your feet."

No kidding. A heart attack about now wouldn't surprise me. I headed for the couch.

The minute I sat something clicked inside me. Why was I acting like this just because she'd shown up? I wasn't the scared child I'd once been, trembling in my mother's presence for fear of the next cutting remark. It was high time I got over that.

My mother took a seat in Ryan's armchair and looked me over. For a split second some emotion—reticence? fright?—flicked across her face.

Or had I imagined that?

"Lisa, what happened to you?" Her voice softened. "Please don't tell me you were attacked a second time."

There it was again, in her tone. My mother was actually afraid for me.

It took a moment to gather myself. "Nothing like that." I rubbed my palm over the couch cushion. "I . . . had a medical procedure, and I'm still recovering."

"What kind of—"

Another knock at the door. Mom's head swiveled toward it. "You expecting someone?"

"Sherry."

"Oh." A terse response that dripped with the memory of their last caustic exchange at Ryan's funeral. "You should have told me she was coming."

That comment deserved no response.

I walked to the door on wooden legs. Oh, man. My mother was enough, but with Sherry in the room? I opened the door with trepidation. "Hi, Sherry. Guess what? Mom's here."

Sherry's chin dipped. She gave me a look through the tops of her eyeballs.

"Didn't know she was coming." My words turned tinny. "But hey, what perfect timing for the three of us to talk."

My mother turned in the chair, her back regal-straight, and gave my friend a cool nod. "Hello."

Sherry crossed the threshold, glancing from me to her. "Hello, Ms. Wegland." She knew my mother hated being called that. Made her feel old.

"Alice. Please."

I closed the door and ran home the deadbolt. Sherry and my mother eyed each other. Maybe I should just go to bed. Let them fight this thing out.

"Come on." I tugged at Sherry's sleeve. "Sit down with us."

She followed me to the couch. I ended up on the side closest to my mother, sandwiched between them. Terrific.

"Mom just got here. After you called." I shot Sherry a look—*Please be civil.*

"I hopped on the first plane I could." Mom sounded almost defensive. "After that threatening phone call about Lisa today, and her not telling me what was happening—"

"Threatening phone call?" Sherry rounded her eyes at me.

"It wasn't really. Well, yes it was." I took a deep breath. Now I'd have to tell both of them everything. I didn't have the strength.

"I *know* it was, since I'm the one who heard it." Mom's tone edged. "Lisa, I expect——"

"Stop." I raised my hand, palm out. Mom's words cut off. I hung there, surprised at my own power. She'd actually *listened*. "Okay." Now what to say? Where did I go from here? "First some ground rules."

My mother's head drew back. "Ground rules?"

At her raised eyebrows, I almost caved. Then steeled myself. "You know fifty percent of what's happened." I pointed at Sherry, then turned to Mom. "And you know hardly anything. I have to fill you both in. And I don't want interruptions. I'm too tired for that. And I *really* don't want judgments."

Sherry gave my mother a hard look.

Mom raised her chin. "I didn't drop my own life and work responsibilities to come here and judge you."

I locked eyes with her, firming my lips. Couldn't she see her mere showing up unannounced was a judgment that I couldn't take care of myself? "Are we clear?"

Mom leaned back with a huff and plopped her arms on the sides of the chair.

"Is that a yes?"

She paused a long beat. "Yes."

I tilted my head. "Sherry?"

"Of course."

Well, just look at me. Handling this situation, even while my insides felt like a limp rag. "Okay." I leaned back against the couch and laced my hands in my lap. "Mom, three days ago I had a chip implanted in my brain. I'd——"

"*What?*"

My hand shot up. Mom froze. I calmed myself, then continued in a rush before she could stop me again. I told her the who, what, where, when, and why. She didn't interrupt again. But she did shoot a glance at Sherry as if to say, *You let her do this?* Sherry ignored her.

"The chip is working." I told Mom how much better I felt. "But in the hospital I started having these strange visions."

I leaned against the couch and took a breath. Tiredness rushed through me, but I beat it back. I told them everything about the murder, my return to Cognoscenti—was that just this morning?—and Jerry and Clair's response. When I told them Cognoscenti said my chip was a placebo, Sherry gasped.

"Yeah. I know. But I don't believe it." I went on to the phone call Mom received, and the call I shot back to Jerry. My conversation with Ice Queen. My searches on the Internet. And my final stunning realization that the gory memories were mine forever.

By the time I finished, my mouth ran dry and my shoulders sagged. And I knew my mother would say I'd gone completely nuts.

Pent-up words clearly beat against her tongue.

"Cognoscenti." The name burst out of her. "That's the company that called, all right. How *dare* they threaten you like that. And through me!"

I gaped at her. Of all the responses she could have shown, anger on my behalf was the last I'd expected.

Mom's lips thinned. "I'll just have to do something about this. Your threat to them wasn't so crazy, Lisa. Maybe we do need the media involved."

"Uh-uh," Sherry said. Mom ignored her.

My mother was publicity director for a large tech firm in Denver. She knew all about using the media. But I couldn't focus on that. I could only think—She *believes* me? I didn't want to move for fear I'd break the spell.

Mom's gaze darted around the room—a clear sign she was thinking hard. Her eyes grazed mine, flitted away, then back. "Why are you looking at me like that?"

My shoulders rose. "I just . . . I wasn't sure you'd believe me."

"Why shouldn't I believe you? My daughter doesn't lie. Besides, it's written all over your face—you're terrified."

This was almost too much to take in. "Maybe I *am* going crazy. Having panic attacks, like Jerry said."

Sherry grunted. "Mighty big coincidence, sudden panic attacks right after the surgery."

Mom pressed her hand against the top of my knee. "I knew before I got here you were in trouble. That's why I came. That phone call was clearly threatening. Companies don't make calls like that unless they're in major hot water. I thought you'd gotten into some whistle-blowing situation. And basically, you have. But I'm here to help you now. I'll find the right investigative reporter—"

"But you can't. Don't you see how Cognoscenti would roll over me? They're too big, and I'm nobody. I don't want my face splashed all over the media as some half insane woman who's mad that she got a 'placebo.'"

"Lisa." Mom leaned closer. "Listen to me. I don't ever want to hear you say again that you're a nobody. You're *not* a nobody. You can accomplish whatever you set your mind to."

My mouth fell open. What had happened to my critical mother? The one who'd always been so disappointed in me?

"Think of all the stories around the world of one person bringing down a company," she said. "Or changing a law. Making some kind of difference. Or a small group bringing down a corrupt government. It starts with a single man or woman who's got guts, and moves out from there. You're telling me you've now got emotional strength you didn't have a week ago. Do you really believe that?"

"I—yes."

"And didn't you go through all the trouble of a brain implant in order to change your life? So you could forge ahead with whatever you need to do? Which in this case means stopping a company before it hurts other people."

I managed a tiny nod.

"Then why aren't you willing to do that?"

Because I was petrified. Because I didn't know what was happening to me.

My mother pressed harder against my knee. "Lisa. You have a choice here. For once in your life, fight."

Sherry stiffened. "She *has* fought. She's dealt with more than you—"

"I didn't mean that." Mom glared at Sherry, spots of color forming on her cheeks. "I know she's dealt with a lot. And she did show courage by getting the implant in the first place. But now it's time to use it."

I felt suddenly light-headed. Where had my energy gone? Up to the ceiling maybe. Spread out on the floor. My vision started to blur.

"Lisa." Mom grabbed my chin. "Do you *want* to keep being a victim?"

My bleary eyes fought to focus. "No."

"Then don't be." Mom stuck her face inches from mine. I could smell her powder. "The Empowerment Chip has worked, but it's got a major flaw. Cognoscenti has lied to you and threatened you. Clearly they've got something to hide. And you may be the only one outside the company who knows it."

The world dulled. "I need to go to bed."

"Fine. I'll carry you there myself. Just tell me you're going to fight this thing. I'll be right by your side."

Oh wonderful.

"Tell me, Lisa."

"Uh-huh." My words almost slurred. "Okay."

My mother shot me a keen look, then let go of my chin. She stood. "Come on." Her voice gentled. "I'll take you to bed."

I turned toward Sherry. "You—"

"She can let herself out." Mom held out her hand to me.

I winced at her curt dismissal of my best friend. Sherry's mouth was pinched. But I had no energy to deal with this tonight. "I'm sorry, Sherry. I'm so tired. Can we talk tomorrow?"

"Yeah. Sure." She stood.

As my mother helped me to my room, I heard the apartment's front door open and close.

TUESDAY, MARCH 13

Chapter 15

I WOKE TUESDAY MORNING REFRESHED FROM A NIGHT OF deep sleep. I couldn't even remember dreaming. And no new visions of a murdered woman had run through my head. No black suitcase.

Except for the memory of my mother's, rolling through my front door.

I groaned. My first thought was to burrow my head beneath my pillow. Stay in bed all day. Instead I pulled myself up and slipped into a robe.

Stumbling into the kitchen, I found Mom already dressed and looking perky, sitting at the table. Her makeup was just so, as was her hair. Didn't she ever just wallow around in her pajamas? Spread before her were my notes on everything I'd seen in the murder visions. I headed toward the coffee she'd made and poured myself a cup. Sat at the table opposite her. Should I say something about Sherry? I didn't want to start an argument first thing in the morning.

"Those aren't complete." I gestured toward the notepad. "The final visions I told you about last night—I saw them just before you came."

She peered at me. "You feel better?"

"Yeah."

"Stronger?"

I couldn't feel any worse than last night. "Uh-huh."

"Good." She got up, fetched a pen, and returned. Pushed the last page of my notes toward me. "Add what's missing."

I gave her a hard look.

"What?"

"Mom. You don't need to command me like some sergeant. I hate it when you do that."

Whoa, Lisa. Had I really said that?

Mom held my gaze, her head at a slight tilt, as if assessing me. "All right." She gestured toward the paper—*so go ahead.*

Well, that was . . . something anyway.

I picked up the pen and forced myself to focus on the last vision—the man's shoes, the garage, the car and its wheels.

Mom read it when I was done. "No license plate?"

"No."

"Make of the car?"

"I don't know. Other than it's a black SUV."

She looked out the window, thinking. I drank my coffee, feeling renewed energy flow through me. My mind ran clearer.

Mom leaned back in her chair. "I'm so sorry about this. These are terrible memories for you to carry around."

"Tell me about it."

"All the more reason to stop Cognoscenti."

"I told you I would."

"You didn't seem to mean it."

Heat rolled through me. "I was *exhausted*, Mom! Cut me a break. I've just had brain surgery. And I've never had someone else's memory of killing a person invade my head."

Besides, she'd showed up at my door uninvited. Why couldn't she at least have called first? This was *my* apartment. My life.

Hurt flicked across my mother's forehead, as if she sensed my thoughts. "What do you want from me, Lisa?"

Oh, man, where to begin?

"Do you want me to leave?"

I sighed. "I didn't say that."

"It's on your face."

I turned to focus on the counter across the kitchen. Of course I wanted her to leave.

Didn't I?

Mom rose. She wouldn't look at me. "I'll go pack my things."

"No. Wait."

She set her coffee cup in the sink, chin high.

"Mom, don't."

She whirled around, a fist grinding into her hip. "I just wanted to help you! I just wanted to help my daughter after all that's happened to you."

"Then *help* me." I stood up, pushing my chair back. "Stand beside me. Not in front, pulling me along. Or in back, pushing me. Don't tell me what to do. Don't make me feel worthless!" Tears crept into my eyes.

Air seeped from her. "Is that what you thought last night?" She waited for an answer, but I couldn't reply. She flicked a look toward the ceiling. "When I insisted you could do whatever you set your mind to—how did that make you feel worthless?'"

My gaze dropped to the table. "It . . . didn't."

"Then what?"

I raised my eyes to meet my mother's. We faced off across the kitchen, across my lifetime. How to tell her of the memories from childhood that would forever pinch my heart? "You haven't seemed to understand me since I lost the babies, then Ryan. Then the attack." My voice thickened. "You kept insisting I move back to Denver. That I wasn't getting on my feet quickly enough."

"I was just trying to protect you. Make you better."

Didn't work, did it.

My mother started to say more, then closed her mouth. Silence filled the corners of the room.

"So." She dropped her arm to her side. "Will my being here help you? Or not."

I searched her face. She still didn't understand, did she? If I told her everything she'd done during my childhood that put me down, she'd never see it that way. But truth was, I didn't know how to fight Cognoscenti on my own. Sherry had her own life, with two small kids. As much as she wanted to help, I couldn't count a lot on her.

My lips curved into a wan smile. "It'll help."

"You sure?"

"I'm sure."

Mom dipped her chin in a decisive nod. "Good." Her back straightened, that all-business aura once again bristling around her shoulders. "Because I've got a plan."

Chapter 16

STEP ONE, MY MOTHER DECLARED, WAS FINDING THE IDEN-
tity of the murdered woman. But only I knew what the woman
looked like. If Mom was to help me find her, we needed a picture.

Mom set her laptop up in the kitchen, telling me to use my own
computer. "No." She caught herself. "I mean—you might want to
use your own computer too, so the work will go faster."

Well, what do you know?

My chin raised in a nod. I stood at the sink, dressed, putting the
last breakfast plate in the dishwasher. Mom had insisted I eat. "What
work exactly?"

"We need to search online for forensic artists in this area who
can sketch the victim's face."

I frowned. "Won't we have to go through the police for that kind
of service?" That's the last thing I wanted to do.

"Many forensic artists are laypeople who contract with the
police. That's who we've got to find. Thank goodness you live in a
big metropolitan area."

Six million people ought to include someone we could use. "But don't they have better things to do than help me?"

"They help find criminals, don't they?" Mom stuck her fist on her hip. "You're looking for a murderer."

It seemed like such a big step, and once we did it, we were committed. "Yes, but—"

"Lisa. You can do this."

We locked eyes. Finally I nodded.

So we got down to work. Over the next hour we followed online hits, reading news stories about various forensic artists who worked on local crimes. Many were police officers. But two were not. Mom called the first one. No answer. She left a message.

I was back with her in the kitchen, mentally beating myself up for being so hesitant. What had happened to the Lisa of yesterday who'd stormed down to Cognoscenti? Who'd given it straight to Ice Queen over the phone? "I'll call the next—"

The SUV's hatchback door yawned open.

I gasped and froze.

"Lisa?" Mom started toward me.

My hand shot up—*Wait.*

The man pushed down the long pull bar of the suitcase. He gripped the front and side handles, grunting. The bag was heavy. He strained it upward, edging it into the hatchback, face up. Pushed it in farther until it cleared the door.

He stood back, panting. Then closed up the car. His eyes swept across the first part of the license plate.

6WB.

The man returned into his house . . .

The scene shimmered, then blitzed away. I found myself staring wide-eyed at a cabinet. My knees turned rubbery. I sank into a chair at the table.

"What happened?" My mother stood over me, hands at her neck.

"I . . . water."

She brought me a glass. I gulped it down.

"He . . . I saw more. It's important." I fumbled for my notes and wrote down the number and letters, my heart still beating double time. "6WB. The beginning of his license plate."

"Oh!"

Oh was right. Finally I had something solid to go on.

But if I found the man, actually proved he was real—then what?

"Did you see the state on the license plate?" my mom pressed.

I thought about it, hoping. "No."

I leaned my head into my hands, the scene still grinding through me. The man had walked out of the garage, back into his house. Like nothing had happened. He'd left her there, shut up in that suitcase.

This man was a monster.

"What else did you see?" Mom sat across from me, leaning over the table.

I told her all of it. "Every time it happens it's so *real*." I wiped away a tear. "I hear it, see it."

Mom watched me. "Do you sense what *he's* feeling about it?"

I hadn't even thought about that. "Should I?"

"You think these are his memories, right? So they should contain more than just what he sees and hears. They should include his emotions."

She was right. My hands clasped, one thumb rubbing over the other. "I don't feel anything he does. Only what *I* feel." Why was that? "I guess my own horrified reaction to it all just . . . overpowers the rest."

"Or he simply feels nothing. A sociopath."

I clutched my temples. "I have to get this out of my head. I can't stand it. What if it plays over and over—forever? And what if this is just one woman in many he's killed, and I start seeing *new* murders?"

That thought withered me.

Mom put a hand on my arm. I blinked at the table, still feeling woozy. A loud car passed on the street below. In the distance a dog barked.

What were they planning against me at Cognoscenti right now? *"Don't do it."* Were they devising ways to keep me quiet?

While my breathing returned to normal, Mom called the second forensic artist—and hit pay dirt. Agnes Brighton was between freelance jobs, she said, and could meet with us in the apartment at one o'clock. After a session of one to two hours, we would have a sketch of our woman. Agnes wanted to know what the woman had done, why we weren't working with the police. "We need more evidence before we approach them," my mother told her. Apparently that was enough for Agnes. They talked for another minute or so, then hung up.

The cost: $300.

I waved away Mom's offer to help pay for it. "It'll come out of the life insurance money. I can afford it."

We had only two hours before Agnes arrived. I went back to bed and slept for forty-five minutes. Yesterday I had way overextended myself. Now I was paying for it.

When I got up I found my mother still at the kitchen table, poring over my notes. She barely looked up at me. "6WB—the first part of his license plate."

Not—*How was your nap? Feel better?*

I sat down at the table.

"You sure it was the first part?" she asked. "Not the middle or end."

I closed my eyes, trying to recall. "It's the beginning." My eyes flew open. "You know what—it sounds like California. I think new cars here start with a six or seven. And that SUV looks pretty new."

My nerves began to vibrate. No, please, any state but California. The man couldn't be that close to me.

"California license plates are long, aren't they? Do you sense how many numbers and letters there were altogether?"

"No." For all I knew there were only five in total, making the plate from some smaller state.

"What was the background color?"

"White." I knew that for sure.

"And the color of the letters?"

"Dark blue."

The scene twitched in my head. The suitcase, lying in that car. Where was he going to take it? What gut-wrenching things would I have to witness next?

"You sure?"

"I know it. Like I was there." I *had* been there.

My mother nodded. "All right then. Let's see if we can find the state." She tapped her keyboard, two furrows between her eyes.

I went to the sink for water.

"Look at this!" She eyed the monitor in triumph. "First site that comes up—'License Plates—1969 to present'."

"For all fifty states?"

"Yes." She tapped the keyboard. "Here's the page for California." She hit the return key as I moved to look over her shoulder. "Here's the last one. But it only goes up to 2007. Guess the site isn't real new." She pointed at the screen. The plate's background was white with dark blue letters and numbers, seven in all. The sequence started with 5, followed by three letters, then three numbers. "Does that look like what you saw?"

Absolutely. Which both terrified and excited me. "It fits. Except by now we're up to beginning with at least six. Maybe seven, I don't know."

Mom considered the screen. "If this is it, he lives in California. And the murder is at least as recent as whenever the number six license plates started."

I sank into the chair beside her, unable to respond. If Mom hadn't shown up, would I have figured this out on my own? It was one thing to believe the murder was real. But to *prove* it . . . Maybe I didn't want to go through with this, especially if the man lived in California. Maybe I should just let it be.

Mom checked the kitchen clock. "We've got an hour until the artist comes. Let's divide up the states and see if any others could be a match."

Hope stirred. Maybe one would match. I'd take Maine. Or Florida.

I returned to my computer, found the Web site and started with New Hampshire. Mom began with the *A*s. After searching for some time, Mom found no states that could be a match. In my states, Virginia plates had a white background with dark blue writing, but the first three places were all letters. Only West Virginia plates used the same colors, with the format of a first number followed by two letters. But the plates also had a yellow line just above the letters and numbers. I couldn't remember seeing anything like that. In fact I remembered the starkness of the white background.

"It has to be California." I was back at the kitchen table, a hand at my forehead. Not liking this at all.

Mom nodded. "Makes sense I suppose. The company's here. Easier for the data to wind up on a chip from someone nearby."

"But who knows where the chip was manufactured? Could have been anywhere." My voice wavered. I needed to pull myself together. "Anyway, *how* did the memories get on the chip in the first place?"

My mother pushed her lips together. "It had to have been a mistake. That murderer certainly wouldn't want anyone to know what he's done. Much less see it all in living color. But how a glitch like that happened, I can't imagine."

We exchanged a long look.

Someone knocked on the door. Mom's face brightened. "Our artist is here." She rose.

"Check through the peephole first."

She waved a hand at me—*of course*.

A minute later Agnes Brighton entered the apartment—a woman in perhaps her midsixties with short gray hair and a weathered face. Dark, intense eyes. She stood tall and stocky, with determination, and carried a sizeable portfolio. She set it down on my kitchen counter, sticking her hand out toward me. "Hi. I'm Agnes."

"Lisa Newberry." I shook her hand.

She looked around. "You want to work at the kitchen table?"

"I guess. If that's comfortable for you."

"Oh, I'm fine. Question is, will you be comfortable?" She peered at me. "You're the one describing the face, right?"

I nodded. "I'll be fine there."

"All righty, then. Let's get to it."

Mom and I exchanged a glance. This was a no-nonsense woman.

"Would you like something to drink?" Mom asked as Agnes carried her portfolio to the table.

"No thanks. I'll be concentrating." She took a seat.

Stiffly, I sat across from her. What if this didn't work? What if I couldn't describe the face I kept seeing?

What if it *did* work?

Mom took the chair between us. Agnes began pulling out various pencils, a large book of some kind, and an eleven-by-fourteen-inch pad of paper. "First, as I understand it, you are not a victim, correct? The face you're about to describe to me is not linked to a traumatic event in your life?"

I hesitated. Seeing the murder was traumatic, but I knew what Agnes meant. This was nothing like trying to tell the policeman about the man who'd attacked me. Then I'd been besieged by fear yet had nothing to tell. I'd never even seen his face. "That's right."

"Good. Makes it much easier on you." Agnes flashed me a smile, softening her face. She set out more pencils. "I'm going to be using a technique called a composite-specific interview." As if by habit Agnes's voice had fallen to a comforting cadence, one that would soothe a victim. "I'll draw the basic proportions of the face as you remember them. Then we'll layer in the details using pictures from the FBI *Facial Identification Catalog.*" She tapped the large book. "At first I'll just let you talk. Tell me everything you can remember. Then we'll work from there. Just relax. We'll do fine together."

I nodded.

She waved a hand over her ready materials. "This pad I use is of Bristol paper. It's a smooth finish, which allows me to draw with more detail than a rougher paper would. These pencils are both hard and soft lead. I'll use the more rounded ones for the initial phase, then the finer points for the details. A couple of erasers here, a soft rubber eraser and a harder one." She pointed them out, then smiled at me again. "The tools of my trade. That"—she tapped her head— "and the knowledge up here."

Agnes opened her pad of paper. "At first while you talk I'll take notes. A picture will begin to form in my head. Then I'll get it on paper. So—you ready?"

I took a deep breath. "Yes."

Silence fell over the three of us. I closed my eyes, sitting very still, and relived the beginning scene of the murder. The living room with large couch and matching love seat. The seascape painting and hardwood floors. Chinese rug. Glass coffee table, white marble fire-place. The woman storming in.

"She's small, maybe around five two. Narrow shoulders and slim. Very pretty. She has dark, shiny hair to her shoulders. Parted on her right side. The hair's straight. She has wispy bangs cut with that uneven stylish look."

The scene began to play. *No, no.* I fought it, tried to push rewind. It didn't work.

The woman started yelling, threatening. The man's hands shook with anger. He surged toward her, reaching for her throat . . .

My body heated up. I clutched the sides of my chair.

The woman drew closer, her brown eyes widening . . .

Stop, stop!

Vaguely I heard my mother whisper to Agnes, "She's reliving it. Just let her go."

"Reliving what?"

I squeezed my eyes tighter, focusing on the woman's face. "She . . ." I swallowed. "Brown eyes. Arched eyebrows. She has no wrinkles. Maybe . . . late thirties? Her cheeks are well defined, with curves under them. Sort of like little rounded apples. Her face is oval. The nose is . . . I don't know, not anything unusual. Straight. Right proportion. Her mouth too, except that her lips are kind of full."

I sat stiff-backed, hearing my own pulse in my ears. Straining to see anything else. But nothing came.

My eyes opened. I licked my lips. Agnes was busily scratching notes.

"I'll get you some water." Mom pushed back her chair. Concern etched her forehead.

Agnes sat back with a loud exhale. "Well. That was great." She frowned and started to say more, then apparently thought better of it. "I can see the woman forming in my mind already." She switched to a pencil with rounded tip and began to draw.

Mom set a glass before me.

"Thanks." I drank it down.

Over the next forty-five minutes Agnes drew, occasionally stopping to ask me questions. How far apart were the woman's eyes? How wide was her forehead? Each time I would close my eyes and refocus on her face before answering. My mother sat without a word, eyes flicking from Agnes to me. I couldn't begin to guess what she was thinking. Deep inside, did she wonder if this woman in my head existed?

Finally Agnes set down all her pencils. For a long moment she eyed her drawing, almost as if she didn't like what she saw. "All righty." She looked up. "I'm ready to show you what I have so far. Remember we'll refine from here. Okay?

I nodded. My heart picked up speed.

Agnes turned her pad of paper around. I stared at a rough drawing of someone who looked like the woman in my memories. The woman who was now dead. "It's almost her, but not quite."

"That's fine." Agnes sounded as if she expected the response. "Let's fix it."

She opened her FBI book. One by one we went over the woman's features as Agnes showed me different eyes, noses, mouths, and jawlines. Did the woman's look more like this—or that? Surprisingly my answers weren't difficult. The more we refined, the more I believed the process was working. My pulse slowed as I concentrated with all my might.

Agnes drew some more. When she finished she again stared at the result, a slight frown on her face.

She turned the pad around. "How's this?"

My mother leaned toward me, focusing on the drawing.

Oh. My mouth opened. It was exactly right. The woman I'd seen stabbed and strangled. Dumped in a suitcase. "That's her." My words came out breathy. "You . . . that's amazing."

Agnes gave a slight nod. She turned the pad a little, giving my mother a clearer view.

Mom shook her head. "She's beautiful."

Was beautiful.

Agnes twisted the drawing back toward me. "You sure you're satisfied?"

"Yes."

Agnes flipped the sketch back toward herself. "Well, first time this has happened." She looked at me, eyebrows raised. "I recognize this woman."

Chapter 17

 IT TOOK A MINUTE FOR AGNES'S WORDS TO SINK IN. "YOU *know* her?"

Mom stared at the artist, eyes round.

Agnes bit the inside of her cheek, focusing again on the draw-ing. "I don't actually know her. I've seen her. I'm sure I've seen this face." She frowned at the pad of paper, then shook her head. "I just can't remember where."

She was real. This woman was *real*. Vindication burst in my chest. So much for Jerry's "panic attacks." So much for my needing a psychiatrist. *I* was fine, it was the chip. That killer's memories were on *my* chip, and now they'd invaded my brain.

Cognoscenti had done this to me.

I wanted to scream. I wanted to tear off my own head.

"Did you see her in this area?" Mom pressed.

"I . . . don't remember. It could be that I just saw her picture, for all I know."

"When?" Mom's voice was sharp. "Recently?"

Agnes's mouth worked as she thought. "I just don't know. I think fairly recently. But . . ." She lifted a hand. "Maybe it'll come to me."

How could she be so cavalier about this? "It *has* to come to you. You *have* to remember!"

Mom patted my arm. "Calm down, Li—"

"But this is . . . everything. She's real, Mom! We have to find out who she is."

"I know, just—"

"Why?" Agnes's gaze bounced from my mother to me. "What has she done?"

"Been murdered." My voice clenched.

"What?"

"She's *dead*."

Agnes looked at me askance. "She's dead."

"Yes!"

"How do you know that?"

"Because . . ." I ran a hand across my forehead. "I saw it."

"You witnessed the crime?"

"Yes." Sort of.

Agnes nodded, as if she now stood on familiar ground. "But you didn't tell the police?"

"Not yet." Mom gestured toward Agnes. "That's why we called you."

Agnes thought that over. "Do you know who killed her?"

"No," I said. "We have to find out who she is first."

"I see." Agnes tapped her finger against the table, as if she didn't see at all.

I bounced one fist on top of another. "Are you sure you didn't see her picture as the victim of a crime?"

Agnes shook her head. "That I would remember." She stuck a hand in her hair. "Do you want to do a sketch of the perpetrator?"

"Not right now." Mom's tone was smooth. She stood. "Lisa, you want to get your checkbook so we can pay Agnes?"

My mother to the rescue. Good thing, because my throat had closed up. The woman was real. She'd been choked and stabbed. Stuffed in a suitcase. And I knew every detail of her murder.

"Lisa?"

"Yeah." Robot-like, I rose and headed for my purse, sitting on the counter. I filled out a check with a trembling hand. We had to find this woman now more than ever. To think we were so close . . .

Agnes busied herself with putting the pencils away in her portfolio. A dozen more questions must have bounced in her head, but she said nothing.

"Thank you." I handed her the check.

She gave me a little smile, akin to one she'd give to a slow-witted child. "You're welcome." With care she pulled the drawing from her pad of paper and slid it onto the table. "Hope this is helpful to you."

"Oh, it is." Weakness fluttered through me. I needed to eat again already. "More than you can know. Just please—if you remember where you saw her, call us right away. Okay?"

The artist searched my face. "I'll do that. And here." She slid a small case from her portfolio and took out a card. "If you need me again."

"Thanks."

Mom and I walked her to the door. As she stepped out into the hallway something crinkled underneath her shoe. "What's this?" She lifted her foot.

The three of us stared at the floor. A plain white envelope lay there, with my name written in block letters.

Cognoscenti. It had to be from them. Heat swept through my veins.

Before I could stop her Agnes bent over and picked it up. "Looks like this is for you." She held it toward me.

I didn't want to touch the thing.

"Thanks." Mom reached for the envelope, her facial muscles tight. "I'll take it."

Agnes slipped it into her hand. "Nice meeting both of you." She nodded at me.

I managed a tight smile.

Agnes headed down the hallway. Mom closed the apartment door.

We looked at each other, then at the envelope. Mom held it by the corner with her thumb and forefinger.

She spun on her heel and headed toward the counter. Dropped it on the hard surface. "You have some cleaning gloves?" She walked around the counter.

"Under the sink." My heart spasmed. I clutched my hands together and pressed them against my mouth. Someone had been *here*. Right outside my door. Of course they'd had my address for weeks now. But to know someone had come right up to my apartment . . .

Mom pulled a pair of yellow gloves from the cabinet and snapped them on. "Agnes's prints are already on the envelope, and mine are in that one corner. Don't you touch it at all."

I stood back from the envelope, not even wanting to get close.

Mom took a knife and slid it open. She pulled out a single piece of plain paper and looked at it. Her eyes flashed. "It says 'You'll be sorry, Lisa.'" She held it up for me to see.

My skin sizzled.

Mom growled in her throat. I knew that angry sound from childhood. "Who do they think they *are*, trying to stop us like this." She dropped the paper onto the counter and hit it with her fist.

Us. I licked my lips, staring at the words. If Mom weren't with me, I'd be coming unglued right now. "What do we do?"

My mother's mouth firmed. "We keep on, that's what. Every

time they do something this stupid it only makes me want to fight back."

Really? I just wanted to run to my bedroom and slam the door.

"And when the time is right, this little note will be one more piece of evidence for us."

I shivered. "I doubt they left fingerprints."

"You never know." Mom stuck a yellow-gloved hand on her hip. "Where are your plastic bags?"

I pointed to a drawer. She marched over and yanked out a large bag. Slid the envelope and piece of paper inside and sealed it. She placed it on the counter. "There." She took off the gloves and threw them back into the cabinet.

"What if they come after me?" My tone sounded dead, like the days just after my attack. What had happened to my new strength from the Empowerment Chip?

I clutched the counter, my body swaying.

"Lisa." Mom laid her hand on my arm. "Go sit down. I'll feed you something."

She led me to the table, where I slumped into a chair. The eyes of the murdered woman stared up at me from Agnes's drawing. I could almost feel her pleading for justice. I turned the drawing over. "Why am I so tired?"

Mom moved the drawing to the counter, setting it beside the bagged message. "It's only been four days since your surgery. You're not back to normal yet."

She fussed about the kitchen, making me a sandwich. I sat like a zombie, hearing myself breathe. When she set the food in front of me I ate every bite. Then I needed to lie down.

"Go ahead, take a nap." Mom put my plate in the sink. "I'll get online and see if I can find anything more."

What else could she do right now? But I couldn't argue. I headed toward bed on wobbly legs.

I stretched out on my back and closed my eyes. But my mind rebelled, kicking up a dust storm of memories and fears. Ryan's car accident, the attack, my miscarriages. After the last one I'd lain on the bathroom floor, my heart and body bleeding. I'd so wanted children for Ryan. For us. A child would have been someone to nurture. An extension of my husband to make me whole.

From deep inside a voice whispered, "*Can any other person really make you whole?*"

"I guess not, God," I whispered. But sometimes it was easier to believe that.

This was something I'd have to deal with. If I was going to build a new outward life, I'd have to work on the inside, too. But right now I was facing so much already. Right now I just felt crushed and exhausted.

God, help me, please. When I can handle it.

Drowsiness cold-drizzled over me. I slipped under the covers and burrowed down. The world fell away.

Another nightmare bared its fangs and hissed into my sleep.

Chapter 18

I WAS INSIDE THE KILLER.

Through his eyes I saw his arm slam the SUV's hatchback shut, sealing the black suitcase inside. He exited the garage, back into his kitchen. Then—a glass under the sink faucet, filling with water. He brought it to his mouth and drank, gazing through the window at his expansive backyard. To his left the sun had half disappeared below the horizon.

The dishwasher opened. He put the glass inside. Brought up his left arm to glance at his watch. The time read 5:48.

He turned toward the door leading to the garage. I saw it approach, heard his footsteps. He opened the door and returned to the car. Slid into the driver's seat. I saw a beige center console. When the engine started, a dashboard full of digital readouts lit up. It included a GPS.

The man's finger—my finger—pushed a button, and I heard a garage door begin to open. He backed out, pausing at the end of the driveway to close the door. The three-car garage was painted off-white. Small windows ran across each door close to the top. The man had exited from the door on the far right.

His car backed out onto the street. For a second he looked at his house. A magnificent two-story colonial, with a large front porch and pillars. Lots of windows with shutters in dark green. A curving front sidewalk lined with multicolored flowers. Three birch trees.

He drove down the street, expensive homes slithering by the passenger seat window. He hit an intersection and turned right onto a road with mature trees on either side. Houses were set back from the road behind large walls and gates. Glimpses of the homes showed they were expensive.

I saw an intersection ahead—wider, busier. Trees now canopied the road. The man reached the intersection during a green light and turned left. Businesses glided by. A Jack in the Box on the right. Jewelry store and an exotic car dealership on the left. A number of blocks later, just before an overpass, he veered right onto another major road, merging into traffic. Lots of cars. Stop lights. Then he hit the freeway.

Abruptly the scene switched to night. A speedboat skimmed over black water. The suitcase lay on the floor of the boat.

The engine cut. The boat gently rocked. The man's arms—my arms— reached for the suitcase. He hauled it up and over the edge of the boat. I heard a large splash.

He gazed into the water. In the darkness I could just make out one side of the suitcase sinking. It upended itself, then disappeared under water—

I awoke with a start, muscles twisted. Sweat dampened my back. My eyes locked onto my bedroom ceiling, my pulse clanging. The moment pulled me apart, half of me still in the dark boat, the other screaming to escape to reality.

It was just a dream . . . But of course it wasn't. We knew the victim was real. This had *happened.* I could still feel the rock of the boat, hear the splash of the suitcase going into water.

But . . .

I checked the clock by my bed. Five fifteen. I'd slept over two hours.

It took awhile to sit up, then stand. My mind buzzed with the pictures. The house, the boat. Sunset, the time. More details to help me find the man.

My feet took me into the kitchen. Mom still sat before her computer, as if she'd never moved. She barely glanced at me. "I've been looking for pictures of women in this area through local newspapers. Haven't found her. It's a needle in ten haystacks."

I sprawled into the chair opposite her. She looked up and me and stilled. "What's wrong?"

In my mind the suitcase splashed into water. "I had another dream. I saw so much. Maybe too much. Maybe it's just my brain, trying to fill in details. But all of it felt so real."

"About the murder?"

"Uh-huh."

"I've never heard you doubt any of the details you've seen before."

"I don't really doubt these either. It's just . . . there's so many."

She thrust the pad of paper toward me. "Can you tell them to me? And write them down. Then we can look at all of it."

"Okay."

The details sputtered out of me. Once I put them into words, any doubts of their being real faded. They still pulsed in my head as I wrote them. The car, the house. The boat. The splash of the suitcase. He'd *dumped* her in the water. What kind of man would do that? She was still out there, somewhere. She was someone's sister, daughter, maybe a mother. Someone's friend. I couldn't let her stay there, abandoned.

Or had she been found?

I finished writing. Filled a glass at the sink. I pictured the man in his own kitchen, doing the same thing. Saw the silver faucet, his hands—

My head jerked up. "The ring."

"What?"

I faced Mom. "The dragon ring on his right hand. When he was at the sink he wasn't wearing it."

"You sure?"

"Positive."

She frowned. "But you definitely saw it when he killed her?"

"Yes. And when he zipped up the suitcase."

"What about when he was closing the SUV doors. Did you see it then?"

I tried to remember. "I don't think so. The last time I saw it for sure was when he closed the bag."

"But didn't he take the suitcase to the garage right after closing it?"

"I thought he did." I pressed a hand to my cheek. This couldn't be right.

I leaned against the counter, my stomach in a knot. Once more I went over the scenes. Putting the woman in the suitcase. Closing it. The dragon ring was on his finger. I clearly remembered that. Wheeling the bag to the car. And suddenly—no ring.

Maybe all the details weren't reliable after all. Which meant my brain *was* making some of them up. But which ones? And why?

"This is a mess, Mom." My throat tightened. "We can't know what to believe. Maybe the woman's not even real after all."

"We know she is. Agnes recognized her."

"Maybe she's mistaken. All the faces she's drawn."

"All the faces she's drawn makes her more reliable. She *knows* eyes and noses and mouths."

Tears splintered my vision. I didn't want to do this anymore.

Mom got up. "You hungry?"

Like I wanted food right now. I shook my head. "Did you eat something?"

"Yes, while you were sleeping." She focused across the room.

"You described all those roads and businesses. I wish there was a way we could find out where that is."

"Yeah."

"We know the license plate is from California. Still, it's a big state."

A sudden thought flashed in my head. I pictured the man's car on the road. Veering onto another. Hitting the freeway . . .

Oh.

Slowly I set down my glass. That road. Just before an overpass. And those businesses he drove by. The car dealership and Jack in the Box. I'd been there.

I looked at Mom, my face slack. "It's Woodside Road."

"What?"

I closed my eyes. "He starts on his own street, then another one I don't know. Then he turns left. And he passes those businesses. I think they're on El Camino. After that he veers onto Woodside. Which leads to Freeway 101."

Mom took a breath. "Where is all this?"

"Just a few miles from here!"

I sagged against the counter. Maybe my brain had pulled these details from my own experiences. But if it hadn't . . . that killer lived *right here.*

"We should drive there," Mom said. "See if everything fits."

I managed a nod. "If it does, maybe I can figure out the street he turned off of to get to El Camino. And if we followed *that* road . . ." Could we find his own street. His *house?*

The thought terrified me.

"Let's do it," Mom said. "We might also be able to figure out when the murder happened."

I blinked at her. "How?"

"You said he looked at his watch. It was 5:48, and the sun was setting. And now you think he may live in this area." She sat down at her computer. "If we could find some website that tells the time of sunset in a location on a given day . . ."

How had she even thought of that? I moved to the table. "You think there is such a site?"

"You can find anything on the Internet."

Mom typed in *sunset times* and hit enter. One hundred thirty-six thousand results came up. I took one look at that and sat down. Mom clicked on the first link: www.sunrisesunset.com. Together we peered at the site. The directions were simple. First, name the state. Mom clicked on California. Then find the town. "What should I put in?"

"I don't . . . just do Redwood City for now."

She clicked on Redwood City. Then we had to name a time. First she tried the current month, March. Sunset times were later than 5:48. Looking at the calendar the site created, we could see that sunsets changed about one minute a day. Except that daylight savings time had just begun the previous weekend, setting time forward an hour.

I leaned closer to the computer. "Go back to February."

With a few clicks we could see the results. The sun set in Redwood City at 5:48 on Thursday, February 16. Nearly a month ago.

Mom looked up, grinning. "That's it! We could be off a day or two. But if he lives around here, this gives us our time frame."

Could this be true? We'd really found the time of the murder?

If my brain hadn't made up details on its own.

If it hadn't, that man was here. So close to me.

Mom glanced at the clock. "It's 5:40. Let's go check out those roads. It'll be dark before we know it."

"Uh-huh." But I couldn't move. No way. I could only think of that man, living right here . . .

"Lisa? Think you should get some shoes on?"

I blinked at my mother. She was trying so hard not to command. "I don't know if I can do this."

She patted my arm. "Sure you can. Don't you want to know the truth?"

Yes. No.

I licked my lips. "The not knowing is killing me."

Mom nodded, as if to say—*there's your answer.* The response rolled around my brain.

I got up to put my shoes on.

As we left the apartment I glanced at Agnes's drawing of the woman, lying on the counter. Beside it lay the Cognoscenti note. How much did they know at that company? Was someone there trying to cover up a murder?

My mind snapped to the suitcase sinking into black water. If that woman was still there, she deserved to be buried with dignity. Her family needed to know where she was. If she'd been found, they deserved justice.

And I just might be the only person who could make sure they got it.

Chapter 19

WE HEADED FOR MOM'S RENTAL CAR, PARKED ON THE street in front of the apartment building. She would drive; I'd navigate. Mom had suggested we take my digital camera. It sat in her purse.

As I walked to the car, clutching my notepad and pen, anxiety clawed my chest. I glanced all around. Whoever had left that note at my door—was he still here, watching us?

"You'll be sorry, Lisa."

Sorry for what? Going to the media about Cognoscenti? Which I wasn't about to do. Or sorry for investigating this murder?

I slid inside the car and locked the door.

Mom put on her seat belt. "Where to?"

How about anywhere but here? "Go to the next street and turn left. A few blocks down we'll hit El Camino. Turn right to go south."

I'd been down El Camino plenty of times since Ryan and I moved to the area. It was a major road, stretching from up toward San Francisco all the way down to San Jose. One town blended into another along El Camino, with an endless stretch of businesses.

Ryan and I had first driven it south from Redwood City to explore Stanford shopping center in Palo Alto.

Mom reached El Camino and turned right. I gripped the paper and pen, praying all the way. Cars flowed by us on the multilaned road. I wanted to turn around, see if anyone was following us. More paranoia. Maybe the depression was coming back. Maybe I really did get a placebo. *And* my brain was making up details—which could be called panic attacks. I was worse off than ever after the surgery. Totally headed for disaster.

I might as well curl into a ball and give up right now.

Mom glanced at me. "You okay?"

"Yeah."

We approached Woodside Road. After the underpass I looked back, peering at the exit I'd thought was in the dream. And there it was, just like I remembered. "There!" I pointed behind us. "That's the road he took. It goes to 101."

"You sure?"

"Mom, I *know*."

But had my brain just made this part up—or was it true?

I turned around, concentrating on the businesses we passed. "See that fancy car dealership? That was in the dream too. And there's the jewelry store."

"Wow," Mom said. "This really isn't far from you."

Way too close.

"There's the Jack in the Box." I pointed left.

My mother nodded. "Where do you think he turned off that residential road?"

"I don't know. But probably not far."

We passed into Atherton, where expensive houses were set behind walls and large trees, like in my dream. I studied each road going off El Camino, looking for the intersection where the man had turned. Nothing fit. We passed Tuscaloosa. And then I saw it. We were approaching the stoplight at Atherton Avenue. Opposite that street rose a beige stucco wall. That wall seemed to leap out at me. "That's it! Just before he turned, his car was pointed at that wall."

"You sure?"

"Yes! Go right."

Mom got over in the far right lane and turned onto the avenue.

My pulse skittered. "The town of Atherton. I should have known. All those big houses."

"Expensive area?"

"Yeah."

My mouth dried out. Important people lived in Atherton. Execs in Silicon Valley, doctors, attorneys. One of *them* was a cold-blooded killer?

A tree canopy covered the first part of Atherton Avenue. I hung on to my seat. "See the trees? This is *it*."

"Okay." Mom sounded grim.

Then came the walls and more trees on either side, shielding large homes. I'd seen that, too. I needed more eyes to take it all in. I needed bigger lungs to *breathe*.

I saw no roads off to the right, only to the left. "Okay, go slow. I need to look up each street." I perched on the edge of my seat, holding on to the dashboard as I peered left. A lot of the streets ended in short cul-de-sacs. That didn't look right. "No," I said at the first one—Odell. And the second—Mercedes. And the third and fourth—Stevenson. We drove by a fifth and sixth. A seventh. Had the man passed this many streets? They all looked too narrow. The one wide road had a median, and I hadn't seen one of those in the dream.

With every wrong street we passed, my muscles drew up tighter. This should be working.

An eighth street. A ninth and tenth.

"It's not here." My voice was thick.

"Maybe we haven't gone far enough."

"He didn't pass that many turn-offs." I slumped back in my seat.

Mom turned onto the next lane and pulled over to the side. She put the car in Park. "Let's think about this. You remember what the house looks like?"

Off-white, two-story. Large porch with pillars. Dark green shutters. Lots of flowers and three birch trees in the yard . . .

"Yeah, but who knows if it's right. If we can't find the street . . ."

"Well, we've come this far. Let's go up each street, even if it doesn't look right. Maybe we'll find the house."

We wouldn't. Then what? We'd never figure this out. Mom might as well go back to Denver. And I'd keep turning in circles.

"Okay, Lisa?"

"Sure. Whatever."

If only I'd never heard of Cognoscenti.

Mom pulled a U-turn and got back on Atherton Avenue. We wormed our way back toward El Camino, taking each road either to its dead end or its first intersection with another street. None of the houses matched. They weren't even close. All of them were set back from the street behind walls and gates. The man's house hadn't been like that. Neither had his neighbors'.

I dug my knuckles into my chin. Maybe I'd seen the house in a magazine somewhere. Seen the woman's face there, too. Some obscure actress.

Jerry was right—I needed a psychiatrist. I had to understand what was happening to me.

We turned off one of the lanes back onto Atherton Road. Some distance down I could see the El Camino intersection. "Mom, it's not here."

"Let's keep trying." Mom turned onto the next street, the wide one with a grassy divider in the middle.

"This can't be it." I just wanted to go home. "I never saw a median."

But the houses here were different. They were spread apart on large lots but without front walls. Looked more like what I'd seen in my dream. Newer homes, the trees not as large. But a median . . . ?

We saw no one out in their yards.

A house on the left jumped out at me. My heart stopped. "There it is!"

"Where?"

I couldn't believe it. *"There!"*

Mom pulled over to the right curb, opposite the house. We gaped at it. I started to shake. This was the place. The porch and paint color, the flowers and trees. Three-car garage. Everything fit. I even recognized the windows going across the tops of the garage doors.

"You sure?" Mom's voice was a whisper.

"Positive." My heart thumped. Even the sun was setting to the left of the house, like in my dream. This *was* it. A woman had been *killed* in that house. I could practically see through the walls, picture the living room and kitchen. The floor where she died.

"But the median . . . Why didn't I see that in the dream?"

"You probably just saw the man's car drive down his side of the street."

Maybe.

Our white car suddenly felt like flaming red neon. What if the man looked out his window right now and saw us? "We have to get out of here."

"I know." Mom leaned toward her window. "See a street number?"

No. And I didn't care. "Just go! He could come out any minute."

"There. On the mailbox. Ten."

Ten, fine. "Turn around."

"You need to write it in your notebook."

Now? "I'll remember it. Just get us out of here."

"Did you notice the street name?"

"No!"

"We'll get it on the way out." Mom thrust the car into Park.

"What are you doing? Mom!"

"Where's my purse? I need the camera."

"We *don't* need a picture. Every detail's in my head."

"It's not in mine. Where's the camera?"

I squirmed around, frantically looking for Mom's bag. She'd tossed it into the back seat. I heaved over and picked it up. Fumbled around inside for the camera. My eyes snapped toward the house. Still no sign of the man. But he could be watching us right now. If he saw me, if he knew, Mom and I were both dead. This was a man who would stalk us. Who would make sure we never opened our mouths.

"Lisa, hurry."

My fingers kept scrabbling. *Where* was the camera?

There. I yanked it out and turned it on.

Mom tensed. "Oh, no."

I checked the house—and saw the middle garage door opening. My fingers froze.

Mom shoved the car gear into Drive, her foot on the brake. "Take the picture, hurry."

The door was now half open.

My hands started to shake. "I can't, just go!"

"*Take* it."

Twice I tried to aim the camera. On the third try I pushed the button. *Click.*

Mom lunged toward me. "Get your head down!"

Holding our breath, we bent low over the console, as if peering at a map. I rolled my gaze up toward the house. The garage door stood wide open.

"Get a picture of the car when he comes out."

"No, Mom, what if he sees me?"

"Lisa, *do* it."

"But I can't . . ."

A car started backing out. My heart slammed into my ribs. But the car wasn't a black SUV. It was a red sedan.

"Is he coming out?" Mom hissed.

"Yes."

"Take the picture."

I aimed the camera and pushed the button.

"Take another one."

I tried, but my fingers had gone numb.

"Here, give it to me." Mom stuck out her hand. I shoved the camera into it.

The red sedan backed into the street and sat parallel to the house. I ducked down more. In that second the driver turned toward us. An elderly man. White haired. Was *that* him?

"He's looking!" Fear stretched my words.

"Keep your head down." Mom swallowed hard. "Tell me when he turns away. I'll get another picture. "

He kept staring at us. Time stopped moving. If he came over here . . .

The man looked up toward his visor and pushed a button. The garage door began to close. I managed a breath. "Take it, quick."

Mom pointed the camera behind her with one hand and pushed the button. No telling what she got.

The man drove off down the street.

Air whooshed out of me. I thought I was going to faint. "He's leaving."

Mom dropped the camera in my lap and checked in the rearview mirror, then headed up the street. She passed two paved turn-offs cutting through the median and drove to the end of the cul-de-sac. Only then did she turn around. By that time the man's car was gone.

I could hardly feel my body. "Get off this street. Please."

We passed the killer's house without stopping.

"Was that him?" Mom's voice was clipped. "I know you've never seen him but . . . did you *feel* it?"

I was still trying to get enough oxygen. "Give me a minute."

At the end of the road I managed to notice the street name. Amethyst Lane. Number ten. I wrote the address on my notepad.

The killer lived here. Just a few miles from my apartment. This was all *real*. I couldn't wrap my head around that.

Mom drove slowly down Atherton Avenue, not wanting to catch up to the man's car. But he was long gone.

I sagged back in my seat and tried to calm my pulse.

"*Do* you think that was him?" Mom asked again.

"I don't know. He came out of the middle door in a red car. In my dream he came out of the right door in a black SUV."

"So he has two cars."

I closed my eyes, picturing the scenes in the garage. I'd never noticed a red sedan there. But the man had been focused on the floor. I hadn't seen the rest of the garage at all. Just like I hadn't seen the median on the street. Still . . .

"I don't think that was him."

"Why?"

"He's too old."

"How do you know how old he is?"

"I've seen his hands. They're not an old man's hands."

"Maybe the guy's in great shape. He did pick up that woman."

I winced. "Maybe. But it doesn't feel right."

What if he wasn't the man? What if the killer didn't live in that house at all? I'd be back to square one, all the more confused.

We drove the rest of the way home in silence. My thoughts continued to whirl. The right house but the wrong man . . . That made no sense. Plus there was that disappearing dragon ring.

We reached the apartment building. Mom pulled into a space on the street and cut the engine. I walked on wooden legs up the stairs and to my door. Mom held all our things as I pulled the key out of my pocket. Once inside we bolted the lock.

I made for the couch and sank into it. Massaged my temples. Were we closer to the truth—or worse off than ever?

I heard Mom plop everything down near the kitchen. Then she gasped.

The hair on my neck raised. "What?"

She pointed. "The drawing. And the note. Didn't we leave them here on the counter?"

The cut of her voice brought me to my feet. "I saw them there when we left."

Mom's face paled. "They're gone."

Chapter 20

I STOOD BESIDE MY MOTHER, GAZING AROUND THE kitchen. At the table, the counters, even the floor. No drawing. No bagged note.

"Maybe they're in your bedroom. Or mine." But I didn't believe it. I'd seen them on the counter as we left. I'd bet on that.

Had someone been watching my apartment building, just waiting for us to leave?

My hands fisted. If someone had done that, he'd violated my private space—and my mother's. Without her, I'd have been beyond petrified. She could have stayed in Denver, but she'd come here to help me. Stepped into my life, and now look what had happened. She wasn't even safe in my own apartment.

What if that someone was still here?

"We should leave," Mom said. "Call the police."

"And tell them we're missing a drawing? They'll want to know what it is."

Mom twisted her lips.

"I'm checking the bedrooms."

"No."

I turned toward her and spread my hands.

"Not alone, you're not."

"Come on, then."

We ventured into her bedroom first. My legs trembled, but my outrage outweighed the fear. The drawing and note weren't there. Not on the bed, the dresser, or anywhere near the computer. And no one hid in the room. I eyed the closed closet door, nerves spitting. He could be in there. We could have surprised him . . .

Before I lost courage I strode over and flung the door open.

Mom gasped.

I shrank back, cringing. But the closet was empty.

Breath returned slowly. I sagged against the wall, willing my legs to stop shaking.

We forced ourselves into my bedroom next. Then the bathroom. We found nothing. And the drawing and note were gone.

Nothing else had been touched. My purse still sat on the kitchen counter, with cash and credit cards. In my bedroom what jewelry I had was untouched. My wedding rings still lay in the drawer. *Thank heaven.* I put them on.

We stood back in the living room, not knowing what to do. Mom pressed a fist against her jaw. "How stupid I was not to make a scan of that drawing!"

"It wouldn't matter. He'd have just taken that too."

"But if I'd hidden it . . ."

"Why would you do that? How could we have known?"

Mom licked her lips. "Why didn't he take our computers? At least mine, if he wanted to see what we've been up to online. It's so easy to grab."

I had no idea.

She looked toward the door. "Your lock hasn't even been tampered with. It looked perfectly fine."

"Maybe he has a key." The mere idea unglued me.

"Or he's a very good lock picker." Fear shone in Mom's eyes. Either scenario left us easy targets.

I shuddered. "When we left I didn't bolt the door from the outside. I should have done that."

"Who knows if it would have helped."

If he'd have gotten through the deadbolt I'd be trembling all the harder. "So what now?"

"Call the police."

"Mom, no. And tell them what? That the only two things missing are a drawing and a threatening note? We don't even have proof they existed."

"We have proof of the drawing. Agnes can vouch for that. As for the note, at least she can say she found the envelope. And I still have the recording of the other threatening message on my phone at home."

"You didn't erase it?"

Mom shook her head. "Something told me not to."

My body swayed. I headed for the couch and sank into it.

"You know what else?" Mom came to stand before me. "I can even play that tape for the police from here. I can call my answering machine remotely."

"You're kidding."

"Want to hear it?"

I shot her an incredulous look. "Why didn't you tell me? If it was Jerry Sterne or one of the other interviewers, I'll know the voice."

She screwed up her face. "Of course. I don't know why I . . ."

Mom hurried to the phone. She punched a few numbers, listened, then hit a few more. "Here." She walked the receiver over to me.

I pressed it to my ear. Heard a click, then a clipped, unfriendly male voice: *"Alice Wegman, I'm calling from Cognoscenti in California, regarding your daughter, Lisa Newberry. I have a crucial message for her:* Don't *do it*."

The line went dead.

I pulled the phone away, veins sizzling. No wonder Mom had hopped a plane. That voice clearly meant me harm.

But it didn't belong to Jerry Sterne. Or anyone else I recognized.

Mom took the phone from me and set it on the coffee table. "Know who it is?"

My head shook.

She sat in my armchair and stared at the floor. "I'm telling you, we should call the police."

I still couldn't imagine it. "If we do we'll have to tell them *why* . . . everything. And they won't help. Cognoscenti warned me the company will say I'm some crazy, vindictive woman."

Mom was already reaching for the phone. "Even if they don't believe us now, we can at least get it on the record for later—when we know more about the murder."

"*Wait*, Mom." I leaned forward. "Don't."

Her arm hung midair. "We have to do this. If we don't, and we later claim someone broke into your apartment, the police will want to know why we never reported it. It'll be one more thing to make them suspicious of our story."

I bit my lip, wavering. But an unfamiliar stubbornness rose up. "This is *my* apartment. My life. You can't make this choice for me."

My mother and I faced each other, gazes locked. I could see the indecision in her eyes.

Slowly, she put down the receiver.

I exhaled. Pressed a hand to my temple. Something major had just happened here, but I didn't have time to examine it.

A minute ticked by. My mother waited.

I picked up the phone.

Chapter 21

WITHIN HALF AN HOUR A POLICEMAN STOOD AT MY DOOR. Waiting for him, I'd nearly cancelled the report a dozen times. Things were spiraling way out of control. Once the police were brought in, everything would change. I couldn't call the shots anymore.

Ted Bremer, the policeman, was tall and big-boned with short salt-and-pepper hair. Around my mother's age. His brown eyes seemed to drill right through me, taking in my bandaged head. That cop aura hung about him, confidence mixed with wariness. I wanted to take back the report more than ever.

My arm waved him inside. Mom stood back, sizing him up. As soon as his gaze landed on her she broke into an endearing smile. "Thank you for coming. We're so grateful for your time." She held out her hand. "I'm Alice Wegman, and this is my daughter, Lisa."

The policeman shook Mom's hand. "Officer Ted Bremer."

Mom gave him a gracious nod. The policeman's eyes lingered on her, clearly impressed. Maybe my mother would charm him into believing us.

"Officer Bremer, we have a story to tell you." Mom spread her hands. "I admit it's rather unusual. But what can we do; facts are facts."

Bremer pulled a pen from his pocket. "Let's start at the beginning. You reported a break-in?" He tore his eyes off my mother and looked around the apartment.

"That was me." I threw Mom a sideways glance. I'd made the move to call the cops; now she needed to let me do the talking.

"And nothing missing but two important documents, you said?"

"Right."

The policeman gestured toward the door. "No sign of forced entry there."

"No."

Bremer nodded. "I'll check the windows. Not as likely, you being on the second floor. But we'll look at everything."

I hadn't even thought of windows. But a man on a ladder in this neighborhood—in daylight? No way.

"What were the documents?" Bremer asked.

Here it came. I swallowed. "Want to check the apartment first? Because the explanation's going to take awhile."

Bremer's eyes flicked from me to my mother. She gave him an encouraging nod, as if he should take his cues from us. But he merely shrugged. "All right."

He found nothing, of course. No evidence at all that anyone had broken into the apartment.

We sat at the kitchen table. I tried to tell Bremer only part of the story, but the sketchy details didn't make sense. Bremer asked hard questions and little by little pulled it all out of me. My surgery and confrontation with Cognoscenti, my memories of the murder. How we'd narrowed down the general date of the crime. And now we knew *where* it had happened, unless I was totally wrong about the house.

Bremer took lots of notes, his face a mask.

My throat had run dry. "Do you know about this case?" Surely Bremer did. Surely he could tell me who the people were. "I haven't watched local news in a long time. Maybe somebody found the suitcase. Or maybe the woman's still missing."

He hesitated, then shook his head. "Atherton's not my jurisdiction."

"But it's so close! You must have heard something."

"No. Doesn't mean it didn't happen. But I don't watch local news either. I *live* it every day. And I'm busy with my own caseload."

I surveyed him. Was he telling the truth?

Why had I called the police? I didn't even trust this man.

Bremer moved on with more questions. He asked Mom to call her answering machine so he could listen to the "don't do it" tape.

Would he believe even that? He could claim we'd staged it.

I pulled out my camera to show him pictures of the man's car and house. I saw the last two photos, and my heart sank. "Oh, no." I looked at Mom. "We never got the man's face."

Her eyes closed briefly. "How about the car?"

"Sort of, but not good enough." The picture of the car backing out had been aimed too high. The license plate was cut off. And Mom's shot of the car's side only included the back seat to the rear bumper.

I had managed to take a decent shot of the house.

Bremer looked at the pictures. "What's the address?"

"Ten Amethyst Lane. In Atherton."

"Would you e-mail those pictures to me?"

For whatever good they would do. But I nodded. He gave me his e-mail address.

The phone rang.

"Go ahead." Bremer gestured toward it.

I stood, wrung out, and walked to the counter. The ID signaled Sherry. Great time for her to call. "Hi." I turned my back to the policeman.

"How *are* you?"

"Okay. Listen, I really want to talk to you. But a policeman's here. We had a break-in, and—"

"What?"

"—we're giving him information. I'll have to call you back."

"Are you *kidding*? Was anything taken? Are you okay?"

"We were gone."

"A break-in. I can't believe it. Do you think it has anything to do with . . . everything?"

"Yes." My throat clogged. "But I can't talk right now."

"Oh, Lisa!"

"I'm not alone. Mom's still here."

"I'm glad for that."

"Yeah."

Sherry breathed over the line. "Call me back soon as you can." She sounded frightened. "Please."

"I will."

We hung up. I shuffled back to the table. Mom cast me a look, as if Sherry was an intrusion. I glared back. We were all in this together, like it or not. Mom had to learn to deal with my best friend. I *missed* Sherry.

Bremer tapped his pen against his notes. "I'll need the contact information for the forensic artist."

My mind blanked. "Where did we put Agnes's card?"

"Over there." Mom went to the microwave. The card sat on top. She handed it to Bremer. He wrote down the information, then focused on me. "And you say she didn't see the letter."

Mom opened her mouth. I cut her off. "We didn't read it until she left. But she did see the envelope. Like I said, she found it. It hadn't been there when she arrived."

Bremer's gaze fell back to his notes. He scratched the side of his nose as if trying to make sense of it all.

He raised his head. "You say you're better after the chip implant?"

"Much. Without it I'd be under the covers right now."

Except that—without it, I wouldn't be in this situation.

"But they're telling you it's a placebo."

"They're lying."

The policeman surveyed me.

"There's no point in your calling them. I've already told you what they're going to say. And no doubt they'll come up with some paper to prove it's a placebo, just like they showed me. Doesn't mean it's true."

Bremer tapped his pen some more. "In the end, does it matter?"

"What do you mean?" Mom asked.

"Whether the chip was a placebo or not, you're alleging that somehow it's been tainted with unwanted data. The memory of a murder."

I could just imagine Bremer returning to his station and telling other officers about this report. *"No way you're gonna top this one . . ."*

My back straightened. "It matters if the chip was real, but they're telling me it's blank just to get me to shut up. That means they *know* something's wrong with it."

"But how do you suppose the data got on the chip?"

"I don't *know.*" I shoved my chair back from the table. "I only know what I see in my head! And now it's not just me anymore. Now someone's threatened me—twice. And he's been in my apartment. And now my *mother's* in danger."

Mom patted my hand. "It's okay, Lisa."

"No, it's not." I stood up and paced across the kitchen. "I just want this fixed! I want to understand what's happening."

"Okay." Bremer held up his hand. "I know it's upsetting that we don't have any answers yet."

We. Yet. Two words I could cling to. I dredged myself to a stop and leaned against the sink.

Bremer gathered his notes and placed the pen back in his pocket. "I'll need to get a tech over here to dust your door and the counter for foreign prints."

"Foreign?"

"Not yours or your mom's. We'll have to roll both your prints too, for comparison."

Great. Now *I* would be fingerprinted like some criminal.

"What about your friend Sherry?" Mom raised her eyebrows. "She let herself out of here last night."

And now we had to fingerprint Sherry, too? Double great.

The policeman rubbed his cheek. "If you have reason to believe her prints might be on the door, it would be helpful."

I hesitated, then nodded. "Can you at least send the tech tomorrow? I don't want to stay here tonight."

"That's not typical procedure. We like to gather evidence as quickly as possible. Before it can be tainted."

Like my brain chip. "We won't *be* here to taint it." My voice thinned. "Really, I just can't deal with any more right now."

Bremer took a long breath. "All right." He rose. "I'll contact you in the morning on your cell phone. I'll also be talking to Agnes Brighton."

Mom stood. "What about running the address of that man's house? Surely it won't take you long to learn who lives there. And if he drives a black SUV with a license plate that begins with 6WB."

The officer eyed her, as if she was telling him how to do his job.

My mother caught the look. She poured on the charm once more. "Thank you for coming. So much. I don't know what we'd have done without your help."

"Yes, thanks a lot." I walked him to the door, my skin crawling.

When he stepped into the hall I bolted the door behind him. "Let's get out of here, Mom. I just have to go . . . somewhere."

We threw a few things into a small suitcase. Mom slid her computer into the laptop bag.

Outside the apartment building the night had a thousand eyes. We hurried to Mom's car and locked the doors. Was the man here, somewhere? Watching from a window? Behind some car or tree? My head nearly swiveled off my neck, checking all around.

"Where do you want to go?" Mom started the engine.

"Get to El Camino and turn left. We'll find a hotel somewhere." I couldn't even think of turning right. Of heading one foot closer to that man's house.

On the way I called Sherry and told her everything.

"Lisa." She sounded so scared for me. "This is unbelievable."

Wrong word, but I knew what she meant. "I know. Wish I could see you."

"You want to come over?"

"Thanks, but I know there's no room for us there. We're headed to a hotel. But I miss you."

"Miss you, too."

We fell silent. "Oh, Sherry, do you think you can give the police your fingerprints tomorrow?" I told her why they needed them. "You'll probably have to go down to the station."

"Okay. I can go while Rebecca's in school."

"What about J.T.?"

"I'll figure it out."

I hung up to help Mom find a hotel. We ended up checking into a place in San Mateo with free wireless. We got into our room—and hunger hit. We'd never eaten dinner. No wonder I felt weak. But no way I wanted to sit in a restaurant, where watching eyes could see me. We ordered room service. I lay on my bed, waiting for the food to come, utterly spent. Mom turned on her computer, itching to see if she could find out who owned the house at Ten Amethyst Lane. But she couldn't get on the Internet.

Dinner arrived within thirty minutes. Mom abandoned her work while we ate.

When we were done Mom picked up the tray to set it in the hall. I hung back, hands clenched, while she opened the door.

Was the man out there? Was he in the hotel?

Mom closed the door and bolted it. "All right." She headed back to her computer. "I *will* get this wireless working."

If we found out the man's name, then what? Part of me didn't want to know.

Mom had to talk to the front desk to get on the Internet. By the time she succeeded it was after 10:00. Adrenaline and exhaustion swirled in my veins.

I drew up a small armchair beside Mom at the desk.

"Okay." Her fingers were poised on the keys. "Ten Amethyst Lane, Atherton, California." She typed the address into Google and hit enter. Over 200,000 hits came up.

My shoulders sank. "It's so many."

"We only need one." Mom started with a realty site. Just like that, a picture of the house appeared.

"That's it!" I leaned toward the computer.

Mom looked around the site. It listed features of the property, its selling history and other houses in the neighborhood. We could click and drag on the pictures for a three-sixty view of the street. But we saw no owner's name.

"Maybe the owner isn't public information in California," Mom said. "Do you know?"

I shook my head.

She sighed. "Let's try another one." She opened a city data site for property valuation. Again we saw a picture of the house. "Look." She pointed at the screen. "It was last sold in 2010 for four-point-eight million." She scrolled down the page—and suddenly there it was in bold caps. The name of the owner.

William Hilderbrand.

Chapter 22

I STARED AT THE NAME, BLOOD GELLING IN MY VEINS.

Mom took a hard look at my face. "You know who he is, Lisa?"

My tongue would barely work. "CEO of Cognoscenti. Inventor of the Empowerment Chip."

Air seeped out of my mother's throat.

"You know that letter I got, accepting me into the trial? *He* signed it."

A million thoughts drilled my brain. I didn't even know where to start. "That man we saw at the house. It couldn't be him. I researched Cognoscenti before signing up for the trial. I saw a picture of William Hilderbrand then. He looks like he's in his mid forties."

Mom absorbed the information.

"*Why* is it him?" My voice rose. "I knew when I saw the house that he was rich. But this . . . Hilderbrand's worth *millions*. He'll crush me. I can't imagine the police even approaching him."

This was too much. No way could I handle it.

"And besides, why would *he* kill someone? And how could it end up on a chip in his own company? No wonder they're trying to silence me. It's not just the chip, it's the founder!" I buried my head in my hands.

Had Hilderbrand made that threatening phone call to Mom himself? Had he written that note? Had *he* broken into my apartment? I couldn't imagine it.

But I couldn't have imagined any of this.

A stunning realization hit. My head came up. "I didn't think the killer knew that I know about him. But if it's Hilderbrand, he does."

He would kill me too.

It was surprising I was still alive.

Mom drew a long breath. "Maybe he doesn't know. Maybe it's what we thought before. You threatened Cognoscenti, so they're fighting back by insisting your chip is blank. They want to shut you up. But they have no idea about this murder."

"But I told Jerry and Clair about it. If Hilderbrand heard that, he *knows*."

Exhaustion and fear clawed me. Every bone in my body felt beaten. I fell back in the chair. "I have to stop. I can't fight this man. Whether Hilderbrand knows now or finds out later—I'm dead."

His hands around her throat . . . Grabbing the knife . . . The suitcase sinking in black water.

I had to leave town. Right away, with no forwarding address. I could call Jerry Sterne and apologize, tell him everything was fine now. It would be a message to Hilderbrand that I was backing down.

Maybe, just maybe, he'd leave me alone.

But I knew he wouldn't. Every minute he'd think of me, still alive, knowing the truth that could bring him down. I'd jag through my days, wondering when he would show up. Grab me in a parking lot one night.

How could I live like that?

I curled up in the hotel chair, darkness crusting around my head. I should just let it smother me. Maybe I was *meant* for depression. Meant to lead a miserable life. Maybe the brain chip *was* a placebo. And now even the power of suggestion was slipping away.

"Lisa." Mom put her hands on my shoulders. "It'll be all right."

I shook her off. It *wouldn't* be all right. And I didn't want to hear platitudes. Somehow I managed to push to my feet. "I'm going to bed." My voice cracked.

Mom let me go.

Soon I huddled on my side, the covers over my head. I could barely breathe like that, but I didn't care. All I could do was pray. *Please, God, take it all away.*

But I heard no response.

WEDNESDAY, MARCH 14—
THURSDAY, MARCH 15

Chapter 23

WEDNESDAY MORNING I WOKE AT 8:30, BLEAK AND SORE. All night I'd dreamed about Hilderbrand killing the woman. Putting her in the suitcase. Dumping her off the boat.

I turned over in bed to see Mom at her computer. Dressed and in makeup as usual. I buried my head beneath the pillow. *No.* No more digging online for me. No more trying to fight Cognoscenti, chase down justice for an unknown victim. I just needed to get out of the Bay Area.

Somehow I'd learn to deal with the memories. Maybe in time they'd fade.

"Lisa, get up." Mom's voice sounded grim. "I found something."

I groaned.

"You'll want to see this."

No, I don't.

"I found a picture of William Hilderbrand."

"I've already seen his picture."

"Bet you haven't seen *this* one."

I should at least get up. I had to go to my apartment and start packing. What about all my furniture? Maybe I should just leave it. Get out in a hurry.

Where would I go?

Mom would drag me back to Denver.

"Lisa."

"Yeah, Mom, I hear you."

With a heavy sigh I forced myself from bed. Stumbled over to the desk and fixed my eyes on the monitor.

Mom pointed. "Look."

It was him, all right. A confident-looking man with sandy hair, dressed in a black tux and bow tie. His arm was draped around a beautiful dark-haired woman in a floor length gown.

I froze.

"It's her, isn't it." Mom looked up at me.

I nodded, speechless. Stepped back to collapse in the armchair.

She lay dead on the kitchen floor, blood oozing from her mouth . . .

In the picture with Hilderbrand she looked so *alive*.

He folded her body into the suitcase. Zipped it closed.

I screwed my eyes shut against the memories. "Who is she, where are they, when was it taken?"

"At some charity ball in Palo Alto last year. The caption says her name is Patti Stolsinger."

Patti Stolsinger. Patti Stolsinger. The name rolled around on my tongue. Who *was* she?

Waves lapped against the boat beneath the black sky. The water looked even darker, ready to swallow her whole. He lifted up the suitcase and slid it over the edge of the boat. It hit with a splash . . .

I rubbed my eyes. Silence ticked in the room.

One end of the suitcase dipped underwater. It sank until it disappeared.

I leaned forward and stared at Patti's face. Was she still at the bottom of some cold lake? The Bay? Or had her body been found, leaving her loved ones desperate to find the killer?

Now I knew the truth. She *was* real. Could I walk away from this? From her?

I gazed at Patti's face. She looked back at me, pleading.

Mom's fingers tapped the keyboard. "Here's another picture of Patti in a society page." Mom spoke quietly, as if our room had become a memorial. "'Patti Stolsinger of Atherton and Marian O'Neil of Palo Alto, admiring a flower centerpiece at the Black and White Ball.' That was in 2010. No sign of Hilderbrand."

The Black-and-White Ball. I'd heard of it—a big charity event for the rich.

The picture of Hilderbrand and Patti still vibrated in my head. How did he go from that to murder?

Mom tilted her head. "If they were dating, he should be a suspect."

You'd think so. But then, he was William Hilderbrand. "Keep looking. There has to be something about her death. Or disappearance."

Mom clicked more keys. "There are a lot of hits to go through."

I lay back in the chair and stared across the room. Voices passed our door in the hall. Children. A mother calling for them to slow down.

"She's a researcher in a biotech company." Mom's voice remained low. "Named Biocent."

On the kitchen floor, she groaned. He grabbed a knife and knelt above her . . .

My cell phone went off. I jumped, my thoughts wrenching from the scene. It had to be Sherry. I pushed out of the chair to answer. Her ID showed on the screen.

"Hi, Sherry."

"Hi. You okay?"

"Yeah."

"You don't sound it."

I wanted to tell her—*We found him. We found her.* But I stopped myself. Maybe she shouldn't know. It might only put her in danger, too.

Would I have to leave town without even saying goodbye to my best friend? Immediate tears filled my eyes. I blinked them away and made my voice sound normal. "I just got up. We're still at the hotel. What's up with you?"

"I have a couple hours this morning while J.T.'s next door for a play time. I can go down to the police station and give them my prints."

"Oh, good."

"Who should I ask for?"

"Ted Bremer, but he may not be on duty yet. Anyone at the station can probably take them."

"Okay."

"Call me after you've done the fingerprints. I'm sure your husband's thrilled you have to do this."

"Jay's very worried about you."

"Probably worried I don't cause *you* trouble."

"Lisa, you're my friend."

My heart panged. "I know."

"Actually he said—Can your mom hear?"

I glanced at Mom, hunched over her computer. "No."

"Jay said something interesting about her. 'Cause you know how well he remembers the scene at Ryan's funeral."

Didn't we all. Mom had been at me to move home, insisting I wasn't strong enough to make it alone in California. Sherry got madder every time the woman opened her mouth. Then Mom added I didn't have any friends here to help me.

"*I'm* helping," Sherry shot back. "A lot more than you, if you want to know. I don't put her down every chance I get. No wonder she doesn't want to move back to Denver. *You're* there."

Whoa. I'd never heard Sherry talk to anyone like that. Mom had gone crimson and stalked from the room.

I sat on my hotel bed, facing away from my mother. "What'd he say?"

"That it's a good thing she showed up. It would make you stronger."

What was *that* supposed to mean? Mom always had a knack for cutting me down, and he knew it. "Well, he's a man. They see things weird."

"Yeah. I suppose."

We fell into silence.

"Sherry, I need to go."

"Okay. I'll call you when I'm done at the station."

I dropped the phone on the bed and stared at the wall. Jay's words rattled around inside me.

"She bothering you?" Mom's tone accused.

I stood up and faced my mother. "She doesn't bother me, Mom. She's my friend."

My mother eyed me, then gestured toward her computer. "I'm still looking." As if I should have no doubts as to who was really helping me here.

I squeezed the back of my neck. Had this day only just begun? I pictured Sherry at the police station, talking to Officer Bremer—

A horrible thought crashed into my brain. It struck so hard it weakened my knees. "Oh, no."

Mom frowned at me. "What is it?"

I sat back down on the bed. Focused on the brown coverlet as snatches of our meeting with Officer Bremer replayed in my head. The way he'd hesitated when I asked if he knew a case that would fit my memories . . .

Of *course* he knew. With Redwood City just one town over from Atherton? He had to.

And I'd stupidly told him details about the murder. Details no one should know—unless they were *there.*

"Lisa, *what?*"

I felt sick in my stomach. "He thinks I'm involved."

"What? Who?"

"Bremer. He thinks I'm involved in her murder." I shook my head. The whole thing seemed so obvious. How could we have been so naïve? We'd handed the police every reason in the world to suspect me.

"Where did you get that idea?"

Was Bremer talking to Atherton police right now, planning their next move?

Now I *couldn't* leave town. That would only make them all the more suspicious. They'd just track me down, drag me back. I was trapped here, between Hilderbrand and the police.

The realizations fell like muddy raindrops, clogging my head. I couldn't begin to think what to do next.

"Turn off the computer." My words sounded off-key. "I don't want to see any more. I don't want to know."

"We gave them evidence, Lisa. We *have* evidence that we're telling the truth."

"Not nearly enough!" I threw out my hands. "Think like a cop. We could have staged the break-in and the phone message. We could have slipped the envelope onto the hallway floor as we let Agnes inside. There's nothing to prove we're telling the truth. We are stupid, stupid, *stupid!*"

"But why would you want to kill that woman? You don't even know her."

I laughed. "Convince them of that."

Suddenly my mother's face was the last thing I wanted to see. She'd gotten me into this mess with Bremer. Practically made me call the police. I slid off the bed and headed for the bathroom. "I'm going to take a shower." Hot enough to burn away my thoughts. Convince me I was wrong.

It didn't work. The hot water only weakened me. I needed food again. But no way. I did not want to sit down and eat with my mother.

Come on, Lisa. Calling the police was your decision, and you know it.

By the time I emerged from the bathroom Mom had packed up her laptop. She took one look at me and declared I needed breakfast. She was reading my mind again. I hated that.

"I don't want anything."

"You *need* it."

I shook my head.

"Look. I drove us here. And I'm not driving you home until you eat."

I leaned against the wall, tears pooling in my eyes. I couldn't deal with this. A murder, the police—and my mother, too?

How had I gotten here? My whole life was falling apart.

Mom slipped her arm around my shoulders, her voice gentling. "Come on, honey. You're just feeling overwhelmed right now. It'll pass. And you'll be better if you eat. We'll talk this through."

I had no more strength to fight her. Next thing I knew, she was leading me down the hall to the restaurant.

We chose a booth in the corner. I faced the wall, not wanting to even look at other people. What was wrong with me? Where was the determination I'd had two days ago?

Mom folded her hands beneath her chin. "You will get through this. We *will* figure it out."

God, please make that true.

I played with my fork, trying to think of something good. "I haven't had any new memories in over twenty-four hours. Maybe they're done."

"Hope so."

The waitress took our orders and poured coffee, trying not to look at my bandaged head. I doused my drink with cream. Mom and I couldn't seem to find any more to say to each other.

"Why did you come, Mom?" The words slipped out of me.

Dismay flicked across her face. "Why are you so surprised I want to help you?"

That question had a thousand answers.

My throat clutched. "You told me I needed to draw my picture better."

"What?"

"When I was five. That picture I made for you. You didn't say thank you or that you liked it. You just told me how to *fix* it. I couldn't do anything right."

Mom's lips creaked open. She gazed at me, lines crisscrossing her forehead. "You did lots of things right."

"You sure didn't make me feel like it."

Her focus danced around the table, as if a response might lie in the plates and silverware. "Is this what you were talking about yes-terday? About making you feel worthless? I really . . . I don't even remember that picture."

Don't remember? The memory had carved itself into me.

"I'm sorry, Lisa. I truly am."

The apology floated by me, a milkweed on the wind. My gaze dropped to my lap. She didn't even *remember?*

"I never meant to make you feel like you couldn't do anything right."

All these years I'd cowed beneath this memory and many oth-ers. While my mother had no clue? Did she think she'd raised me well? Didn't she wonder why she had so much self-esteem while I had none?

And then I saw it. Just like that. I'd let these memories shape my life. And who had it hurt?

Me.

The thought sent me reeling.

"Lisa, do you hear?"

I looked at my mother as if for the first time. "Yeah. I hear."

We fell silent again. I took a drink of my coffee, the heat and taste of it anchoring me.

Mom pressed her fingers into the table. "Whatever I've done, whatever I've said to you, now or years ago, was to help you. I just want to make you better."

Make me better. Hadn't she said those same words yesterday morning?

I set down my coffee cup. "Mom, *you* can't make me better. You, or anyone else on this earth. *I* have to make myself better, with God's help."

Mom gazed at me, then nodded. "It's so hard to watch your child suffer. You'd do anything to make it go away."

That made no sense. "When you pointed out the flaws in that drawing, you *made* me suffer."

My mother looked away. "That's the irony, I suppose. In trying to prepare you for life so you'd hurt less . . . I hurt you."

It was a major revelation for her, and it played across her face. I didn't want to pursue it, afraid I'd just rub it in. She already looked pained enough.

The waitress appeared with our food. Somehow I forced it down. It tasted like glue. Mom and I talked little. My thoughts fixed on our conversation and what she might be thinking.

"I'm sorry," she said eventually. "Really I am."

"It's okay, Mom."

We could talk about it no more. The whole thing needed time to settle.

I found myself wondering about the break-in and Officer Bremer. Where was he right now? What was he doing?

And where were Mom and I supposed to sleep tonight? At the hotel I felt like a refugee. Discarded. Helpless. If I couldn't leave town, on my own turf at least I could fight.

But fight how?

"I'm going to call the apartment manager to get my lock changed," I told Mom as we headed back to the room. If the lock had been picked, it may make little difference. But it was something to do.

"Sounds good."

We packed up and checked out of the hotel. The whole time I felt our conversation shimmer between us.

On the drive back to Redwood City my cell phone went off. It was Sherry again, telling me she'd been fingerprinted. "If I ever hold up a bank, they'll know where to find me."

I tried to laugh. "Thanks for putting yourself through that. We're on our way home."

"You sleeping there tonight?"

"I can't stay away forever."

"But won't you be scared?"

Petrified was more like it. "I'll work through it."

Sherry made a sound in her throat. "That chip was no placebo."

"Thanks. I needed to hear that."

I hung up—and my phone rang again. Maria Delgado, a tech from Redwood City Police Department, was on the line, wanting to come over to dust for fingerprints. "Can you give us half an hour?" I asked. "We're just now headed back."

Delgado agreed.

We drove up to the apartment building, and fear immediately descended. It wrapped around my throat as we neared my door. Mom and I shot each other a look. I took a deep breath and unlocked the door. Eased it open.

The living room looked as it had when we left.

I stepped inside, and Mom followed. She rolled in the suitcase and bolted the door. Together we checked the bedrooms. Everything seemed fine.

I called the building manager and asked to have the lock changed. Today. "Just in case the guy somehow got hold of one of my keys and made a copy," I explained. Herman Walters was a good man. Ryan and I had called him before when we'd had a problem with a leaky faucet, and he'd been very responsive. Herman promised to have a new lock for me by late afternoon.

Officer Maria Delgado showed up, a full-figured woman with dark hair and large eyes. "I hear you had a problem here yesterday." She stepped inside, carrying a kit with her equipment. "Sorry to hear that. Let's see what we can do to catch the bad guys."

I hid my surprise. Either Bremer hadn't told her his suspicions that I'd made all this up, or she was a very good actress.

Maybe they needed to go through this drill just to cover their bases. To prove there were no "foreign fingerprints."

At the kitchen table Delgado rolled Mom's and my fingers in black ink and then onto paper, creating crisp replicas of our prints. Delgado smiled. "If only the ones we get from suspects were that perfect."

With efficiency she dusted the door handle and surrounding area, inside and out. She picked up some "pretty good prints." But they could easily be ours. Next she moved to the counter, dusting in the area where the stolen documents had been. Mom hovered on the kitchen side, watching her every move.

I wandered the living room, scenes from Patti Stolsinger's murder scrolling by. "Is Officer Bremer on duty?" I asked Delgado.

"He'll come in at 5:00."

Had he talked to Jerry Sterne and Clair Saxton? Had they filled his head with the insistence that my chip was a blank? That I was just out to get the company?

How much did Jerry and Clair really know about Hilderbrand?

Delgado finished her work and packed up her tools. She shook my hand, then Mom's. "Someone will get back with you when we know more."

They wouldn't find anyone else's prints. "Thank you for coming."

One o'clock rolled around. Then 2:00. I tried to take a nap but couldn't sleep. I resorted to cleaning my bathroom. Then the kitchen. Anything to keep busy while we waited for the next shoe to fall.

"Bremer's going to arrest me, Mom."

"No he won't. I won't let him."

Uh-huh.

Time ticked, and my nerves scissored. When Bremer came on duty he would be after me. He'd call me down to the station. I'd have to explain the inexplicable.

No need to worry about sleeping in the apartment tonight. I'd be in jail.

Mom cleaned as well. And did some ironing. I wouldn't let her even turn on her computer. Call it denial or what you will. I just couldn't face any more.

Sometime after 3:00 Herman Walters showed up. Herman was in his late sixties, tall and white-haired. Mom answered the door. I stuck one of Ryan's old baseball caps on my head before leaving the bedroom, in no mood to explain my bandage.

By the time I greeted Herman, Mom was already working her charm. "Thank you very much for coming so quickly to help my daughter."

"No problem, ma'am, no problem at all." He beamed at her.

Herman set about his work. When he finished he gave me two new keys. "There you go. I hope this keeps you safe."

"Thanks. Me too."

Five o'clock arrived. I pictured Bremer coming on duty. Picking up the file with my name on it.

At 5:45, my cell phone rang. I was in the kitchen, heating some soup. My movements stopped.

Mom bit her lip. "Want me to get it?"

Wouldn't matter who answered. I shook my head. With reluctant fingers I picked up the receiver. The ID told me what I already knew. "Hello?"

"Miss Newberry, it's Officer Bremer."

My heart stopped beating. "Hi."

"I'd like you to come down to the station. I need more information about the alleged break-in at your house and the other details."

Alleged. The word reverberated. "You want my mother to come, too?"

"That would be helpful. The station's at 1301 Maple, on the east side of 101."

"We'll find it." How calm I sounded, while my world fell away.

"Can you get here soon?"

"We'll be right down."

On the way out the door I gazed back at my apartment.

When would I see it again?

Chapter 24

IN THE CAR MOM AND I TALKED LITTLE. I GAVE HER THE police station's address, and she keyed it into the rental car's GPS. The directions took us across El Camino, then past Freeway 101. I spotted the station ahead. "There it—"

He drove through the darkness on the freeway, exit signs sliding by.

I stilled, my hand hanging in the air.

I saw Holly . . . Harbor . . . Ralston.

I braced myself. Please, no more. After so long? When would these pictures ever stop?

The scene faded.

My hand dropped to my lap.

"Lisa!" Mom's voice was sharp. "Did you see something?"

Holly, Harbor . . . I knew those exits. "He went north on the freeway."

Mom turned into the parking lot for the police station, a tan building with green trim. "Hilderbrand?"

I latched my mind back onto the scene. "I just saw a flash. He was driving up 101 after getting on at Woodside Road. I saw signs for exits just north of here. But . . ."

Mom pulled into a space and cut the engine. I couldn't move. Something wasn't right . . .

"But what?"

Anxiety spread through my chest. What was I not getting? It felt like something so obvious. "I don't . . ." I squeezed my hands into fists, picturing the man in his kitchen. Looking at his backyard. Driving away from his house—

The sun had been setting.

I leaned back in my seat. That was it. The time on his watch had read only 5:48. But that didn't fit with what I just saw.

"It shouldn't be dark." My gaze fixed on the dashboard. "He left his house, and the sun was setting. It was still light when he drove up Woodside Road. But then he gets on the freeway, and in two minutes it's totally dark?"

This new memory couldn't be right. It didn't make sense at all.

"Is that what you just saw? It was night time?"

"Yes."

Mom pulled the keys from the ignition. "What does this mean?"

"I don't know." Heat flushed my cheeks.

"Maybe what you just saw happened on a different day."

I rubbed my forehead. "I guess."

I gazed at the police station. Somewhere inside it Bremer waited. I couldn't let this new thing throw me. I had to get hold of myself.

"Come on." Mom touched my arm. "We'd better go inside. We can figure this out later."

I threw her a look. There wouldn't be a *later*. "Yeah."

We got out of the car.

In the lobby I sidled up to a reception desk and told the woman Officer Bremer was expecting us. She motioned us to some chairs to wait. Mom sat. I wandered around, my mind churning.

All too soon Bremer strode in, extending his hand. "Ms. Newberry. Ms. Wegman. Thank you for coming."

I shook his hand, not a bit fooled. This was no friendly visit.

"Come on back." He led us through a door, down a hallway and into a small, windowless room. Nothing in it but a table with three chairs. Mom chose one and sat straight-backed. Wary. I sat next to her, Bremer on my left. Near him lay a thin manila folder. I glanced up—and saw a camera mounted near the ceiling in a corner. Pointed at me.

"Sorry this isn't exactly a room with ambiance." Bremer clunked his chair closer to the table.

My gaze moved from the camera to the folder. What was in there?

Mom patted my hand—an action I knew she wanted Bremer to see. "Sorry if we're a little quiet. We're still nervous from yesterday. We stayed at a hotel last night, and today we had the apartment lock changed."

Bremer nodded, his expression impassive. "Glad to hear about the new lock."

He leaned back in his chair. "All right, last night after I saw you I was able to investigate your situation." Bremer looked at me. "As you might guess it didn't take long to run the address in Atherton that you gave me and come up with the owner's name."

My muscles wouldn't move. Mom said nothing.

"The owner of that property is William Hilderbrand, CEO of Cognoscenti."

I forced myself to look straight back at Bremer. "I know. We did an online search last night."

"Were you surprised?" Bremer's eyes were like lasers.

"More like stunned."

"Because the man that you say killed someone runs the very company that performed your procedure? The procedure you claim is flawed."

I could feel my chest rise and fall, but oxygen didn't seem to reach my lungs.

Bremer's gaze flicked from me to Mom and back. My mother stared at him levelly, daring him to continue.

The officer leaned an arm on the table. "I was able to contact Agnes Brighton last night. She did confirm that you hired her to do a composite drawing. She also confirmed finding the envelope outside your door."

Well. That was something.

"Ms. Newberry, I'd like you to tell me again about these 'memories' or visions you've been having."

My shoulders slumped. "*All* of it? Everything I told you yesterday?"

"Just start at the beginning. We'll work from there."

I glanced at the camera. Surely it was running. My story would all go on film. Every self-incriminating word.

Maybe I should walk out right now. Demand a lawyer.

But I'd already told Bremer everything. He had it all in his notes. Like it or not, I was in this thing up to my chin. Wouldn't demanding an attorney make me look all the more guilty?

"I don't have to talk to you."

Bremer kept his poker face. "Is there some reason you don't want to?"

Other than the fact that I didn't trust him one bit?

"We spoke for quite awhile yesterday."

I shrugged.

"She's been through a lot," Mom said. "She—"

"It's okay, Mom."

"But you—"

"It's *okay*." She couldn't get me out of this. No "protecting me from suffering" now.

Bremer sat casually, as if we weren't engaged in a war of wits. "It really would help to hear your report again."

Scenarios spun through my mind. Walking out of there. Leaving town. Hiding from Hilderbrand and maybe even the police until . . . what? When would this all end?

Another strained minute passed. Something within me thrashed . . . then fell away.

I heaved a sigh—and started to talk.

First came the dream (or was I awake?) in the hospital. Then the other visions. The suitcase. The black SUV with its partial license plate. Hilderbrand's drive from his neighborhood. I didn't tell Bremer about the new memory I'd just seen—day suddenly becoming night. Or how the dragon ring was on Hilderbrand's finger—then it wasn't. Sometimes Bremer asked questions. My voice sounded factual, emotionless. Why should he believe me? By the time I finished, it seemed so outrageous I hardly believed myself.

"And that's everything."

Silence clung to the walls of the room. Outside the door male voices grew near, then receded down the hall.

The officer shifted positions. "And you say you didn't discover who this man was until last night. After I was at your apartment."

"Yes. When we were at the hotel."

He tapped the table. "Do you intend to sue Cognoscenti?"

"No."

"What do you want from them?"

"The truth."

"And what is that?"

"I don't know, because I don't understand everything that's

going on. Partly that there *is* something wrong with the chip they put in me. They need to own up to that before this product goes on the market."

"But they say the chip they gave you was a placebo. In other words, completely blank."

"They're lying."

"They also told *me* it's a placebo."

My eyebrows raised. "You talked to them already?"

"To Jerry Sterne. Today. He confirmed your participation in the trial, and the outcome. He also faxed me a copy of the document about your chip."

Coldness sank through me. Mom made a disgusted noise.

Bremer watched me intently.

When I was in third grade a much larger girl coaxed me into getting on the playground seesaw. We pushed up and down for awhile, then she used her weight to sink to the ground. I hung in the air, helpless, as she laughed at me. Now I hung there again, Cognoscenti and the police on the other end.

They'd never believe me. I was caught. Meanwhile there was a killer out there.

"He also told me, Ms. Newberry, that at your last meeting you threatened to call the police."

My heart skipped. "Maybe I did. I don't remember."

"And you said you'd sue Cognoscenti."

I shook my head. "I didn't mean that."

"It appeared to him that you were very upset at the company because you'd received a placebo and were threatening to derail the trial."

Mom smacked the table. "*They're* the ones who were threatening. It was that very day someone made that phone call to me. You heard the tape."

Yeah, wait a minute. I was the victim here. "I was *not* threatening to derail the trial." My voice rose. "I went there for help. They refused it. Then they pulled me from the trial and sent me packing. *Then* someone from the company called my mother, and later left another threatening message outside my door. After that they broke into my apartment to get rid of the evidence. And to terrify me."

Bremer made no response. I seethed all the more. "Listen to me, please. You've got to look into this murder. Because the man who did it runs Cognoscenti. He's surely heard all my details of *his* crime. He knows *I* know."

Bremer let the last sentence echo. He put a fist against his hip. "The results came back from the evidence the tech collected at your apartment. We found no foreign prints."

"He was probably wearing gloves."

"And there was no evidence of forced entry."

"But he got in, didn't he. And I wasn't there to open the door for him."

Bremer rubbed his eyebrow. "I want to believe you, Ms. Newberry, I really do. But I'm having a hard time putting this together. I can find no physical evidence that anyone was in your apartment. And the alleged reason you give for the break-in—the theft of that written message—can't be substantiated either. No one claims to have seen the actual message but you and your mother. And Mr. Sterne denied any knowledge of someone at the company contacting you, either by phone or in writing."

"So—what?" My mother's tone was pure flint. "We're just making all this up?"

Bremer spread his hands. "Are you?"

"That's ridiculous!" She huffed back in her chair. "My daughter's never given the law any trouble in her life. Nor have I."

"Look." I forced my words to a simmering calm. "The main thing is—there's a killer walking the streets. And now I even know who he murdered. Her name is Patti Stolsinger. We matched her picture on the Internet. I'll bet you know her identity already, don't you. And you're just leading me on here. But I'm telling you—now Hilderbrand surely has his sights on *me*. I'll end up dead, too."

Bremer surveyed me, then opened the mysterious folder. He drew out a single sheet of paper and flipped it toward me. "That her? The woman in your 'memories'?"

It was the same picture we'd seen online. Hilderbrand's arm around Patti. Sadness hit me. She'd been so unsuspecting. Did he know then what he was going to do?

I nodded.

Bremer stabbed me with those eyes of his. "You're sure."

"Yes."

"Patti Stolsinger. Age thirty-eight."

Yes, yes, *yes*. How many times did I have to say it for the camera? "Have they found her?" The question snagged in my throat.

"Found her?"

"In a lake somewhere? In the Bay?"

He raised his chin. "No."

So she was still there. The knowledge made me want to weep. All this time. How long had it been? Was there anything left of her?

I licked my lips. "Look, I know I can't prove how I know all this. But that woman deserves justice. And I want to be safe. You've got to look at William Hilderbrand."

"Ms. Newberry." The officer bounced a fingertip against the table. "I have to tell you, I'm confused. I really don't know what to do with what you've told me. As I said, we investigated the alleged break-in and found no evidence. Now you insist this is the woman you've 'seen' murdered—in memories emanating from the chip implanted in your brain."

How crazy he made it all sound.

This was it, wasn't it? The moment when he arrested me. I would definitely need an attorney now. Where to find one? Would they let me out on bail? Only to return to my apartment, where I was a target for a maniac?

Bremer gestured toward Patti's photo. "I discovered that Miss Stolsinger resides in Sunnyvale. I called that department to ask if they had any kind of open case on her. The answer was no."

What? "You mean they don't even know she's missing?"

"I had the department do some checking. They tracked down her place of business as Biocent, also in Sunnyvale. The officer went to the company, asking to speak with Miss Stolsinger. She was in her office."

The words iced the blood in my veins. I gaped at him.

Bremer spread his hands. "That's the main source of my confusion, Ms. Newberry. You insist that this woman"—he reached over and pulled the drawing toward himself—"has been murdered and dumped in the water somewhere. But I can assure you of one thing. She is very much alive."

Chapter 25

I BARELY FELT THE CAR SEAT UNDER ME, BARELY HEARD THE sounds of traffic. All I could do was stare through the windshield of Mom's rental car, my mind numb.

What can you do when truths you *know* have been ripped away? Have been balled up and set on fire?

I'd walked out of the police station on robot legs, the world tilted. Imagining the snide laughter of officers behind me. *"Crazy Lisa Newberry. Should be locked up."*

"Maybe it's the wrong woman." Mom gripped the steering wheel, her back not touching the seat. "She just looks like the one in your visions."

"No. It's *her*."

How many times had I seen Patti Stolsinger—shouting . . . choking . . . dying? I knew that face like I knew my own. It. Was. *Her*.

We crossed El Camino. My fingers dug into my legs. I didn't want to go home. What was I supposed to do? How was I supposed to live?

"You might as well go back to Denver, Mom." My voice brittled like dry leaves.

"I can't leave you now. Not like this."

Like this. Spinning with no place to land.

"You've already missed two full days of work. They must need you."

"You need me more."

My chest collapsed. I folded over and leaned my head on the dashboard. "I'm going *insane.*" The awful word dropped onto my knees. Rolled off to the floor. "What did Cognoscenti *do* to me?"

Mom held my shoulder. "No, you're not. There has to be an explanation."

I cushioned my head with both hands. My brain geared on, running scenes of the murder. *No!* I wanted to scream. Jump from the car and tear down the street. I wanted to lay my own skull open, rip out the cursed chip.

"Lisa, hang with me." Fright zigzagged Mom's words. "Please. We'll do . . . something."

But there was nothing we could do. Nothing.

I reared up with sudden force. "Maybe Bremer's lying. They didn't talk to her at all."

"Why would he do that?"

"I don't *know.*" I pressed my fingers against my temples. "Maybe Cognoscenti got to him. Bribed him."

Mom's silence shrieked.

She didn't believe me anymore, did she? Thought I'd gone mad, just like the police did.

We reached my apartment building. Mom parked and turned off the engine. I gazed up at the second story. Had I really once had a life there? With a husband—and sanity?

"You will get through this, Lisa."

I gazed at the floor.

"Come on, let's go inside. I'll fix you something to eat."

Her panacea. Like I could stomach anything right now.

My door opened with a loud *click*. The sound sliced right through me.

The sun was setting as we got out of the car. Somehow I made it up the stairs.

Woodenly I used my new key to open my apartment door. All fear of another break-in had withered. They'd trashed my brain. What difference did it make if they trashed my home?

I went to the couch and sat down. Deep inside a voice chanted, *"He's lying, he's lying, he's lying."*

I *couldn't* be completely crazy. How had I known Hilderbrand's house? His car? Although Bremer had never confirmed the SUV or its license plate. But I'd bet I was right about that, too. The knowledge was stitched in my gut.

Just like the knowledge that Patti was dead.

Next thing I knew I was on my feet. I strode into the kitchen and yanked open a drawer, snatching out the phone book for Redwood City down to Sunnyvale.

Mom hovered by the counter. "What are you doing?"

I smacked down the book. Flipped through the residential section. Maybe, just maybe . . . I found the S's, my finger running down Ste . . . Sti . . . There, a listing! I couldn't believe it. Stolsinger, Patricia. 617 Nickle Street.

"Get me some paper and a pen." I pressed my finger against the letters as if they'd disappear from the page.

Mom brought them to me. I wrote down Patti's address and phone number.

My hands flipped the large book shut. "I'm going to see her." I headed toward my purse.

"Lisa, that's not a good idea."

"It's a *very* good idea. Because I don't believe she's there. She's *dead*."

"Lisa, don't."

I whirled on Mom. "I'm going! You stay here. *I'll* figure this out." I slung my purse over my shoulder and made for the door. On the way I scooped up Ryan's baseball cap, lying on the coffee table, and stuck it on my head.

Mom hustled behind me. "What are you going to do once you get there? Knock on her door?"

"Why not?"

"And when she answers?"

"She *won't*, Mom!" I flung open the door. "She's dead!"

"Wait." Mom grabbed my arm. "At least let me come with you."

"What for?"

"I can't let you go out there alone."

Out where? Into the world? Because I just might unleash my insanity upon it? "I don't want you to come."

"You *need* me to come. I'm driving."

"Well, you better hurry up, because I'm not waiting." I stomped out of the apartment and banged the door shut. Forged down the hall. Seconds later I heard my door open and Mom trotting after me.

She caught up, panting. "You could just call—"

"Anyone could answer. How would I know it's her?"

"But you could talk—"

"The person could lie." I carved to a halt. "Look. I *have* to do this. Because I am going stark raving mad, and I *have* to do *something*!" I wheeled away and trounced down the stairs.

Mom followed.

In the car she asked me for the sheet of paper with Patti's address. I handed it over. Mom punched it into the GPS.

I pressed back in the seat, trying to stanch the wild flow of my pulse.

The sky mottled to dark as we headed south on 101. My limbs refused to loosen.

Some time later we exited onto Stevens Creek.

My thoughts had settled to a slow boil. If I found Patti Stolsinger—looked her right in the eye—so be it. I'd deal with the outcome and get on with my life. Probably move—anywhere. Maybe a change of scenery would wipe my brain clean like a white slate. A tabula rasa. Sounded good to me.

The rental car's GPS told us to turn right, left, then right again. The canned woman's voice remained so calm, so factual. As if my universe wasn't tilting on its axis. I wanted to shake the thing and yell, *"Don't you understand what this means to me!"*

We reached Nickle Street.

My nerves began to vibrate.

"Your destination is on the left," chirped the GPS. And there we were, at number 617. A stylish one-story with a recessed entrance and large windows. The house was dark inside. No porch light.

Mom pulled over to the right curb. Streetlights illumed the road. I opened my door. "Stay in the car."

"No—"

"*Stay* in the *car!*" I got out on unsteady legs. My courage nearly failed me then, but I plowed across the street. Up the house's three steps and across the dim porch. The air smelled like jasmine.

A doorbell button emitted a faint glimmer. I pushed it.

Silence. No footsteps. No flicked-on light seeping through the front windows.

I pushed it again.

A car engine thrummed behind me. It came nearer, then slowed. I turned—and a dark-colored Corvette pulled into the driveway.

I froze.

The sports car stopped. The driver's door opened, and an overhead light came on. A dark-haired woman was lifting a purse off the passenger seat. She slid from behind the wheel.

I pressed against the wall of the porch, my heartbeat on hold.

She anchored the purse on her shoulder and crossed behind her car, heels clacking. Aimed for the curb. Streetlight spilled over her face.

Patti.

My stomach fell away.

At her mailbox she pulled open its front lid and withdrew a white bundle. I heard the metallic *clunk* as the mailbox closed.

The woman headed back toward her car. Reached the driveway.

"Patti Stolsinger!" I jumped into view on her porch.

She gasped. The mail fell and scattered at her feet. Patti stared at me. "Who is it?"

"Is it you, Patti? Is it really you?" I hurried down the steps and across the ground between us. The closer I got the less I could deny it. It was *her.*

Shock gripped her face. She shrank away. "Who are you?"

My mind exploded. "*Why* are you here? Why are you *alive*?"

"I don't . . ." She stood four inches shorter than I. Looking so vulnerable. Patti cast wild glances around, seeking someone to help.

I pushed myself in her face, teeth clenched. The bill of Ryan's baseball cap bumped her forehead. "You're supposed to be dead."

"What?" She backed up against the rear of her car. I came after her.

"They *told* me you were *dead*!"

"Who?"

"The memories."

"M-memories?" She was shaking.

"The scenes in my head! The ones that show you choked and stabbed. Stuffed in a suitcase."

Air stuttered from her mouth. She brought up both hands. "Please. I don't know what you're talking about."

"You *have* to know."

"I *don't!*"

I raised a fist. "You better start talking to me."

She ripped her purse from her shoulder. "You want money? Credit cards? Here." She groped in the bag and pulled out a wallet. "Take it all—"

"I don't want your money!" I knocked the wallet and purse from her hand. They spun to the pavement.

"Lisa!" My mother's voice knifed across the street. "Stop!"

Patti jerked toward the sound. "Help me!"

I heard Mom's running footsteps. I didn't care. "I'm *not* going to hurt you. I just want you to talk to me!"

"Lisa." Mom jumped over the curb and pounded up the driveway. She grabbed my arm. "Stop it right now."

Patti pressed herself against the car. "Get her off me."

Mom dragged me away. I fought. She threw both hands on my shoulders. *"No."* We half stumbled backward a few feet. Patti watched in horror.

Mom and I slid to a halt, panting. She still had hold of me. We eyed Patti, and she eyed us.

The night tremored.

Patti regained her equilibrium. "You'd better get off my property. I'm calling the police."

Maniacal laughter burst from me. "Oh, that'll help. We just came from them."

"Lisa, what are you doing?" Mom dug her fingers into my shoulders. "Just look at yourself. She has every right to call the police."

Those words finally got to me. The blaze within me sputtered, then died. My mind began to clear. What *was* I doing? I'd never gone after anyone like that in my life. My arms went limp.

Mom hung on for a moment, then let me go.

I swallowed, trying to find something, *anything* to say. "I'm sorry."

Patti's back straightened. Mom walked over to lift her wallet and purse from the driveway. She held them out. Patti snatched them and dropped the wallet in her purse.

"Please forgive my daughter." Mom backed up, giving Patti space. "She's just . . . overcome. She's been through some traumatic events. And even though you don't know us, we think you may have some answers as to why."

Patti raised her chin. "She assaulted me in front of my own house!"

"I know but—"

"Do you have a twin?" I took a step forward.

"Stay away from me!" Patti jerked back.

"Lisa—"

I stopped. "*Do* you have a twin?"

Patti's face twisted. "No."

"A sister who looks just like you?"

"No. Get off my property right now." Patti shoved the handle of her purse over her shoulder. "I mean it."

"Please." Mom's voice lilted into charm. "Patti. My daughter was sure she'd witnessed you being attacked and murdered. She was so sure and so devastated by what she saw that she told the police. But here you are, alive and well. We're very glad for that. But it's hard to reconcile it with what we've been led to believe."

Patti gave my mother a hard look. "This is what glad looks like?"

Remorse clogged my throat. A whiff of jasmine filtered over me, sweet and so out of place.

"She's just confused, that's all. My daughter's never hurt anyone in her life. Please, just . . . will you give us a chance to talk to you?"

Patti's eyes flicked from my mother to me. I glanced away, saw her scattered mail, and went to pick it up. I offered the stack to her. She hesitated, then took it from my hands.

Realization moved across her face. "*You're* the reason that policeman came to my office today."

I nodded.

She licked her lips. "You really saw someone murdered?"

"Yes." Sort of.

"Why did you think it was me?"

"I saw your face so clearly. Then I found your picture online. With William Hilderbrand." I surveyed her. How would she respond to his name?

"What picture?"

"At some formal event."

Her chin lifted in recognition. "Well, whoever was killed, it obviously wasn't me."

But it *was*.

"So you can go now. And leave me alone."

No way. I'd come this far. "So you know him. Dr. Hilderbrand."

"What's that to you?"

"He's CEO of Cognoscenti. He invented the Empowerment Chip."

Patti shot me a wary look. "So?"

Mom and I exchanged a glance. Clearly she already knew this. "I took part in the medical trial. Had the chip implanted." I lifted the baseball cap and pointed to my bandage.

She pulled her top lip between her teeth. "Did it work?"

A strange question. And something about the way she asked it . . . Did she have some personal stake in the trial? I put the cap back on. "Yes. And no."

"What does that mean?"

Mom shook her head. "Lisa—"

"It cured my depression. And it placed scenes in my head. Of your murder."

Patti's eyebrows raised. "You're crazy."

Tell me about it.

The scene of her storming into Hilderbrand's living room replayed in my head. Her accusations of infidelity . . . "You're dating Hilderbrand, aren't you."

"That's *none* of your business."

"Why can't you stop cheating on me? You're nothing but a liar!"

"But you know he's running around on you."

Mom covered her face with her hand.

Patti stiffened. "Get out of here."

"Aren't you going to ask me how I know?"

She pushed past my mother, clutching her mail. "If you're not gone by the time I'm inside, I'm calling the police." She stalked up the driveway.

"I know what his living room looks like. Beige walls, a marble fireplace. Impressionist painting of the ocean, a glass coffee table. Hardwood floors and a Chinese rug. And his kitchen—stainless steel appliances."

Patti halted, her spine rigid. Slowly she turned around. Her eyes flashed. "So that's what this is about. You're one of them."

"No."

"You've been in his *house.*"

"No."

She strode back toward me, indignation pouring off her shoulders. "Who *are* you?"

"Lisa Newberry. I don't know your boyfriend. I only know that the chip he designed has put pictures in my head. Of you and him. His house. I see them through his eyes. Like they're *his* memories."

Patti hung there, her mouth open, eyes lasering into mine. Emotions trickled across her face like melting water over stone.

Her face blanched. She drew her head back and fixed her gaze on some faraway point. "It's true, then." She spoke half to herself.

"What?"

Her jaw worked. She looked back at me as if deciding what to say. "I've heard rumors that some of the chips . . ."

Mom's lips parted.

"Are tainted?" I leaned forward, my heart tripping over itself.

Patti shrugged.

"*Please* tell me. You have no idea what this has been like."

Patti ran her thumb over the stack of mail. "I don't know. I've just heard Bill mention a few things. But he's not sure what the problem is. If there *is* one he wants to fix it. This company is his life."

Bill. I stared at her, the puzzle pieces in my brain more jumbled than ever. Why was she admitting this? To me, of all people? And why were some parts of the visions I'd seen apparently true while the big one—her murder—was false?

"Lisa went to Cognoscenti." Mom edged closer to Patti. "She told the directors what she was seeing. They insisted her chip was blank and kicked her out of the trial."

Patti shook her head. "I don't think anyone told Bill that."

"Why would they keep it quiet?" Mom looked at her askance.

"I don't know. To protect the chip? Keep the trial going forward?"

I tipped my head to the sky. Stars ghosted the surreal night. What to even say next? I'd spent too many torturous hours believing William Hilderbrand was a cold-blooded killer. He was no *Bill* to me. No CEO kept in the dark.

Patti regarded me. "Are you really telling me you think the chip made you 'see' my murder?"

"I know it's hard to believe but—yes."

"Who supposedly killed me?"

Mom shook her head at me. I ignored her. "Hilderbrand."

"What?"

"It happened in his house. I saw the whole thing through his eyes."

"Through his eyes?"

"Like it was his memory. Somehow put in my brain."

Patti glanced distractedly at the mail in her hand. She stuffed it in her purse. "You mean—you never actually saw him. Saw his face."

I managed a nod.

"So what made you think it was him?"

"Like I said, his house. I saw it in my head. Then I found it in Atherton—for real." I put my hands on my hips. "He owns a dragon's head ring, doesn't he."

"A what?"

"A ring that looks like a dragon's head. Has emeralds for eyes."

"Are you kidding? He'd never wear anything like that."

Wait a minute—*no?* My mouth snapped shut. Then whose ring . . . ?

She ran a hand through her hair. "You say you never saw his face. What if you were seeing through someone *else's* eyes? Someone in his house?"

That stopped me cold.

For a long moment I could only stand there, the question ricocheting in my chest. *God, please let this make sense!* Because absolutely none of it did. I was worse off for coming here.

"Well, you're clearly alive." Mom to the rescue. "So whoever's eyes it was—that person's not a murderer. None of that is even true. What remains is the problem for Lisa—and for Cognoscenti. There's something wrong with her chip. The company needs to accept that and fix it."

Patti took a deep breath, as if confronting a major decision. "I can get you in to see him."

My jaw dropped. "Hilderbrand?"

"Would you want to?"

"*Yes.*"

She nodded. "I'll call him tonight."

"You will? Really?"

"Yes."

"Okay." My voice sounded like a little kid's. I backed off, palms up. How I would ever face the man, I had no idea. "Okay."

Patti aimed me a hard look. "I hope you understand what I'm doing for you both. Getting in to see Bill is like getting in to see the President. He's so busy, and he protects his time. Nobody infringes on it. You understand that?"

"Yeah. Sure."

"And one more thing."

"Uh-huh." My mind was already twirling. I didn't think I could take much more.

"*Don't* lie to him. Don't try to put *anything* over on him. Or I'll tell you something, Lisa Newberry." Patti took a step toward me, jabbing her forefinger in the air. "He'll chew you up and spit you out."

Chapter 26

ON THE DRIVE HOME MOM HAD TO PULL TO THE SHOULDER of the freeway so I could throw up. I stumbled from the car, stomach wrenching. By the time we made it back to the apartment I could barely think straight. All the work Mom and I had done—and we only had more questions. And now I had to face Hilderbrand himself. How would I get through that?

Once home I collapsed on the couch. It was nearly nine-thirty. My body begged for sleep, but my brain wouldn't turn off. Around and around it went over the questions and inconsistencies, a nightmare carousel.

My mother tried to get me to eat.

Mom, really?

Patti was supposed to call when she got through to Hilderbrand. Mom laid the receiver on the coffee table beside me.

The clock ticked. We waited.

We talked about the meeting with Hilderbrand—*if* it happened at all. What we'd say. What questions we wanted answered. "I'm so glad you're here," I told Mom. "I wouldn't want to face that man by myself."

She nodded. "But he's not a murderer, Lisa. You've got to turn your thinking around on that."

Not so easy to do. Even after talking to Patti Stolsinger, being inches from her face, I still saw visions of her lying on the floor, dead.

Sometime after 10:00 the phone rang. My hand snatched it up. "Hello?"

"It's Patti."

Guilt rose in me. "Hi. I'm so sorry again for what I did to you. So sorry."

She made a sound in her throat. "He'll see you tomorrow morning at 9:00. In his office at Cognoscenti. Take it or leave it."

This was really happening. "I'll take it."

Silence hummed over the line.

"He wasn't happy with the way you treated me, you know. And I have to tell you—he's heard your name before. You threatened the trial directors that you were going to sue his company."

"I didn't mean it."

"Let's hope not."

Mom watched me, biting one side of her cheek.

"Look, Patti, I'm sorry. Really. I know I scared you."

My mother nodded her approval.

"So make it up to me. Tell Bill what he needs to know. Work with him."

What he needs to know. My fingers tightened on the phone. These people didn't care about me. They just wanted to protect their company. A company and a product potentially worth millions of dollars. Maybe a billion.

If Hilderbrand wanted to destroy me, he could.

"Okay. I will."

Patti clicked off the line.

I pulled the phone from my ear and stared at it. "I can't believe this," I whispered.

Mom leaned toward me. "Are we in?"

"We're in."

For the next two hours Mom and I planned the meeting. We listed questions we wanted Hilderbrand to answer. Where are the chips manufactured? Who could be responsible for my tainted product? Were other trial members complaining of similar problems? Patti had hinted that they were. Bottom line I still wanted the two things I'd always wanted: proof that the chip was responsible for the scenes in my head and assurance that it wouldn't go on the market until it was fixed.

Looking back I think: how very naïve.

But as Mom and I talked, something else happened. A different kind of feeling grew between us. Even though she'd been a lot of help the past two days, it wasn't until that conversation that I really started to see us as friends. Yes, she'd made mistakes in raising me. But she'd never meant to hurt me, only build me up. I'd made the mistakes worse by clinging to those memories as an excuse for my poor self-esteem.

Sherry's words came back to me: *"Jay says it's a good thing your mother showed up. It'll make you stronger."*

Was this was he meant?

Mom and I sat on the couch as we talked. When we were through I leaned over to hug her. She hugged me back, a little awkwardly maybe, but she did it. "Thank you again for being here," I said. "I know it can't be easy leaving your job this long."

She waved a hand. "You know how many sick days and personal days I've accumulated over the years? They owe me."

"Did you tell them you were sick?"

"I told them my daughter needed me."

And I did.

Sometime after midnight I crawled into bed. Tired as I was, I still couldn't sleep. I lay there praying, thanking God for sending Mom to help me. We'd need that charm of hers in our meeting with Hilderbrand. I'd probably be tongue-tied for most of it. Mom and I had become a team.

You and I are a team, too, God seemed to say.

I smiled. Of course, I knew that.

Didn't I?

Then a moment came back to me—a fleeting realization from my stay in the hospital. At the time I'd been too drugged and amazed at my lack of depression to grasp it. Now I saw it clearly. God *had* been there every minute of my grief-stricken days. He really had. My lack of feeling Him didn't mean He'd abandoned me.

The thought so drenched me with warmth I could hardly stand it. All those days and nights I'd felt so alone—I'd been *wrong?*

I started to cry. *I didn't know, God. I didn't. But how could I have doubted You?*

Then I saw the rest of it—the answer to my own questions—and the tears gushed. How could I have doubted? Because I'd believed my own emotions, that's how. My own unstable, ever-changing emotions. There I'd been, Lisa Newberry, one person among billions on this Earth. And I'd based the universal Truth of God's love for His creation, His nearness to me, on how I *felt?*

For a long time I couldn't move. My body felt pressed to the bed, even while the new knowledge filled me with lightness. God had *never* left me! It had just been *me,* stuck in my own narrow-minded, unseeing view of the world. I never needed to think that way again. If I went through new hardships—and life seemed to be full of them—I didn't have to trust my feelings. I could trust God's word. He said He'd be there. And He *was.*

My nose was running, and my head pounded. I went to the bathroom for some aspirin and tissues. After that I walked my bedroom floor in the dark, asking God for forgiveness. Begging Him to help me do better. He'd shown me this truth. Now I had to use it, live by it. But I was still such a feeble, mixed-up person.

God, I'm going to need all the help you can give me.

I don't know when I finally managed to sleep. Two o'clock, maybe? Three? I do know I drifted off with a peace I hadn't felt in a long, long time.

And I had no dreams about the murder. Not one.

The next morning Mom woke me up at 7:00. Way too soon. But I needed time to get ready. I showered and slipped into a jacket and slacks. Put on makeup and fixed my hair—as well as I could, considering it hadn't been washed and still sported a bandage.

My insides still simmered with all I'd learned the night before. I wanted to tell Mom about it but felt shy. Would she understand? Would she really *get* how deep this was for me? As it turned out, that conversation would have to wait. We spent breakfast again going over our plans for The Meeting. Mom did most of the talking. As for me, panic was setting in. (Those fickle emotions again.) We were going to see *Hilderbrand*. The man who knew I'd threatened to sue Cognoscenti, his company. I'd nearly assaulted his girlfriend. I'd told the police he was a killer. Why should he answer any of our questions? What if all he wanted was my information? Then he'd sweep me under his exquisitely expensive carpet.

Okay, God, this is one of those times. I know You'll be with me.

Mom reached across the table and squeezed my hand. "Don't worry. If you clam up, I'll take over. We'll get through this."

I managed a smile. "Thanks."

At 8:15 the phone rang. I got up to answer it. "That's probably Sherry."

But the ID said Patti Stolsinger. My veins chilled. Was she cancelling the meeting? I threw Mom a wild look and picked up the phone. "Hello?"

"You're going to see Bill, right?" Patti's voice was hard.

Not even a hello from her. If *she* was this bad, what would Hilderbrand be like? "I . . . yes. At 9:00."

"Fine. I forgot to tell you one thing. It's nonnegotiable."

"Okay."

"Come alone."

Chapter 27

 I DROVE TO PALO ALTO, MY BACK WOODEN. I COULD hardly feel my hands on the wheel.

"Come alone."

No way did Patti Stolsinger forget to tell me that last night. She'd seen firsthand how much my mother's presence stabilized me. Hilderbrand had planned Patti's last-minute call just to put me off balance.

It was working.

Mom had wanted to at least ride along with me. I told her no. What if Hilderbrand looked out his window and saw her? Would he cancel the meeting out of spite?

I pulled into a space in the Cognoscenti parking lot—and my gaze fell on a black SUV close to the building. Its license plate started with 6WB.

The sight rattled me. Hilderbrand's car. One more thing the scenes in my head had gotten right.

On shaky legs I entered the office building. Richard Mair, my old friend the security guard, was expecting me.

With camera watching, I hung the mandatory name badge around my neck and signed myself in. He looked on impassively. If he was surprised at my entrance to the holy ground of Dr. Hilderbrand, he gave no sign.

Mair told me to wait in the area with the couches. I followed his pointing finger but couldn't manage to sit.

My pulse flip-flopped.

I thought of the previous night, one without nightmares. Was that because of all my revelations? Or were the memories really going away? If I'd just waited this thing out, maybe it would have disappeared on its own. I wouldn't be here right now, my stomach tight and skin all pebbled.

"Ms. Newberry?" A female voice spoke behind me. I turned to see an impeccably suited woman with stylish red hair. "Dr. Hilderbrand will see you now. Follow me, please."

No greeting, no handshake. Not even an introduction of herself. Hilderbrand's administrative assistant?

I followed the woman to the elevator. We rode to the top floor in silence. As we exited she motioned to turn right. "It's down at the end of the hall."

My feet shuffled me over the carpet, a lamb led to slaughter. Ahead of us, massive double doors of carved mahogany drew near. I could almost feel their weight as I approached.

The woman knocked.

"Come in." A voice filtered from beyond. She pushed back one door and gestured me through with her arm. I stepped over the threshold into a breathtaking office with windows on three sides. Beyond them lay a view of the Bay.

The door whooshed closed behind me.

Hilderbrand rose from his seat at a huge, ornate desk. He was taller than I'd expected, a wide-shouldered man with sandy hair and an undeniable air of self-confidence. He wore a dress shirt and tie. A suit jacket hung from an exotic coat rack in the corner.

An expanse of blue carpet separated us. I didn't move. He liked this, didn't he. Watching me sweat.

Something shifted within me. Sweating or not, I *deserved* this meeting with His Highness. After all his chip had put me through?

"Come in, Ms. Newberry."

The voice sounded vaguely familiar. Could it be the one that shouted, "Shut up!" to Patti in my visions? I crossed to stand before Hilderbrand, chin high.

He indicated a chair on my side of the desk. "Please. Sit down."

I obeyed.

"Would you like something to drink? I'll have Nancy bring it in."

So that was her name. "No, thank you."

He sat. His chair was high-backed brown leather, the front of its arms studded with brass. Hilderbrand's keen eyes looked me over. I forced myself to gaze back.

One side of his mouth turned up. "So you're the one who wants to sue Cognoscenti."

Why had I ever said that? "I have no intention of suing you. That was said in the heat of the moment, when your trial directors wouldn't listen to me."

My voice sounded steady. Maybe I could really do this.

"And what were you trying to tell them?"

"That your Empowerment Chip is both miraculous and flawed."

His eyebrows rose. "Quite a combination. Let's start with miraculous."

"It worked. Incredibly. It cured me of my depression."

"I'm very glad to hear that."

So he wasn't going to claim it was a placebo?

"And . . . flawed?"

"It has data on it. Some man's memories. I thought it was you because he's in your house. And he's killing your girlfriend."

Take that, Hilderbrand. Didn't expect me to be so direct, did you?

He rested an elbow on his chair. He had to know the gist of my story already, through Patti. Even so, did I see a slight twitch in his jaw?

"Sounds like you've got quite a tale to tell, Ms. Newberry."

"My name is Lisa."

"Lisa, then." His eyes narrowed. "Before we continue let's get something clear. Our conversation is between you and me—only. I expect it to stay that way. If you repeat anything I say here, I will deny it. There will be no way for you to use this meeting to discredit me or my company. Understand?"

"I don't want to discredit your company. I just want answers."

"*Do* you understand?"

"Yes." Arrogant man. He knew I'd been to the police. What made him think they hadn't sent me in here wearing a wire?

Hilderbrand surveyed me. "That door you came through." He pointed behind me. "If you were carrying a recording device of any kind, you'd have tripped a sensor."

I held myself very still. *How* did he do that?

Hilderbrand offered a chilly smile. "Experience has taught me how to interpret people, Lisa. You're not one who hides her thoughts very effectively."

Wonderful. Now he was a psychic, too.

"And, of course, I read a lot. I do love a good spy novel." He leaned back and laced his hands. "So. Tell me your story."

My story—the one I'd told to Mom and Sherry, then to Officer Bremer—twice. By now I nearly had the words down pat. There was nothing to do but begin again.

"It starts in the hospital last Friday, after I woke up from the surgery . . ."

Bit by bit it spurted out. The first vision—or dream, whatever it was. The following ones, when I knew I was awake. More scenes after I got home. The sounds and sights of a horrible murder. How Mom and I had found Hilderbrand's house. How we'd found Patti Stolsinger. The threatening messages and the break-in.

Somewhere along the way Hilderbrand's poker face wavered. Oh, he tried to remain stiff-backed and aloof. But I saw that flex in his jaw again when I described the inside of his house. I saw that slow breath when I told of the stabbing. Patti Stolsinger's dead eyes. The suitcase disappearing into blackness.

By the time I finished, my throat was dry. I asked for water. Hilderbrand paged his assistant, and she brought in a glass with ice. We waited until she'd left the room to continue.

Hilderbrand swiveled his chair to stare out the side windows. I sipped my drink.

"Did you tell me everything?" he asked.

"Yes."

"Every vision you had, every detail?"

I thought about it. "Yes."

He turned around to face me. "The dragon ring is an odd touch."

Was *that* all he could say? "Patti said you don't own one?"

"Not my style."

He tapped the arm of his chair. "First of all let me say I'm very sorry for what you've gone through."

Finally. A stiff apology, but it was a start. I nodded.

"Second, you need to know neither Jerry Sterne nor Clair Saxton knew about this. They could only think you were having psychiatric problems."

No, they could have believed me. "They told me my chip was a placebo."

"That's what the documentation they received said. They had no reason to question it."

"But that documentation was false, wasn't it."

Hilderbrand tipped his head back and regarded me through lowered eyelids. "Yes."

The stunning admission knifed through me. I bled vindication, but it soon clotted to anger. "So who lied? The vice president?"

"He knew nothing either."

"Then who?"

"I did."

I gripped the arms of my chair. *"Why?"*

Irritation twinged across his face. "You can drop the self-righteousness, Ms. Newberry. Look at it from my perspective. I'm in the midst of a multi-million-dollar trial. I have a participant who's spouting wild accusations against the product, threatening to derail the entire process. I chose to shut you down swiftly and efficiently until I could look further into the matter."

"You didn't look into it! You just left me out there to hang."

"How do you know that?"

I swallowed. This was too much. Somehow I had to keep my wits about me. Suddenly I remembered where I'd heard his voice. "You called my mother, didn't you? That was *your* voice. And you sent that note. Did you break into my apartment to get it back, too?"

He seared me with a glance. "Do I look like a lock picker to you?"

A lock picker. So that's how he'd gotten in—whoever he was. Which meant my new lock was no help at all.

Another thought surfaced. "Wait—it *was* you. Because the drawing of Patti disappeared. You recognized it."

Hilderbrand merely lifted his shoulder.

I glared at him. This was my *life* we were talking about. My sense of safety in my own apartment. I wasn't going to let this man intimidate me. *He* was the one in the wrong.

"So." I spread my hands. "Now what? You going to deny the chip is bad?"

He shifted in his chair. "No. Most of these visions, or memories, as you call them, are ridiculous. But a few things you said are right. Like the description of the inside of my house."

Another surprising admission. I waited for him to say more, but he held out for my next move. What a chess game we played.

But games took two, didn't they. Fact was—he needed me, as much as he might despise being in that position. Above all else, he wanted to protect his Empowerment Chip.

"How did my chip get this tainted data on it?"

"I have no idea."

"You must think something."

He rubbed a finger along the edge of his desk.

"Where are the chips manufactured?"

Hilderbrand looked up. "I won't discuss that with you."

"Well, wherever it is, someone there had to have done this."

"Agreed."

"But how? They got a lot of stuff right. Like Patti's face."

"Look at all they do with computer graphics in movies these days."

That stopped me for a moment. I should have thought of that. "*Why* would they do it?"

"I have enemies, Ms. Newberry. The technological race to understand and harness the brain has been akin to that of mapping the human genome. Any man who's accomplished what I have in this field, who's on the brink of an earth-shaking product, has enemies."

"But they knew the inside of your house."

"Bothersome, isn't it."

I wanted to shake the smugness right off his face. Hilderbrand couldn't be feeling so sure of himself. He had to be scared to death of losing the "race"—and zillions of dollars.

"Are other people in the trial complaining of problems?"

"Also something I'll not discuss."

"Patti said you'd heard rumors."

"Did she now?"

My mouth snapped shut. Had I just gotten her in trouble? Well, so what? She hadn't been very nice to me, either.

I leaned back and folded my arms. "If you're not going to talk to me, why did you even ask me to come here?"

"I wanted to hear your story."

Uh-huh. Just as I thought. And I shouldn't have come so easily. Should have realized how much he needed my details. I could have insisted on a few quid pro quos up front.

But it wasn't that simple. I needed Hilderbrand as much as he needed me. "So what are you going to do about everything I've told you?"

He breathed in, his nostrils flaring. "I'm going to get to the bottom of it."

"I don't want your chip going out on the market with this kind of flaw."

"And you think *I* do?" He looked toward the ceiling. "Talk about lawsuits. That would decimate the company." Hilderbrand slow-swiveled to focus out the window once more. "And that's where they made their mistake." He spoke almost to himself. "Tainting a chip that was in the trial. If they'd waited until it was on the market . . ."

The thought suspended in the air.

An odd thing happened then. A shift in positions. I'd spent a lot of dark hours believing William Hilderbrand was a cold-blooded murderer. I still didn't like the man, but now I knew he wasn't a killer. In fact, he'd been wronged, as I had. By a twist of fate we faced a common enemy. "They didn't *want* to see the chip on the market. They wanted to kill it before it ever got there. And that would have been a tragedy. Because it *works*."

Hilderbrand turned and regarded me for a long moment. "Do you want to help get the Empowerment Chip back on track?"

I gave him a wary look. "Yes."

"Then let me take your chip out of you."

My eyes rounded. Cognoscenti had circled back to *this*, after ignoring my pleas for it?

"To put it plainly, Ms. Newberry, I need it. I need to study it in order to understand how this was done. And most of all, I need to catch who did it."

Like I was going to trust this man now. "But you're talking a second surgery for me."

"Isn't this what you demanded just a few days ago?"

"That was before I learned that taking it out wouldn't help. The memories are now mine. In the circuits of my own head."

He raised his chin, as if surprised I knew as much. "True. But you mentioned the visions came in sequence, bringing further details each time. How do you know that's over? You could be facing more horror."

"I haven't had any new memories in over twenty-four hours." Well, not really. I'd had the last one on the way to the police station.

"And that's long enough to make you think this is over forever?"

I licked my lips. I didn't really believe that. The chip could be loaded with a dozen murders, for all I knew. A hundred. It may have just gotten started.

"Lisa, I need the chip. I'll give you a new, viable one. I'll inspect it myself. And you can go on with your life, free of depression. The memories are now yours, yes. But you've seen they're wrong. You don't need to fear them. And in time they'll fade."

True or not, they still filled me with dread. But to think that bad chip could be out of me. That never again would some gory scene screech my world to a halt. What if I had one of those visions while I was driving?

"Cognoscenti will finance the procedure, of course." Hilderbrand steepled his fingers. "And we'll pay you a half million dollars for your inconvenience."

My neck thrust forward. A *half million dollars?*

"I'd insist that you sign some legal documents first, pledging not to disclose our agreement or sue the company. And you'll not be allowed to discuss your experience with Cognoscenti in any way with anyone."

A half million dollars. I couldn't get past that. Five hundred thousand dollars—for one week's setback in my recovery. That money, plus the two hundred thousand from Ryan's life insurance, would fund a new life for me. I really could walk away from this. Vindicated *and* compensated. And emotionally strong enough to fight whatever lingering memories played in my head . . .

Hilderbrand raised his eyebrows. "Do we have a deal?"

But how could I trust him? What if he told the surgeon to let his knife "slip" while I was under anesthesia? He could get his chip *and* get rid of me.

"I don't know."

"Really." Hilderbrand cocked his head.

I caught myself twisting my hands and forced them apart.

"What's the problem?"

Hilderbrand had mentioned legal documents I'd have to sign. Which meant I would need a lawyer. "I'd want something in the contract, too—to the effect that if anything happens to me during the operation, all bets are off. My attorney goes to the police with our contract. And the media. He talks to anyone who'll listen. They'll know you killed me. Cognoscenti won't survive."

He sighed. "Ms. Newberry, I'm not a murderer, remember? *Why* would I want to kill you?"

I had no answer for that.

"Even if you can't believe *me*, do you think a surgeon or

anesthetist would risk his career to harm you? We want you well. And we want the chip."

I took a drink of my water.

"So I pose it to you again. And remember, half a million dollars is on the table. Money I can remove any time. *Do* we have a deal?"

I put the glass down. Shifted in my chair. If I did this, Hilderbrand would get away with everything. Lying to me about the placebo, making threats, breaking into my apartment. Which would really chafe me. But if I didn't do this, I'd never prove all that anyway. I'd already tried with Bremer, and look how far that had gotten me.

"Ms. Newberry?"

"One million," I heard myself say.

Hilderbrand's mouth slowly twisted. "Why, Lisa. You had me fooled. I never thought you'd be one to dig money out of this unfortunate situation."

"I'll put the other five hundred thousand in savings. When the chip comes on the market, I'll donate it to needy patients who can't afford the surgery." In essence, force Cognoscenti to give away a few of their own chips.

William Hilderbrand managed a smile. "A worthy cause." He thought it over. "One million it is."

"One more thing."

"You might stop while you're ahead."

Oh, no. I would make *sure* this product was perfect. "If the Empowerment Chip hurts someone like it did me, I can disclose our agreement. I'll tell the world my story."

I doubted Hilderbrand would ever let it come to that. He *would* catch the culprit and fix this—his fortune depended on it. All the same, a little more pressure never hurt.

He waved a hand. "Easily agreed. That's not going to happen."

"And a final point."

His jaw flexed.

"I want to hear what you find on the chip. And when you catch the person who did this to me."

"That is not information you need to know, Ms. Newberry."

"You telling me I don't deserve it, after what I've been through?"

No response.

I shrugged. "That's my deal, Dr. Hilderbrand. Take it or leave it."

To quote his girlfriend.

Hilderbrand put two fingers against his upper lip. Moved a pen around on his desk. I waited.

He pressed back his shoulders. "Agreed. I'll hear no more demands."

"Fine." My voice nearly squeaked. Had I done the right thing?

We looked at each other, wary partners. I let out a breath. "I guess we're done."

"Not quite."

He wanted to go over details so we'd have no surprises later. When the surgery would be performed. (As soon as possible, perhaps Sunday.) How I would sign the papers. (In his office, with attorneys present.) He would have the documents drawn up by tomorrow. If I wanted my own lawyer, I needed to find one fast.

By the time our meeting was over, I felt completely drained. Hilderbrand and I stood. He held out his hand. For a second I cringed from it, the hand I'd believed had killed Patti Stolsinger. Then I managed to shake it.

Back in my car I wanted to call Mom immediately but resisted. What if Hilderbrand was watching the parking lot from his office window? I didn't want him seeing me on the phone. I would drive home, tell Mom in person.

When I got to the apartment, she met me at the door. "What happened, what happened?"

I led her to the couch and sat her down. Went over everything. She managed not to interrupt. But as I told her of Hilderbrand's and my agreement, her face began to pinch. When I was done she sat back, staring at a cushion.

"*What*, Mom?"

She took my hand, clearly trying to be gentle. To not judge. "I hope this is right, Lisa, I really do. But . . . I don't think you should do this."

Chapter 28

MOM AND I HAD TO TALK THIS THING OUT. SHE DIDN'T TRUST Hilderbrand. Well, neither did I. But I explained to her again that our agreement left him no wiggle room. All the same, my mother's reaction made me wonder what I'd done.

We moved into the kitchen, where she made sandwiches. The food did not go down easily.

"I can still change my mind," I said for the tenth time. "I haven't signed anything yet."

"I know."

"But I want that chip out of me—now. And the only way to replace it with a good one is to go through Cognoscenti."

Mom cut the crust off her sandwich. "That's the part I don't like."

"Can you think of an alternative?"

She put down her knife. "No, that's the thing. Other than leave the chip in place. But I'm with you—you don't know what it will do. Like you said, just think what could happen if you had a vision while you were driving. You could be killed."

In a car accident. Like Ryan.

"Nothing's going to happen to me, Mom. Hilderbrand won't let it—his company's at stake."

Concern still lined Mom's face. "So you're going to do this?"

I sighed. "I think so. I just . . . can't keep dealing with new memories. I can't relax, wondering what's going to hit me next."

My mother nodded. "I have another issue, if you go through with this. I'm leading training sessions at work all next week. I have to be there."

"That's okay."

"I don't want to leave you if you're having surgery."

"I'll be in the hospital recovering anyway. The last time I didn't even have visitors."

"That was because of the trial. They'll allow you visitors this time. I should be there. And I'd certainly want to be here when you come home."

My mother couldn't put her life on hold for me forever. "Look, I'll be fine when I come home. I managed for two days without you before, didn't I? Basically I'll just sleep a lot. And Sherry will be around if I need her."

My mother gave me a look.

I sighed. "Mom, you have to get over this thing with Sherry. She's a really good friend to me."

"She accosted me at my own son-in-law's funeral."

I ran my tongue underneath my top lip.

Mom eyed me askance. "What's that look? You think I deserved it?"

Oh, boy. "I . . . no."

"You sound so positive."

I pushed my plate away. How'd we get into *this* so fast? "Look. Remember what you said about criticizing me during my childhood? That you were only out to protect me?"

"Yes." Mom drew out the word.

"Sherry was just trying to protect me, too. You were coming on pretty hard about my moving back to Denver. She knew I didn't have any strength left."

"I knew that, too. It's why I was trying to help you!"

I gazed at her. Slowly her expression flattened. "But I wasn't helping, was I."

"No."

Mom leaned back in her chair and stared out the window. Emotions fluttered across her face.

"It's okay, Mom."

"I'm sorry. Again."

"It's okay." I reached over and rubbed her fingers. She wasn't the only one who was learning things about herself. "Let me tell you what happened to me last night."

I told her all the amazing things God had shown me. As I described it, the emotions welled up in me all over again. By the time I finished, both of us were crying. We'd hardly touched our sandwiches.

"Thank you for sharing that with me." Mom wiped her cheek. "I needed to hear it."

I nodded, my throat tight. I wasn't sure where Mom was with God. Maybe she wasn't as far away as I'd thought.

We managed to finish eating. With the last bite of my sandwich, I suddenly remembered—*attorney*! My gaze flew to the clock. One thirty. So much time I'd wasted. I shoved my plate away. "Mom—I have to find a lawyer. Now."

"Oh, right." She looked at her watch. "Better do it right away."

My first thought was to call Sherry. Jay would probably know someone through the investment firm. But there was so much to tell her. That would take a long phone call, and I didn't have time for that. I glanced at Mom. She was rinsing our dishes in the sink, her back to me. "I'm going to call Sherry. I think she'll be able to help with an attorney."

"All right." No argument. Not even a tensing of her shoulders. It was a start.

Sherry's daughter, Rebecca, would still be at school. J.T. may be taking a nap. I crossed to the counter for the phone and punched in her number. One ring—and she answered.

"Hey!" Her voice sounded breathless. "I've been thinking so much about you. What's happening?"

"Everything."

She sucked in air. "Oh, no, now what? You okay?"

"Yes. There's a lot to tell, but I don't have much time right now because I need you to help me with something. So just hang with me." As my mother would say.

"Okay."

"So here goes. First, we found out who the murderer and the victim are in my visions."

"You're kid—"

"Then we talked to the police, only they didn't believe me, because the victim turned out to be alive. So the killer obviously turned out not to be a killer. And did I mention he's the CEO of Cognoscenti? So I went to see this woman for myself—Patti, the one we thought was dead—at her house and nearly assaulted her. Mom held me back. Then I went to see Hilderbrand, the CEO. And in a couple days I'm going to have *another* brain surgery to take out my bad chip and put in a good one. So I need a lawyer. Can you help with that?"

Stunned silence.

Maybe I'd gone just a little too fast?

"Lisa."

"Yeah."

"I'm a little . . . Can you give me a few more details? And by the way, I'm now sitting down."

"Okay. But first, the main thing. Do you think Jay knows an attorney who could look over a legal document before I sign it?"

"What kind of legal document?"

"An agreement between me and Cognoscenti to take out the chip and pay me a million dollars. But there are some stipulations."

"A *million* dollars?"

"Well, he offered half a million. I got him to raise it."

Mom shot me a smile.

Another long pause. "Lisa, you are beyond . . . something."

Yeah. Something. "Does Jay know an attorney?"

"I don't know. I can call him."

"Can you do it now? I need one fast. The documents are supposed to be ready tomorrow."

"Tell you what. I'll find you an attorney. On one condition. Since you're suddenly into negotiating and all."

"Okay."

"You come over here, sit down, and tell me everything."

"What about the kids?" This was hardly a story for little ears.

"Rebecca's going home from school with a friend. And J.T. just went down for a nap."

Sherry deserved to hear what had happened. And I really wanted to see her. Plus . . . I looked at my mother. "Okay. One thing—Mom's coming with me."

Mom stopped her work and eyed me.

"Your mother's still there?"

"Yes. And it's good. And you two need to see each other."

"Really."

"We'll be over in fifteen minutes. You call Jay, okay?"

I hung up.

Chapter 29

SHERRY AND JAY'S HOUSE WAS A BASIC THREE-BEDROOM, two-bath starter in a well kept San Carlos neighborhood with good schools. They'd gotten it for a bargain at $690,000.

Memories hit as Mom and I walked up to the porch lined with potted flowers. Ryan and I used to love coming here. We'd eat dinner with Jay and Sherry, and play with the kids.

It seemed a lifetime ago.

I knocked softly, remembering that J.T. was sleeping. Sherry opened the door right away.

"Come in, come in." She hugged me. Even managed to smile at my mother. "I found a lawyer for you."

That was Sherry, true to her word.

She led us into the living room. Mom and I settled into the familiar soft couch. Wow. It had been a long time since I sat there.

"Want something to drink?" Sherry remained standing. "Coffee, tea?"

"None for me, thank you," Mom said. "We just had lunch."

I shook my head at Sherry. "Thanks, no."

"Okay. I'll get that information for you." She headed into her kitchen.

In the corner of the living room stood a large basket filled with J.T.'s toys. A tiny teapot and cups sat on the fireplace hearth. Mom pointed to it. "You used to do that, Lisa. Have tea parties."

Sherry returned, holding a piece of paper. "That's Rebecca's favorite thing these days. We have a little party every night before she goes to bed. Jay pours."

Pain cut through me. Someday I would have that. A husband and kids and tea parties. Someday.

Sherry winced, as if she knew what I was thinking. "Here." She handed me the paper. "His name is Rocky Rhodes."

I looked at her sideways. "Rocky Rhodes?"

She shrugged. "I didn't name the guy. Jay says he's good. The investment firm has sent a lot of work his way. You'd better give him a call now 'cause you might not get through at first. Jay says to tell the guy he referred you." She sat down in the rocking chair she'd inherited from her mother.

I looked at the piece of paper. "Is Rocky a nickname?"

"I don't know."

What mother with the last name of Rhodes would name her son Rocky?

"Maybe he's a son of the sixties," Mom said. "Hippie parents facing hard times."

Sherry laughed. "Hah, that's good. Or maybe they loved the ice cream flavor."

Mom smiled.

Well, what do you know.

I pulled out my cell phone to call Rocky Rhodes. Some female assistant took the call, saying he wasn't available. But the attorney knew Jay well, and she was sure Rhodes would get back to me as soon as he could.

"It has to be in the next few hours, or I'll need to contact someone else."

"Okay. He'll call you."

I set the phone in my lap and looked to Sherry. If this didn't work, I was in big trouble. "How long do you think I should give him?" It was now after 2:00.

"You don't have time to wait," Mom jumped in. "Keep looking."

Sherry threw her an irritated glance. "No, give him at least an hour."

Here they went again. Another minute and they'd be out-and-out arguing. I put a hand over my eyes, suddenly exhausted. I was tired of being caught in the middle.

Mom touched my arm. "What's the matter?"

I sat back. "Look, you're my mother, and Sherry's my best friend. And I really don't like you snipping at each other. So guess what—I'm not leaving here until you two work this out."

There. Deal with it.

They looked at each other. Mom took a breath. "Lisa and I have learned quite a few things about each other and ourselves in the last few days."

Sherry's eyebrows rose. "I'm glad to hear that."

"I'm sorry for what I said to you. At the funeral."

One thing about Mom, she never danced around. I bit the inside of my cheek, eyeing Sherry.

She pressed her lips together. "And I'm sorry for what *I* said. I shouldn't have come at you like that."

An awkward silence followed. Or maybe simply . . . a readjusting. My eyes flicked from one woman to the other.

Mom slipped into a tight smile. "Well then, that's that."

Sherry nodded. "I guess it is."

That was *it*? All the ill will—fixed with two simple apologies?

Clearly it was easier to make up with someone other than your own mother. Mom and I had taken a number of days to even begin sorting through our issues. We still had a lot of work ahead of us.

Sherry hit her palm against the arm of the rocking chair. "So, Lisa. You going to tell me what in the world is going on?"

Another wave of tiredness hit. But I'd promised Sherry. "It started from seeing the outside of the murderer's—well, what I thought was the murderer's—house in my visions . . ." I detailed how we'd found Hilderbrand, then Patti Stolsinger. Our meeting with Officer Bremer and his shocking news—Patti was alive. I wasn't too happy having to tell Sherry how I'd behaved at Patti's house.

"*You* did *that?*" Sherry gaped at me.

"I was . . . overcome."

Sherry tilted her head. "I can understand that. But I understand Patti's reaction too. She had no idea who you were. Imagine if some stranger came at *you* like that."

"Yeah, I know."

My story continued. Meeting with Hilderbrand, and finally, his and my agreement. "Which I'm not supposed to be talking to you about, by the way."

Sherry shrugged. "You haven't signed the document yet. But yes, I'll keep it to myself."

Mom tipped her head. "Won't your husband be curious?"

"Don't worry, he won't tell anyone either."

"But that's one more person who would know the details of this agreement." Mom frowned at me. "Lisa, if this leaks out, Cognoscenti could pursue you for their money back."

"It's not going to leak out, Mom. Sherry and Jay won't tell anyone."

"Just make sure you don't." Mom eyed Sherry.

Oh, no, not again.

Sherry gave my mother a long look. "You can trust us. Alice."

A fluttering beat ticked by. I almost hoped J.T. would wake up and interrupt us.

Mom nodded. "I'm sure we can."

Sherry seemed to accept that. She shifted her gaze to me. Some new thought flitted across her face. "One thing I don't get. Didn't you say Hilderbrand told you even his vice president didn't know you were being lied to about the placebo?"

"Yeah."

"But the vice president is in charge of the trial."

Jerry Sterne and Clair Saxton had said as much. "True."

"So . . . even the guy in charge of the trial doesn't know who received a placebo and who didn't?"

I had to think that one over. "Guess not."

Mom was frowning at the coffee table.

"So it must have been Hilderbrand himself who chose which patients got the placebo and who got the real chip," Sherry said.

Mom looked up. "No, it would have been done in some random fashion. But maybe Hilderbrand alone had the information on who got what."

I shook my head. "Why does it matter, Sherry?"

"Probably doesn't. I just find it interesting that the CEO himself is the only one who knows who got real chips in the trial."

"He's not just CEO, though. He's the inventor. The Empowerment Chip is *his* baby. And his potential huge fortune. He has to make sure the trial goes right."

Which was why Hilderbrand was paying me a million dollars so he could inspect the chip someone had tampered with. What *would* he find on the thing? And whatever it was—would it lead him to who'd—

He washed the red-stained knife in the sink.

"Oh . . ."

Blood ran down the blade and into the stainless steel, crimson on silver. It mixed with the water and swirled into the drain . . .

I wrenched back to Sherry's living room, my muscles tight.

"Lisa?" Mom touched my arm. "What happened?"

I swayed, still seeing the blood. I knew it wasn't real. Patti *wasn't* dead. Still it seemed so . . . "I just had—"

A clump of blood stuck to the top of the blade, just below the handle. He rubbed it with two fingers.

A thump sounded behind him. He whipped his head around. Patti lay on the floor, still. Eyes open. Another sound. His eyes flicked to the refrigerator. He breathed out, long and low. "Ice maker."

He turned back to the knife . . .

The scene faded.

I swallowed and blinked hard. My eyes stung with tears. All that *blood*.

"You all right?" Mom asked.

"Can I have some water?"

Sherry scurried into the kitchen. She brought back a glass, and I drained it. She took the glass from my trembling fingers. "What'd you see?"

I collapsed back against the couch and told them. I could still see the blood whirling in that sink. Made me shudder.

Mom put her arm around me. "I can't wait till this is over for you."

I nodded weakly. *This* was exactly why I needed to get rid of that chip.

Sherry pressed her hands against her cheeks. "This is terrible.

You looked absolutely . . . kidnapped. Like your mind was totally somewhere else."

It was.

The water hissed. He held up the knife, inspected one side, then the other. It was clean.

He laid it on the counter. Washed his hands. Blood on his left wrist caught his attention. It had splattered all the way up to the bevel of his fancy gold watch. A Rolex. He grabbed a tissue and wiped it off. The blood disappeared. Beneath it was a readout of the date.

Monday, March 19—

The cell phone in my lap rang. I jumped, my body tearing back to the present. The cell went off again. I gawked at it.

"Better answer." Mom picked it up. "It may be the attorney."

I shook my head, trying to clear it. Half my mind was still staring at that watch . . . *Monday, March 19.* I took the phone from Mom and read the ID. *Rockland Rhodes.*

Rockland. That was even worse than Rocky.

I punched on the line. "H-hello?"

"Lisa Newberry?" He introduced himself. "I hear Jay Grubacker referred you. You're in need of an attorney immediately?"

That watch . . . A gold Rolex. Different than the one the man was wearing before.

"Yes. I need someone to look over a legal document before I sign it. It's with a company called Cognoscenti."

"Ah, yes."

Oh, no, was this a conflict of interest? "Have you worked for them?"

"No. But I've heard of them."

He asked me what kind of document. I told him.

"You mean it's a settlement, then?"

I hadn't thought of it that way. "Sort of."

"How much money is involved?"

"One million."

"Ask him his fee," Mom whispered.

"What would your fee be for reading the document?"

"For settlements it's a standard twenty percent."

What? I pulled the phone from my ear and looked to Mom. "He wants twenty percent."

She huffed. "Give me the phone."

I shoved it into her hand. Fine, let her deal with it.

My mind returned to the bloodied watch. The date on it. A different watch than before.

Why?

"Mr. Rhodes? Hello, I'm Lisa's mother. Look, we're only talking a couple hours' work on your part. I realize there's a standard fee in settlement cases, but Lisa's done all the work here. All you have to do is read over the document."

I could hear Rhodes's voice filtering from the phone. "I understand that, but it's also a last-minute case, and I have a lot of things going here."

Mom's eyes narrowed. "Are you in a large firm? Perhaps you can give it to an associate. We'll pay $200 an hour."

Two hundred an hour? I mouthed to Sherry. She nodded as if that was normal.

Well, it was better than $200,000.

Mom went on. "I know Jay will be very happy to hear you're helping Lisa, since his firm sends you so many clients."

Mr. Rhodes paused. "I'm sure I can find someone to help."

Sherry raised one eyebrow and tipped her head toward my mother—*She's good.*

"Great. That's wonderful." Mom looked pleased with herself. "I'll hand you back to Lisa to work out the details."

And so I had an attorney. By the time I got off the phone, Rhodes had agreed to do the work himself for a flat $5,000. Probably more than my mother would have wanted me to pay, but I didn't care. He gave me his fax number and his cell. I was to call as soon as I heard the document was ready. I hung up and sagged back against the couch. "Thank You, God."

"Better thank your mom too," Sherry said. "Nice amount of pressure in the right place, Alice."

"Yeah, Mom, th—"

The watch was clean. Time: 5:35. Date: Monday, March 19.

He picked up the knife. Dried it off on a paper towel. It slid into its place in the wooden block without a sound.

He turned back to the body . . .

"Nnno." I bent over, pressing my hands against my head. "Go *away*."

Mom held my shoulders. "It's still happening?"

I nodded. My heart beat in my ears. I waited for more.

Nothing came.

Slowly I straightened. Licked my lips. I was so tired. "I think it's done." What day was this—Thursday? I had to wait three more days for the surgery? I wanted it *now*.

"What's the date?" I blurted.

Mom eased her hands away. "The fifteenth."

Hilderbrand, at his sink. Cleaning off the bloodied watch . . .

March 19.

Four days from now. The realization hit me in the chest.

"What if we were off in our calculation of the day, Mom?" My words croaked out. "Maybe it happens next week."

Sherry frowned. "What happens?"

"The murder."

Silence from both of them. They must have thought I'd lost my mind for sure this time.

I squeezed my eyes shut. "I mean, it doesn't really happen. I know that. None of this is real. But I just saw the date on his watch. A different watch. Monday, March 19. Plus, the time was a little different—5:35. But it's all fake anyway. So it doesn't matter."

But it did.

But it couldn't.

But it *did.*

My teeth clenched. I just wanted to run away from my own brain.

"Come on, Lisa." Mom tugged at my arm. "Let's get you home."

"Yeah, okay." But my legs felt weak as we walked to the door.

Sherry hugged me tight. "You sure you're all right? 'Cause you're scaring me."

I was scaring myself. "I'm fine."

But that date . . .

"Call me tomorrow. After you hear from Hilderbrand. Okay?"

"I will."

Mom helped me to her rental car. On the way home my cell phone rang again. It was Hilderbrand's assistant, saying the documents were done. Did I want her to fax them to me? I gave her Rhodes's number.

"Look," I asked her, "if we sign these documents tomorrow, can I have the surgery on Saturday?"

"Surgery?"

So the assistant had no idea what the contract was about.

"Just ask Dr. Hilderbrand. Tell him I want the procedure done on Saturday. I need it as soon as possible."

"All right."

"When can we meet him to sign?"

"Just a moment, please." I heard the shuffle of paper. "He's free tomorrow at 11:00."

Exhaustion clawed at me. "Okay. I'll see if that works with my attorney."

By the time we walked into the apartment it was almost 3:30. My legs were rubbery, and my head pounded.

Mom set our things on the counter. "Go take a nap."

My shoulders felt so heavy. Those visions took everything out of me. I wanted them *gone*. "I have to call Rhodes first. Tell him the papers are coming. And see if 11:00 tomorrow is okay."

"I'll do it for you. Go to bed."

No energy to argue. I stumbled to my room.

Please let the surgery be Saturday, I prayed as I fell asleep. I didn't care that I'd have to be cut open again. Stay in the hospital. Start recovery from scratch.

I just wanted that wretched chip out of my brain.

FRIDAY, MARCH 16

Chapter 30

ON FRIDAY MORNING WE MET AT HILDERBRAND'S OFFICE at 11:00—me, Rocky Rhodes, Hilderbrand, and his attorney, Matthew Lundgren. Rockland Rhodes turned out to be a silver-haired man with a gentleman's aplomb and the eyes of a shark. I was glad he was on my side. Lundgren stood much shorter than Rhodes, thin-boned and long-fingered. But every bit as keen.

Rhodes had pored over the document last night, and we'd discussed it. He had a few tweaks, but nothing major. Hilderbrand had done a good job of covering everything he and I talked about. Including the part that cancelled all secrecy about the contract if anything happened to me.

One change we had put in writing last night—that the surgery be done one day after the deal was complete. Rhodes had faxed his changes back to Hilderbrand, who responded a few hours later. Everything looked good.

So here we were, ready to sign. Tomorrow I'd be back in the hospital. Getting rid of my chip. I hadn't even had time to get the stitches taken out from the first surgery.

The four of us gathered around a small conference table in Hilderbrand's office. Outside the CEO's windows the sky strutted a clear slate blue. The Bay shone beyond. This time around, the office looked less intimidating. A little.

We wasted no time in getting down to business. There were four copies of the contract—one for each of us. I signed on the lines reserved for my name. Hilderbrand followed. The attorneys signed as witnesses.

Just like that, the deal was done.

Hilderbrand handed me an envelope, unsealed. Inside it—a cashier's check from Cognoscenti for $1 million. Autographed by the CEO himself.

I stared at the piece of paper, not quite believing it was real.

"Thank you, Ms. Newberry." Hilderbrand gave me a rather mocking smile. "Don't forget half of that goes to help future Empowerment Chip patients."

"I won't." The language hadn't been in the legal papers, but I intended to keep my promise anyway, whether Hilderbrand believed me or not.

He nodded. "May you have a swift recovery from your procedure. And I hope you enjoy the new life our Empowerment Chip gives you."

Sounded like some sort of political speech. "Thank you."

"I suggest you stay an extra day in the hospital," Hilderbrand added. "We'll pay for that. Since it will be your second surgery in eight days, you'll probably appreciate the added rest."

By that point I felt numb. I could only manage a nod.

Out in the parking lot, I thanked Rhodes more than once. He said he'd send me the bill. We shook hands and parted.

I walked to my car on legs that felt light for the first time in days. After all that had happened, this had gone so easily. I was almost done with the horror. One more surgery, yes. And that wouldn't be fun. But Hilderbrand was right. After that my whole new life awaited.

On the way back home I stopped at my bank to deposit the check. When the teller saw the amount of money involved, her eyes widened. But she managed to keep her business-like cool.

Sitting in the bank's parking lot, deposit slip in hand, I called Sherry and told her it was done. She was happy for me—sort of. She also had to admit she was still scared.

"I know. Me too. But when it's all over, I'll be so glad."

Mom was waiting anxiously as I walked into the apartment. I spread my arms and turned around. "Do I look richer?"

"No." She smiled. "But you do look relieved."

That was an understatement. I could *breathe.* "Let's go out to lunch. At a really nice place. I'm buying."

We ended up at Evvia Estiatorio, a Greek restaurant in Palo Alto. I couldn't remember ever eating Greek cuisine, but the smell of the food wafted out onto Emerson Street. We followed our noses inside.

Ordering took my full attention. So many interesting dishes to choose from. I looked over the menu, feeling new wonder. A whole world of experiences lay before me. I had so much to look forward to. So much to *live.*

Hard to imagine just eight days ago I'd been immobilized with depression.

We ordered. The server brought the first course.

"I'm so sorry to leave you on Sunday." Mom took a bite of her classic Greek salad. "But I don't know what else to do."

"We already discussed this. I'll be fine. I won't even come home from the hospital until Monday. Maybe even Tuesday."

Mom winced. "At least I can be there when you wake up from the surgery. And the next morning."

Her flight to Denver left Sunday afternoon.

"I'll be fine, Mom. Really. You've done so much being here for me this week. *That's* when I've really needed you. Look at all you helped me do. We found Hilderbrand. And Patti."

Alive.

Monday, March 19.

We fell into silence as we concentrated on our salads. Or maybe we were thinking of how far we'd come with each other the past few days.

Mom's expression changed, as though she'd decided to tackle a heavy subject. "When you've recovered, do you think you'll end up moving back to Denver?"

At least it was a question, not a demand. And the subject didn't bother me at all. "I don't know. Maybe. I have the money to go anywhere now. But why go to a place where I don't know anyone? Doesn't appeal to me."

Sadness washed over me. If only Ryan were still alive—*and* we had this kind of money. We could buy that house we'd dreamed of owning. I'd plant my flowers and bushes all around, front and back.

"You have plenty of friends you left behind in Denver."

Maybe. "I've lost touch with most of them this past year."

Mom tipped her head. "Well, at least come visit when you're better, okay? Your friends would love to catch up with you, I'm sure."

"I will. I'll do that." For the first time in years the thought of visiting Denver and staying with Mom felt good.

By the time we left the restaurant, closing out the lunch crowd for Evvia, it was almost 3:00. I didn't even feel tired.

Later that afternoon I spoke with the hospital, going over details about the surgery. I already knew the drill. No food or water after midnight. Report to the hospital at 8:00 a.m. Mom would drive me. And whatever day I was discharged, Sherry would pick me up.

All my plans were in place. How perfect they sounded. The final closure of my week of terror, and my months of depression. I didn't want to dwell on the surgery itself—too much angst in that. So I focused on my future. On hope. This time, I didn't even stop to wonder—

What if something goes wrong?

SATURDAY, MARCH 17—
SUNDAY, MARCH 18

Chapter 31

FITFUL RAIN FELL AS WE DROVE TO THE HOSPITAL ON Saturday morning. Fear tried to work its way up my spine, but I wrestled it down. As I checked into the hospital, slipped out of my clothes and into a gown, I fought to stay calm. And I prayed a lot. I didn't doubt my decision. But facing the surgery sent a hum through my veins.

Mom stayed with me until the last minute. Before we parted, she patted my arm. "I'm proud of you, Lisa."

I looked into her eyes, startled. She'd never said those words to me. "Thank you." I wanted to say more but . . . couldn't.

They wheeled me into the operating room.

One of my surgeons was the same as before—Dr. Rayner, the gray-haired sixty-something with a round face. The second was someone new. Dr. Edward, a younger man with eyes that reminded me of Ryan.

"Take good care of my brain, Doc." I lay on the table in the operation room, looking up at the white ceiling. My words trembled.

This had to be the worst time, just before going under anesthesia. Every doubt gripped me in its tentacles.

"Don't you worry." Dr. Edward smiled.

"So you're back for more." Rayner stuck a needle in my arm. "Must have liked it so much the first time you wanted another round."

Sure. Something like that.

Did he wonder why I was back? Surely this wasn't normal. But maybe Cognoscenti paid him to do the procedure and not ask questions.

I closed my eyes against the room's brightness. Whatever flowed through the needle was already working. My mind fogged. "Where's the chip?"

"We have it."

"Take care of that, too." The words slurred.

"Okay, Lisa, here we go." The mask came down over me.

This time I didn't fight it. The world thickened . . . gelled. Blackened.

Chapter 32

 SOUNDS WASHED OVER ME. LOW VOICES. THE SWISH OF A curtain.

My eyes opened. I lay under a blanket.

Thoughts firmed slowly.

The chip.

My surgery—it was done already? Like before, it felt like no time at all had passed.

Maybe they didn't do it. Maybe something happened. They lost the new chip. They couldn't find the old one in my brain.

That was too terrible to dwell on.

I lay there, brushing an imaginary fingertip over my mind. Had the depression returned?

No.

Could I sense the old chip?

I pictured the terrible scenes I knew so well. Patti being choked. Stabbed. Her body in a suitcase. The bag splashing into water. They were still in my head, but no new scenes came. I felt only peace.

Thank you, God, for helping me through.

Time ebbed and flowed. A nurse came to check on me. Then I was in a private room, the bed elevated. Mom appeared.

"Lisa. You okay?" She patted my hand through the blanket.

"Mm-hmm."

"How does your brain feel?"

Almost sounded funny. "Fine." My tongue was thick. The room oozed cotton. "Did they . . . gimme drugs?"

"You're doped up, all right. Just sleep it off. I'll be here."

"No, first I havta talk to Sherry."

"I've already called her. She knows you're okay."

"I wanna talk to her."

Mom got Sherry on the line and handed the phone to me. My arm felt heavy to lift. "Hi, Sher."

"Hey, there. Sheesh, you sound half dead."

"Thanks. Back at me. Back atcha. Huh?"

Sherry laughed. "Smarter than ever, I see."

"Uh-huh. Think I need sleep now."

"I can believe that."

"Bye." I closed my eyes. Vaguely, I remember Mom hanging up the phone.

For the rest of the day I floated in and out of sleep. By dinnertime I felt more alert and was ready to eat something. I wanted to shout with relief. But I could only lie there, trying to take it all in.

My mind was so quiet.

"Did they have to shave more of my hair?" I asked Mom. She'd stayed all day to watch over me.

"I don't know, you're bandaged. But I doubt it. Except the stubby growth from the past week."

I struggled with a bite of soup. "Maybe when it grows back I'll get some highlights. Maybe go blonde, what do you think?"

I'd never even considered coloring my hair before. It was a good sign.

"I think you'd look beautiful in any hair color." Mom smiled. "Except maybe pink."

"Okay, purple then." I took another bite and smiled back. "This worked, didn't it."

"Looks like it."

Wow. "We did it, Mom. We really did it!"

Now I just had to recover. And I had plenty of money to help me. It was almost more than I could grasp.

"*You* did it," Mom said.

Evening came—and still no blaring new scenes of murder. Mom and I talked and watched some TV. "I can't believe how . . . blissful I feel," I told her. "This is amazing."

I slept through the night.

Late the next morning Mom returned. Her suitcase was packed and sitting in the rental car, she said. From the hospital she would go straight to the San Francisco Airport. "I wish I didn't have to say good-bye." She leaned over to brush a fingertip across my check.

"Me too. But I'll visit you soon."

"Promise?"

"As soon as I can travel."

She hugged me good-bye. A real hug. When she left, the room felt empty.

After lunch Sherry called to check on me. "I talked to your Mom this morning. She's still giving great reports."

"Yeah. I'm good."

"Want me to come visit?"

"I'm not much company. Still sleeping a lot, or staring at the TV. But the drugs have worn off, and I'm not letting them give me any more."

"Does your head hurt?"

"Yeah. But not bad."

"Wish I had your level of pain tolerance."

I heard a kid wail in the background.

Sherry sighed. "Great. J.T. just woke up for some reason. I only put him down ten minutes ago."

I pictured J.T. with his curly hair and blue eyes. Chubby little hands. I couldn't wait to see him and Rebecca as soon as I felt better. Would he even remember me?

The crying grew louder. "Sorry, Lisa, I need to go. I'll call you tomorrow. And we'll need to figure out what time on Tuesday you want to come home. I have a tentative babysitter for J.T., but she needs to know when."

Suddenly Tuesday seemed so far away. I didn't want to stay in the hospital that long. "I want to go home tomorrow."

Sherry hesitated. "Really? I thought you'd be spending an extra day."

"I could. But I don't want to. Or need to. I'm feeling ready to go."

"Well, okay."

She sounded a little reluctant. "Can you come get me tomorrow?"

"It's just that the babysitter isn't available then."

Oh. That was a problem. The hospital was no place to bring a toddler.

"But don't worry, I'll figure it out. If you want to come home tomorrow, I'll make it happen."

Yes! "Thanks so much. You're amazing."

"Yeah, well. So are you, Miss Two-Brain-Surgeries-in-a-Week."

I smiled and hung up the phone. Soon I drifted off again.

Sometime later a knock on my open door tugged me from sleep. Light footsteps followed. My eyes blinked open. Of all people, Patti Stolsinger gazed down at me.

Oh.

She was wearing the blue silk top. The one in my visions. The one I'd seen stained with blood. My body went rigid. That top. One more detail that was *real*.

"Hi," she whispered.

I lay still, mouth hinged open. Highly aware of my weakness. Why was she here? "Hi."

She bit her lip. "Don't worry. I'm not here to argue with you."

Good thing. She'd win.

"Can I . . . talk to you for a minute, Lisa?"

I nodded.

She set down the purse slung over her shoulder and pulled up one of the yellow chairs. I pushed my sleepiness away. I would need my wits about me.

Patti sat and folded her hands in her lap. "Bill wanted me to come. So I could assure you I don't hold anything against you."

Hilderbrand concerned about *me*? "In other words, *you* didn't want to."

"No, no, I didn't mean that. I did want to. It's just that he suggested it first."

"That's nice of him."

Should I be buying this?

Patti rubbed her palms against her jeaned legs. "After you saw him on Friday and told him the full story, he told it to me. We were both amazed at what you'd gone through. I really had no idea. I knew some of it, of course, but . . . That night at my house, I was too startled to let it sink in."

"I can believe that."

She nodded. "Anyway I just wanted to personally say I'm sorry. I know I wasn't very nice to you on the phone. Now I know none of this was your fault. Actually, we're both on the same side. Somebody tried to sabotage the Empowerment Chip—which hurt both of us."

Yeah, well, it hurt me a lot more than her. But I knew what she meant. Her face and name had been dragged into it. "That's okay. I'm sorry, too. I've never yelled at anyone like that before in my life. I was just . . . beside myself."

"I get that now."

We fell silent.

Patti focused on the bed. "I hope you didn't suffer any more of those horrible visions before you got to surgery."

"A few. They were short."

"Oh, no."

I shrugged. "Apparently I survived."

"But I'm so sorry. What did you see?"

The scenes splashed through my head. "It's not something you'd want to hear."

"It's okay. Bill should know. And I'll . . . deal with it."

I gazed at her. "It wasn't much, really. Just . . . the man, washing blood off the knife in his kitchen sink. I saw his gold watch. Really fancy Rolex. The time was 5:35. And the date was tomorrow."

"Tomorrow?"

"Monday, March 19."

"You mean he had a gold Rolex that shows the day and date?"

"Yeah."

Shock flattened Patti's expression. She looked away.

What was that about? "I'm sorry. I shouldn't have told you."

She managed a wan smile. "Oh, it's fine. I just . . . I'm glad all that's out of your head."

Her stunned reaction ping-ponged in my mind. "Does Dr. Hilderbrand have a watch like that?"

She still wouldn't look at me. "No."

She was lying. It was written all over her face. Pinpricks went down my back. Why would she lie about this? "No?"

Patti shook her head.

He did. He *did*. My heart turned over. I focused on the bedcovers, fighting to keep a calm expression. Hilderbrand owned that watch. It was real, too.

And she didn't want me to know.

What did this mean?

I shifted my position. What to say to keep her talking? "Dr. Hilderbrand has the chip they took out of me, right?"

She turned back to me. "You bet he does."

"Has he examined it in the lab yet?"

"He's doing that today."

Today. What would he find?

What would he think when Patti told him I'd seen his *real watch*?

"He agreed to tell me what he finds out," I said.

"I know."

"Do you think he'll really do that?"

She shrugged. "He said he would."

More than said. It was in the contract. But he'd lied to me before. If he claimed he found nothing, how could I press it?

Patti gazed at the bandage on my head. "How are you feeling?"

"Okay."

"The new chip?"

My lips curved. "It's good. Working well—and no more visions of your murder."

"Well." She shivered. "Glad to hear that."

The blue silk of her top screamed at me. And the watch . . .

"Is it scary to have enemies like that, Patti? Who'd want to bring down your boyfriend's company and involve you, too?"

She looked at her lap. "Terrifying."

She sounded so plaintive. For the first time I felt real sympathy for her. Bad enough that she was dating a man who couldn't be trusted not to cheat on her.

"Why do you stay with him?" The question blurted out. I half expected Patti to get up and stalk from the room.

She laced and unlaced her hands. "I love him."

I watched her face. Waited for her to say more.

"You don't know him, Lisa. I mean, he's brilliant. Look at what he's created. And he's confident and strong. Everything I need . . ."

Except trustworthiness. All the same, I could partially understand. On the outside Patti Stolsinger looked like she had it all. Beauty, health, a good career. But who knew what demons chewed at her self-worth?

My expression softened. "I see." And I did. Not that I thought she was right.

Patti's mouth opened, then closed. A frown flicked across her forehead. I had the distinct impression she wanted to ask me something but didn't know how.

I waited, but she said nothing.

"Don't . . . *settle*, Patti. Confidence and intelligence are great. But they can never beat out reliability. And gentleness." I pictured Ryan.

Patti raised her chin in a defensive gesture—then blinked. Her gaze slipped away. She gave a tiny, defeated nod.

A warning light went off in my head. Was Hilderbrand abusive to her? He seemed like such a hard man. It was easy to imagine him losing his temper, especially if she ever confronted him about running around on her.

The false memories of her murder—did they scare Patti on some deeper level? Maybe she thought they were some kind of sign. And now she knew I'd seen Hilderbrand's watch.

I licked my lips. "Patti, are you afraid of—"

"I need to go." She rose. "I'm sure you should be resting."

No way could I let her leave yet. I needed answers. "Are you okay?"

"Of course, what do you mean?" She busied herself with returning the chair to its position against the wall. By the time she turned back to me, her anxious expression was gone. She gave me a tight smile. "I wish you the best, Lisa. And I'm very glad to hear the Empowerment Chip is working for you."

Clearly I would get no more out of her. But her face and body language had said plenty. "Thank you."

Patti picked up her purse. "Anything I can get you before I go?"

More empty politeness. The vibrations coming off her said she wanted out of there. "No, thanks. I'm fine."

She nodded.

"I appreciate your coming to see me. Hope to talk to you again sometime. You have my number."

She managed another smile. "Bye, Lisa."

"Bye."

When she left the room, the air thrummed.

MONDAY, MARCH 19

AS I CHECKED OUT OF THE HOSPITAL LATE MONDAY MORNING I felt pretty good physically, considering I'd been through back-to-back brain surgeries. But my mind wouldn't settle. I kept going over and over Patti's visit. Something was off. Something important. Like that watch showing today's date. Monday, March 19. Hilderbrand's *real* watch.

Sherry had left J.T. with a pinch-hit babysitter, but not for long. She had time to pick me up and take me home, then had to hightail it back to her own house. Mom had stocked my kitchen before she left, so I'd be set.

In a phone call Sunday night I'd told Sherry about Patti's visit. She was as surprised as I'd been. "I know the watch I saw in that final vision was real," I said more than once. "Even though Patti denied it. I saw it on her face."

"That's really bothering you, isn't it?"

"And her blouse. The one I saw her wearing when she was murdered. It was the same one she was wearing when she came to see me!"

"But, Lisa, you already knew some of the details from those scenes were true. Like Hilderbrand's house and street. And his car."

"But these seem different. I mean, they're personal things Hilderbrand and Patti wear. How could somebody fake that?"

"The same way they faked a lot of other things, like Patti herself."

"Look at all they do with computer graphics in movies these days."

I shut up then. But I hadn't been satisfied.

Now on the way home, Sherry and I rode mostly in silence. I lay back against the head rest, eyes closed. It seemed no time at all before I felt us turn off of El Camino. Soon we'd reach my apartment building. I sat up with a sigh.

"You all right?" Sherry glanced at me.

"Yeah. I'm just tired."

"You're not still worried about Patti's visit and all that?"

This woman knew me too well. "Guess I am."

"Why?"

Good question. What was wrong with me? I'd been through the surgery—again—and everything was all over. Hilderbrand had kept his word. I should be nothing but happy. So what if Patti owned that blue top? So what if I'd seen Hilderbrand's watch?

"Lisa, tell me."

I folded my arms, chilled. "You know how sometimes you just feel things? And you can't prove anything, but you just know. Or maybe you don't even know exactly *what*, but something . . ."

Yeah, like I "knew" Patti had been murdered when she hadn't.

Sherry pulled into a parking spot at the curb in front of my apartment building. Her brow knit. "Yeah."

I looked up at my living room window. Why had I let us get into this conversation? "So there's these . . . things. One is that date I saw on Hilderbrand's watch. Monday, March 19."

"What about it?" Sherry put the car in Park.

"It's today. Why did it show that date?"

She shrugged. "I don't know. Could have been any date, I suppose."

"And why was the watch one that Hilderbrand really owns?"

"Well, you don't really know that, right? Patti said it wasn't."

"She was lying. I could tell that right away."

"Just by looking at her?"

"Come on, Sherry, don't you know when your kids are lying just by looking at them?"

"They're kids, Lisa. Which makes them bad liars."

"So Patti's a bad liar."

Sherry lifted both hands. "Okay."

She wasn't getting this at all. "Also I think he abuses Patti. Or at least he loses his temper—badly. She's scared of him."

"She didn't tell you that either, did she?"

Okay, this was getting just plain irritating.

Sherry caught my expression. "Look, Lisa, I don't know why you're worrying about this now. It's over. You've got a perfectly working chip in your brain, and you don't have to think about those people ever again."

She was right. But I couldn't help it.

Sherry squeezed my arm. "I just want to see you better. It's been a terrible week for you. A terrible *year*. Now you can put it behind you."

I know, but . . . Couldn't she see how all these things were adding up?

To what?

"Yeah, I know. I want to put it all behind me."

She smiled. "And you will. Right now you're just tired. You need to get into your apartment and rest." Sherry turned off the engine. "Come on. Let's get you settled."

I sighed again and got out of the car.

Sherry carried my suitcase up the stairs for me. When we got into the apartment she checked the cupboards and refrigerator, making sure I had everything I needed.

"I'm set, Sherry. Mom already did all that. I know you need to go."

She looked me over. "I don't like leaving you alone."

"I'll be fine. I'm just going to sleep."

She bit her lip. "Call me when you wake up?"

"Promise."

"Yeah? Just make sure you follow through better than last time."

I deserved that. "I will."

She gave me a long hug and reluctantly left.

I bolted the door behind her, wishing I could call Mom and tell her I was home. But my mother was tied up in meetings all day. I'd have to wait till evening.

I turned around and faced my apartment. Nine days ago at this same moment, I'd seen the suitcase for the first time. And I'd begun to go flat out crazy.

Now—blessed nothing.

All the same, for some reason I pictured the eye of a storm. That humming stillness before the world exploded.

Chapter 34

A RINGING PHONE WOKE ME FROM A DREAMLESS SLEEP. I blinked a few times and stretched out my arm, fumbling for the receiver. "Hello?" My voice sounded thick.

"Lisa? This is Agnes Brighton."

It took a minute to place the name. "Hi, Agnes."

"I'm sorry, did I wake you?"

"It's okay." I pushed myself to sit up against the headboard. "I was just . . . resting."

"I am sorry. I'll be brief. You wanted me to call you if I remembered where I'd seen the photo of the drawing I did for you. Your victim?"

My chin dropped. She was a little late. "Uh-huh."

"I remembered where I'd seen her. And by the way, I suppose you know by now a policeman called me about the case."

The case that wasn't, she meant. Although Officer Bremer had probably only asked Agnes questions, not told her the outcome of his investigation. "Yeah, I know."

"Anyway I saw the woman in your drawing about four to five weeks ago at a jewelry store in Redwood City. She was with a man, but it looked like they'd come in separate cars. I was only in there for a couple minutes when she was there. They were looking at engagement rings. She and I left about the same time."

Engagement rings. Patti must have been with Hilderbrand. "What jewelry store?"

She hesitated. "If you hadn't asked me, I'd be able to tell you." Another pause. "Oh, I just can't remember. Anyway, it's on the south end of Redwood City on El Camino, just above the Atherton border."

Hilderbrand's driving route from the murder scenes flashed in my head. He'd passed a jewelry store on El Camino. "Does the building sort of look like a house?"

"Yes. It's on your right when you're headed south."

That was the one.

"Does this help you, Lisa?"

"Yes, thanks." I didn't want to tell her I'd found the woman days ago—alive. Not a conversation I cared to get into. "What made you remember this now?"

"I was in that jewelry store again. They've been fixing a bracelet for me, something I recently inherited. I went to pick it up. And— boom, it hit me. I could picture her at the counter."

The mysteries of memory. "Thanks, Agnes. I really appreciate your calling."

"You're welcome. I'm just sorry to think she's dead. She was a beautiful woman."

Oh, man. At some point I should tell her the truth. "Yeah."

"Should I call Officer Bremer and give him this information?"

But how could I tell her the truth? I wasn't allowed to talk about my experience with Cognoscenti with anyone. And there was no way to explain without doing that. "You've done enough. I'll handle it. Thanks again."

We said our good-byes and hung up. I scooted down on the bed and stared at the far wall.

Patti and Hilderbrand, looking at engagement rings. But here it was—what did Agnes say?—four or five weeks later, and Patti wasn't wearing a ring.

Four to five weeks. Why did that seem significant?

I pushed from bed and headed into the kitchen, where I kept a small calendar in a drawer. I pulled it out and counted back five weeks. And landed on February 12.

Four days before February 16—the original date Mom and I had calculated for Patti's murder.

Yeah, so? The murder never happened. I shoved the calendar back in the drawer.

The clock read 3:35. If Mom was here, she'd be making me eat. I dropped into a chair at the table and tried to clear my head. *Why did Agnes's call bug me so much?*

My last vision had shown 5:35 on Hilderbrand's watch—one I was convinced he really owned. And today's date. *Today.*

Which meant nothing. The first date was clearly wrong. Why shouldn't this one be wrong too?

Because this time I saw his real watch.

What did that matter?

Then it hit me. Hilderbrand had tried to keep me in the hospital an extra day. Until tomorrow. He'd suggested that before he even knew of my final vision about his watch and today's date.

What did this mean?

Nothing, that's what. Thinking about it was stupid.

My head throbbed. I needed aspirin. And something to eat. My legs felt weak.

A jewelry store. Patti had left before Hilderbrand . . .

Why did he stay? Didn't look like he'd bought her a ring. Unless he just hadn't given it to her yet. But Patti hadn't mentioned expecting a ring from him.

But why should she tell *me* that?

Maybe she *was* expecting a proposal from him. Maybe that's why she seemed to be rethinking the relationship.

Had Hilderbrand lied to her? Had he stayed in the store after Patti left to make her think he'd bought her a ring?

What if he had? Why should it even matter to me?

I checked the clock again, and my stomach rumbled. How I wanted to simply eat and rest. But this news, on top of everything else that nibbled at my gut . . .

Patti was in danger. That was the thought I couldn't shake. In fact the more I tried, the stronger I believed it was true. And if I didn't explore this . . . whatever it was, I would live to regret it.

The jewelry store.

Let it go, Lisa.

Maybe I could find something out at that store.

Let. It. Go.

But I couldn't.

So strange, the way that agonizing decision played out. I can't even remember making a conscious choice. Almost like my brain made it for me. I just knew I had to go. I felt it in my gut.

But I wasn't going anywhere without eating first. I grabbed a yogurt from the refrigerator and dumped it in a bowl with some granola. I forced myself to eat it all. My mother would be so proud of me. When I was done I swallowed two aspirin.

Then I went to the bedroom to try to make myself presentable. A little hard, with a bandage on my head, dirty hair, and all the tiredness sagging my face.

Why was I going to that jewelry store? What could I possibly say when I got there?

I fired up the Internet and found the picture of Patti and Hilderbrand that Mom and I had seen. I printed it out in color and folded it into my purse. Just in case. Next thing I knew, I was in my living room, gazing bleary-eyed at the walls. Wondering what was happening to me. Why I had to do this.

Apprehension crackled in my veins. I stepped out of my apartment and bolted the door behind me.

Chapter 35

THE DIGITAL CLOCK IN MY CAR READ 4:19 WHEN I PULLED into a parking spot outside the jewelry store. I gathered my purse and got out of the car. Even though I'd eaten I still felt unsteady. Once I put this thing to rest, I'd go home and go to bed.

So I told myself.

My heart thudded as I entered the store. Two long display cases sat on my left. To the right was a door disappearing into . . . offices, maybe? A thirty-something man greeted me from behind one of the displays. His brown eyes grazed my bandaged head, then slid away. "May I help you?"

Words froze on my tongue. What to say? My conscience twinged at the thought of lying. But I couldn't tell the truth. "I . . . um. I have a friend." I approached him, the case between us. Jewelry with sapphires, emeralds, and diamonds sparkled up from the glass.

"Yes?" He was smiling. That's what salesmen did with customers. All the same he had to wonder. I knew I looked a sight.

I spotted a wedding ring on his finger.

Gently I touched my bandage. "I'm sorry I look so terrible. I just got out of the hospital after a little . . . procedure."

Empathy flicked across his face. "Oh, no problem. Are you all right?"

"Yes, just tired." Might as well milk all the sympathy I could from this married man. Maybe he'd picture his own wife in the situation. "I'll go home and lie down when I'm done here."

"Sure. There's a stool behind you. Would you like to get off your feet?"

I looked over my shoulder. "Yes, thanks." I took the folded picture of Patti and Hilderbrand from my purse, then set the bag on the floor. Pulled the stool a foot closer to the jewelry case and sat.

"So." The man spread his hands. "How can I help you? My name's Michael, by the way."

"Hi, Michael." I worked to keep my fingers from trembling as I unfolded the picture. I still had little idea what I was going to say.

"This is my friend and her boyfriend." I turned the printout to face him and laid it on the counter. "I think they came in last month to look at engagement rings. Do you recognize them, by any chance?"

If Agnes Brighton had given me wrong information, I'd be dead in the water here.

Michael's gaze dropped to the photo. If he knew Hilderbrand and Patti, he gave no sign. "Why do you want to know?"

Here it came. I was a stranger to him, asking about two of his clients. Probably very high-paying clients. If he suspected my intentions, why should he answer?

The lie that slipped out of me materialized from nowhere. "I . . . this sounds silly, but my friend—Patti's her name—isn't wearing a ring yet. Her other friends and I don't want to ask her what's going on, in case it's bad news. But if Bill has bought the ring and intends to give it to her, we'd like to know. Because we need to start planning a party."

My insides cringed. What a lame story. Why should a party be so important that I'd come from a hospital to ask about this today?

But Michael merely nodded. "Bill, you say?"

"His last name is Hilderbrand."

The salesman surveyed me. I forced myself to look straight back at him. My pulse fluttered.

He tapped the counter. "I think I've heard the name. But I took a week's vacation last month to go skiing. Let me see if someone else knows."

Before I could speak he walked to the office door and called through it. "Hey, Dan. Could you come out here for a minute?"

I steadied myself, both hands on the counter. What if Dan was a friend of Hilderbrand's? What if he called the CEO as soon as I left?

Dan appeared in the doorway, a younger man with black-framed glasses. Michael led him down the length of the counter and pointed to the picture. "She wants to know if this guy bought an engagement ring for her friend." Michael indicated Patti's picture. "So she can start planning a party."

Weakness filtered down my spine. I just might fall over any minute. Now I had *two* men to convince.

Dan smiled. "Oh, that's Dr. Hilderbrand." He looked up at me, noticing my bandaged head for the first time. He looked away.

Air knocked around in my lungs. "That's right. His first name is Bill."

Dan's smile widened. The sight of it made me almost giddy. "Well, you might call him that. He's Dr. Hilderbrand to me. One of my regular customers."

My hands gripped the counter. Next time Hilderbrand came in here, this guy would surely mention me. What would Hilderbrand do when he learned I'd been checking up on him?

I had to leave this area. I had to move away.

My dry throat swallowed. "Did he buy Patti a ring?"

"Nah. They weren't seriously looking. Well, maybe *she* was." Dan laughed, then saw my stricken expression. "Sorry to disappoint you."

"Oh. No, it's fine." I slid the photo toward myself. Folded it. "I just . . . I'm feeling a little spent."

I had my answer—so what? Why had I even come?

My ankles trembled as I slid off the stool. I leaned over to pick up my purse and felt my face flush as I straightened. "Thank you for letting me know. Sorry for rushing off. I need to go home and lie down."

"Sure," Dan said. "Hope you feel better."

I made for the door, feeling their eyes on my back. Wishing I could think of another question. But what to ask? My brain had trouble focusing. I was just too tired.

With effort I pulled back the door, hoping I could drive home okay. I had no business being out like this so soon after surgery.

I was halfway out the door when I heard Dan comment to Michael.

"Hilderbrand. That's the guy who bought the dragon ring."

Chapter 36

I FROZE IN THE DOORWAY.

The dragon ring. In a forever second I hung there, my thoughts grinding. Part of me wanted to run. Get out of there before one of the salesmen called Hilderbrand and told him about my questions. The CEO had lied to me about that ring. That made him dangerous.

Didn't it?

Some force beyond myself turned me back. "Oh, that ring." Amazing how casual the words sounded. "The one with the dragon's head? Emeralds for eyes?"

Dan nodded. "You've seen it?"

"Sure have."

"Crazy ring, isn't it. I never pegged Dr. Hilderbrand as someone who'd buy it."

I balanced in the threshold, hearing traffic pass on El Camino. The world out there had turned dangerous again. But I wasn't exactly sure how. Or why.

That dragon ring was real. The image in my head was *real.* Just like the watch. Just like Patti, and her blue silk top, and Hilderbrand's house, and his car . . .

"It is crazy." My breathing shallowed. I needed to sit down. "Did he buy it that day after Patti left?"

"That's why he stayed behind."

The answer spun through me. Somehow I managed to smile. "Sounds just like him." I kept my voice light, lips curved. Felt like they were set in stone. "Well, thanks again."

I stepped outside. The door closed behind me.

Somehow I made it to my car and fell inside. I wanted to sit there and rest my head on the steering wheel. Try to process what had just happened. But I didn't want the salesmen looking through the window and seeing my reactions.

Patti had been shocked that I'd seen that Rolex watch. Now the ring . . .

"He owns a dragon's head ring, doesn't he? Got emeralds for eyes?"

"He'd never wear anything like that."

She didn't know he'd bought it. She had absolutely no idea. What would she think if she learned the truth?

I started the car and backed out of the parking space. The digital clock read 4:40. At El Camino I needed to turn left to go home. But that's not what happened. My hands turned me right. Toward Hilderbrand's house.

Why, I didn't know. I had no idea what I was going to do.

Hunched over the wheel, I drove. I passed over the border into Atherton. Didn't matter. Didn't mean anything. Any time now I could come to my senses and turn around.

My mind churned through the details. Today's date on Hilderbrand's watch. The black suitcase. The hardwood floor of his kitchen, the bloody knife. And Patti didn't trust him.

Patti, choked, stabbed. Stuffed in a suitcase.

Monday, March 19. At 5:35.

"I suggest you stay an extra day in the hospital."

Hilderbrand had wanted me there today. Watched by nurses. Out of commission. Why? What did he plan to do?

A thought hovered before me, one that made no sense: the man in my visions—it was Hilderbrand. In his own house. Standing at his own kitchen sink. Wearing the ring he denied owning.

But how was Patti alive?

An answer came—and punched a hole in my stomach. I gripped the wheel, my limbs going numb. What if the scenes on my old chip weren't memories at all? What if they were *plans*? Hilderbrand, going over and over the act in his head. Some of it was imagined— Patti yelling at him, what she was wearing. But even that was based on truth. Patti did own the blue top. They probably did fight about him cheating on her.

Not memories. Plans.

That would explain the different details. The dragon ring disappearing. Wearing one watch, then another. Details that had changed each time he imagined the murder. But the important parts stayed the same . . .

Monday, March 19.

Hilderbrand planned to kill her *today*.

The thought pressed my foot into the accelerator. I nearly hit the car in front of me. At the last minute I braked, pulse pounding in my ears. Someone honked, and the sound shot through me.

This was crazy. I should get off the road. I could barely pace myself with the other cars. Could barely feel myself sitting in the seat.

But I drove on.

If those scenes were Hilderbrand's plans, how had they gotten on my chip? Had he told someone who turned out to be his enemy? I couldn't believe that. He wouldn't tell his plans to anyone.

What had he thought when I told him about my visions? He must have felt like a truck had hit him. I *knew* what he planned to do. No wonder he wanted that chip out of me. No wonder he paid me for my silence. Now he would kill Patti. Stuff her into a suitcase and throw her in a lake.

Hilderbrand must own a boat.

My head jerked back. Why hadn't I thought of that before? Where was the boat kept? That water would be Patti's grave.

But why kill her today?

Why at all?

How did someone learn of his plans and put them on my chip?

I passed Tuscaloosa. The next street would be Atherton Avenue. I couldn't go to Hilderbrand's house. There was nothing I could do. I hardly felt strong enough to drive.

I should call the police.

Like they'd believe me.

I reached Atherton Avenue. Someone else's hands turned the wheel to the right. The tree canopy threw the narrow road into thick shadow.

I checked the clock: 4:46.

This was outrageous. I needed to turn around. What was I going to do—stake out Hilderbrand's house? And what for? He wasn't really going to kill Patti. Even if he had thought about it, the time could be completely off. And the date. Whoever made that chip had put together random scenes. Had done everything he could to scare Hilderbrand out of putting the Empowerment Chip on the market. The scenes weren't real.

Except details of his house, inside and out. His car. The ring. The watch. Patti's top. How could someone *else* know all those details?

I'd bet anything Hilderbrand owned that black suitcase. The thought sent a shiver down my spine.

The lanes slipped by on my left. Odell. Mercedes. Stevenson . . .

Turn around, Lisa. Turn around!

I glanced in my rearview mirror—and saw a black SUV.

Hilderbrand.

My nerves popped. I hit the accelerator and threw another backward glance. The SUV was some distance away. He couldn't possibly recognize me or my car—yet. I passed Amethyst Lane. By the time I neared the next street I saw him turn onto Amethyst.

I whipped onto the road and turned around.

My heart pummeled my ribs as I eased my car back toward Amethyst. Just before the bottom of the street I pulled over and leaned forward, straining to see up toward Hilderbrand's house. The SUV was idling in his driveway as the far right garage door slid open.

Hilderbrand drove into the garage. The door came down.

It was only 4:49. What was he doing home from Cognoscenti so early? Silicon Valley execs were notorious for working late hours.

Tiredness swept over me. I gripped the steering wheel, trying to think.

The clock turned over to 4:50. Forty minutes from now, Patti would be dead.

It's not real, Lisa!

I turned onto Amethyst Lane. Drove all the way to the cul-de-sac and turned around to come down Hilderbrand's side of the median. Two houses up from his I pulled to the curb. I put the car in Park—and waited.

What now? Would Patti show up?

Why should she?

If she did, I'd . . . do something. I'd have to. The timing couldn't be coincidental. If she didn't, I'd drive home. Take a sleeping pill or two. Or five.

But what if she was already in the house?

I thought that over. Patti didn't live there. Though she could have a key.

Minutes snailed by. Four fifty-five. Five o'clock.

I was wearing a shirt with long sleeves. Too hot. My palms turned sweaty. Breathing came hard. It was more than just tiredness. Scenes from my life flashed before me—the miscarriages, Ryan's funeral. My attack. The depression. Two surgeries. Now I finally had hope for the future. I was ready to start a new life. So why was I here, putting those plans in danger?

But I couldn't stop.

Fear circled me, a vulture looking for carrion. I felt lightheaded. Desperate.

I yanked my cell out of my purse and punched Sherry's auto-call button.

"Lisa, how are you?" I heard J.T. and Rebecca playing in the background. "Are you better?"

"I'm on Hilderbrand's street. Watching his house."

"What?"

"He's going to kill Patti in the next half-hour."

Stricken silence.

"Lisa, get home right now."

"I can't. I have to do something—"

"No! What you have to do is get home and rest. Something's gone wrong. I'll call your doctor—"

"I don't need a doctor, Sherry." Tears filled my eyes. This was about to put me under. "I need help here. What should I *do*?"

"Get out of there!"

"I can't let Patti die."

"She's not going to die, Lisa. Those visions weren't real."

"But they were, just not the way I thought. They aren't memories, they're Hilderbrand's plans. He bought the dragon head ring.

He really has it, and he told me he didn't. He lied to me. Why would he do that, Sherry, why?"

Her breathing vibrated over the phone. "How do you know he bought that ring?"

"I went to the jewelry store where he got it. They told me."

"What? I don't—"

"Just believe me, okay? It's true."

"Whether I believe you or not, you have no business being there."

"The cops for sure won't believe me. If I drive away from here and Patti disappears, I'll never forgive myself. *I* was almost strangled to death, remember? I know what it's like. I can't let some other woman go through that!"

Sherry made a sound of disbelief in her throat. "Even if you're right—what could you do to stop it?"

"I don't know."

"You can't have much strength right now."

"I don't." Tears fell on my cheeks.

"Lisa. Go home. If Hilderbrand catches you stalking him, he'll have you arrested. Is that what you want?"

A blue Corvette turned left onto the bottom of Amethyst. *Patti's car.*

Air stilled in my lungs. She would cut between the median sections not far from where I sat.

I flicked off my car's engine and flung myself over the console, head almost on the passenger seat.

"Sherry." My voice muffled. "She's here. Patti. Driving up the street."

"Oh, no. Lisa, don't—"

"She's come. I *told* you!"

What should I do, what should I *do?*

I heard the Corvette rev up the street, closer . . . closer. I squeezed my eyes shut.

The sound shifted. For a second it seemed to stop. Was Patti staring at my car? Did she somehow know it was mine? Surely she couldn't see me.

I gripped the phone and prayed.

The Corvette's engine receded. Cautiously I raised my head. Patti was headed down toward Hilderbrand's house.

"Lisa, what's happening?"

"She's stopping outside his house." The far left garage door began to open. Patti must have her own remote for it. "She's driving inside the garage!"

"Fine. This is your chance to get out of there without being seen."

I sat up. Turned on the engine and checked the clock. It was 5:11.

Panic swelled in my chest. "He's going to kill her *now*! By 5:35 he's cleaning off the knife."

"Lisa, get hold of yourself. You know this isn't true."

I should know that. I really should. "But they're his plans!"

"Fine. Whatever. Plans can change. Why should he time the murder so exactly? *Think* what you're saying. None of this makes sense."

She was right. It made no sense at all. But here they were at Hilderbrand's house. On this date. At the right time.

"Lisa, do you hear me! Get out of there right now. If Hilderbrand catches you on his property, he'll call the police. You'll end up in jail. Is *that* what you want?"

Why wouldn't Sherry believe me? Why wouldn't *anyone* believe me? If my own mother was here right now, even she'd think I'd gone off a cliff.

"Lisa!"

"Gotta go, Sherry." I punched off the line and threw the cell on the passenger seat.

I watched the door Patti had driven into. It wasn't closing. Was she still sitting in her car?

Maybe she'd left the door open because she planned to leave again soon. But she wouldn't walk out of there, would she. She'd leave in a suitcase.

God, show me what to do!

In my mind I heard the *zzziiip*. Saw Patti's bloody body disappear under the suitcase's cover. Terror flamed through me. I had to stop this.

I drove down the street past Hilderbrand's house. Stopped one door down and cut the engine.

My cell phone went off.

I opened the door and got out of the car on rubbery legs. My pulse whooshed in my ears. Part of me couldn't believe I was doing this.

My phone kept ringing. Sherry, no doubt. I shoved the car door closed.

Up the street I tottered. Turned left into Hilderbrand's driveway. I could see Patti's Corvette parked straight ahead of me. No sign of her.

I crossed the threshold into the garage.

The space next to Patti's car was empty. And to the far right— Hilderbrand's SUV.

Halfway through the garage I stopped, staring at the door that I knew led into Hilderbrand's kitchen. With the stainless steel appliances and hardwood floor. The butcher block of knives to the right of the sink. Patti, stabbed and strangled, would soon lie on the floor. I saw her glazed eyes, the blood from her mouth—and nearly toppled over.

I reached the wall by the door. Leaned against it.

Now what? I couldn't go in there. But I had to. If I didn't, Patti would die. If I did, how could I stop Hilderbrand? I had no strength at all.

Sherry was right. I shouldn't be here.

No, she was even more right than that. I'd gone flat-out insane.

My feet shuffled to turn me around—and I heard it through the door. Patti's voice, yelling the very words I'd heard so many times in my head.

"Why can't you stop cheating on me? You're nothing but a liar! I'll tell them all what you really are. I'll make you pay!"

"Shut up!"

"I'll leave you, how will you like that? You can't kick me around like some dog!"

My brain reeled. I knew what followed. Could see it happening, even now. Hilderbrand's hands closing around her neck—

I grasped the knob of the kitchen door and flung it open.

Chapter 37

 I BARRELED INTO THE KITCHEN I KNEW SO WELL AND SLID to a halt.

The very sight of it flushed me with cold. Like stepping into a nightmare. In a split second I took in the sink, the floor. The sliding glass door out to a lush backyard.

Choking sounds emanated from beyond the room. So loud. Louder than in my visions.

My hand jerked to let the door slam. I stopped, then eased it half closed without sound. My mind shrieked at me to sprint toward Hilderbrand, scream for him to stop. But that would do little good. I had to think.

I had no time to think.

My eyes fastened on the butcher block across the room. I hurried to it and slid out a large knife. It looked like the one Hilderbrand had used.

The horrible choking sounds grew even louder. They filled the house, my head.

I made for the door on the left—the one I'd seen him drag Patti through. Then stopped.

The sounds weren't coming from that direction. They were supposed to come from the living room at the other end of the house. These seemed to come from this side.

A heavy thump. Patti's body hitting the floor?

I gripped the knife handle and ran on cat feet through the door straight ahead.

I hit an expansive hallway. On the far left was a staircase. The sounds were coming from ahead of me and to the right, beyond a large arched entrance. I looked through it and saw carpet. The back edge of a couch.

My heart skidded sideways, and my body shook. I couldn't do this. Hilderbrand would kill me, too.

I *had* to save Patti.

I forced myself forward until I stood even with the door. My gaze swiveled into the room. I knew the scene I would see, was already bracing against it.

Across from me, mounted on the wall sat a huge TV. On its screen—the familiar and horrible sights and sounds from my own brain, the volume turned up high. Patti, lying on the living room floor in her jeans and blue top. Not moving. Hilderbrand's heavy breathing as he bent over her.

But the real Hilderbrand sat on the sofa watching the TV, his back to me. Patti, in a black top, sat beside him, eyes also glued to the scene.

Air backed up in my throat. The knife loosened in my hand.

On the TV screen I saw the next sequence, as if through Hilderbrand's eyes. Up came his arm as he wiped it across his mouth. His breathing steadied.

On the floor, Patti moved.

Hilderbrand cursed and grabbed her feet. Roughly dragged her out of the room—

The real Hilderbrand's arm moved. On the TV the scene froze, as if someone had punched the pause button.

"See." Hilderbrand pointed at the screen. "All these sequences I looped over and over, and that's just how she saw them. But the last one didn't work as well."

What? *What . . . ?*

Numbness spread through my limbs. I don't know how I kept standing. My mind couldn't process what I was seeing. The truth— but not the truth. The scenes were from my brain chip. How could these two people be watching them on TV?

Hilderbrand's arm moved again. The TV scene jumped to life—his hands pulling Patti into the kitchen. Grabbing the knife—the one I now held. Kneeling over her, arching the weapon down toward her chest. He closed his eyes before the blade split her open.

My jaw slacked. He closed his eyes . . .

I'd never seen the knife stab her.

Then a close-up of Patti filled the screen. Blood on her blouse, coming from her mouth . . .

"Ooh, it's so real." The Patti on the couch shuddered and looked away.

My body went limp. Darkness swirled through my vision. Before I could stop it, the knife slipped from my hand and clattered to the floor.

Hilderbrand and Patti whipped around.

For one eternal second, my eyes met Hilderbrand's. *Don't faint, don't faint,* my brain screamed. I had to run. Had to get out of there. Had to . . .

In the same instant I fell, Hilderbrand jumped to his feet.

Chapter 38

"HOW DID SHE GET IN HERE?" A MAN'S VOICE RAGED ABOVE ME.

"I don't know." A female, frightened. "I guess I left the garage door open."

What . . . ?

My eyes opened.

I lay on a hardwood floor. Hilderbrand's house. It all rushed back.

Hilderbrand towered over my feet, Patti cringing away from him. I tried to move but fear weighed me down.

He punched her hard on the shoulder. She stumbled against the wall. "Why did you leave it open?"

Patti's face creased in pain. She held her arm where she'd been hit. "I wasn't going to stay, remember? You're the one who told me to watch that thing with you."

Hilderbrand's face flamed red. He raised his fist. "You've done it now. You have really done it."

Patti's hands flew to her face. Hilderbrand's arm cocked back to punch her.

My limbs unlocked. I kicked him hard in the shin.

"Ahh!" Hilderbrand's arms flew out. He grabbed his shin, then surged toward me, still bent over. His pulse beat a purple vein in his forehead. His lips pulled back. "I'll *kill* you."

"No!" Patti reached for his arm. He shoved her away.

Hilderbrand grabbed my shoulders. Lifted me off the floor. "Get up."

The stitches in my head pounded. I flailed at him, terror spilling from my mouth. *Jesus, help me!*

"Get *up!*" Hilderbrand lifted me higher. If he dropped me now my skull would crack open.

"Leave her alone!" Patti thrust her hands beneath my head.

"Help me get her up." Hilderbrand's teeth clenched.

"What are you going to do to her?"

"What do you *think* I'm going to do?" Spittle flew from his mouth.

"You *can't.*"

"You got a better idea? *You* killed her, Patti. You let her get in the house. She *saw* the tape."

Hilderbrand yanked me all the way up. My legs scrambled for footing. I nearly went back down. Hilderbrand hung on to my arms and pushed me against the wall. He stuck his face in mine. I could smell his breath.

"Why did you come here?"

Words clogged in my throat. In my mind I saw his hands around Patti's neck. Around *my* neck.

"*Why?*"

"I th-thought you were going to kill her."

"Who?"

"Patti."

Hilderbrand smirked. "And why would you think that?"

"Bill, let her go!"

"Shut up, Patti." Hilderbrand eyed me, his head tilted. "Come on, Ms. Newberry." My name sounded like a snarl. "Tell me."

His fingers dug into my arms. My muscles screamed and my legs shook. I was going to faint again.

Hilderbrand jerked me off the wall and banged me back against it. My head rattled. "*Tell* me."

What if he broke my stitches open? "I . . . the date on your watch. Today."

He screwed up his face. "That's it?"

"Huh-uh . . ." The trembling slithered up to my stomach. My chest.

"What, then?"

"You . . . b-bought the dragon ring. You lied."

"How do you know that?"

Would he kill them too? The men at the jewelry store?

My eyelids fluttered.

Hilderbrand shook me. Patti grabbed his arm, trying to pull him off. He elbowed her away.

"*How* do you know, Lisa?" The vein in his forehead still pulsed.

"I . . . just did. The watch date. All the l-lies you told. Your threats." Plus Patti's fear of him. And the jewelry store guys. But I couldn't say that.

"Did *you* tell her anything?" He threw the words at Patti.

"No."

"When you saw her at the hospital?"

"*No.* I only said what you told me to."

Told her to?

Understanding roared through my head. The TV screen. The two of them watching the scenes from my brain . . .

They'd played me. From the very first minute to the last. Both of them. He hadn't planned to kill her today. They'd *filmed* those scenes. Staged everything.

And put it on my chip.

"Looped over and over . . ."

Hilderbrand's fingers dug deeper into my arms. I cried out. "You saw the watch, you said. Today's date. You told Patti."

Tears slipped down my cheeks. My breathing shallowed. "Yes."

"When did you see it?"

When? I tried to remember. My brain slogged through mud. "I don't know."

"After you and I talked?"

"Uh-huh."

"That day?"

What difference did it make? My knees buckled. A wail rolled up my throat.

"Tell me!"

"Yes, later. That day."

Patti cowered back, hands to her mouth. Why wouldn't she do something? Maybe the two of us—

The knife. Where was it?

My terrified gaze rolled to the floor. I'd dropped it when I fell. If I could just get it. If Patti would just pick it up . . .

Fury twisted Hilderbrand's face. *"Why* did it take so long?" He wrenched me from the wall and flung me back again. My body shrieked.

"Wh-what?"

"Stop!" Patti grabbed his arm. Her expression softened to coaxing. "Come on, Bill. She doesn't even know what you're talking about."

"It shouldn't have taken that long! She should have seen that sequence sooner."

"Okay. You'll figure it out." She tugged at him. "Look at the chip again."

"Let go of me, Patti."

"Just calm down."

"Let go."

"But you can't—"

"I *said let go!*" He shook her off.

I searched again for the knife. There. Kicked across the floor, a good ten feet away. Too far from me. Too close to him.

"Bill." Patti looked scared to death. "You have to let her go."

"Go where? Straight to the police? She *knows*."

"She doesn't know. And they won't believe her anyway."

"After all I've done." Hilderbrand raged in my face. "All my research and work. I'm *not* going to let you mess this up."

I swallowed. My arm muscles flamed under Hilderbrand's grip. "Sh-she's right. The police think I'm crazy. They won't listen to me."

Nobody listened to me. Nobody. Now I was going to die.

"Do you have any idea how long I've waited for this? Huh?" Hilderbrand shook me again. "How dare you think you can stop me. You're *nothing*."

"I . . . won't t-tell."

"You're nobody. *I'm* going to change the world." His lips twisted. "Go upstairs, Patti. Get the suitcase."

"What?"

"Get it."

"No, Bill. No."

He growled and shoved me sideways. I stumbled, then banged into the hallway corner. Crumpled to the floor.

The knife lay about eight feet away.

Hilderbrand jumped toward Patti, his back to me. His hands circled her neck. Her eyes bugged, her fingers scrabbling to pull him off.

No.

I fumbled to my knees. If I could just crawl . . .

Patti backed up. Hilderbrand stuck with her, hands circling her neck. "Do you want to die for real, huh? *Do* you? Because it sounds to me like you can't handle this."

She shook her head. Her cheeks whitened.

"Are you with me or not?"

"Y-yes." She panted.

"You sure about that?"

"Yes!"

My knees started to move.

Hilderbrand let go of Patti and pushed her. "Get the suitcase."

She grasped her neck, chest heaving.

"Get it!"

Thoughts swooped and dipped in my mind. *The suitcase.*

Patti sucked in air. "She won't fit in that thing."

The big black one. With the whirring zipper. It had swallowed Patti. But she was much smaller.

I crawled soundlessly. Shaking. My legs wouldn't hold me for long.

"She'll fit when I'm done with her," Hilderbrand sneered.

I moved another foot. My hands trembled against the floor. I could picture the heavy suitcase thrown off a boat. Sinking in dark water. That would be me. *Me . . .*

"Get it *now!*" Hilderbrand yelled.

He wanted Patti upstairs so he could kill me. So she wouldn't have to watch.

Don't go!

She fled toward the staircase.

The knife was three feet away. I heaved toward it—and slipped. I went down, my elbow banging the floor. Electricity shot up my arm.

Hilderbrand spun around.

I rolled to my side and grabbed the knife.

He cursed and strode toward me. I pulled myself up on my good elbow.

His face blackened, his voice low in his throat. "Oh, you have done it now."

On the stairs, Patti turned. Hilderbrand stomped across the hardwood.

The world slowed. My blood chilled . . . turned to slush. Every muscle weakened. A distant part of me saw Hilderbrand close in. Saw the rage in his eyes.

"Lisa, don't!" Patti started running down the steps.

He rushed on. The space between us melted.

Patti hit the bottom stair.

Hilderbrand ground to a halt and raised his foot to kick the knife from my hand.

Inside me a switch ignited, and my icy veins blazed into fire. In one frantic motion I sat up, bent forward and plunged the knife deep in his thigh.

Patti screamed. Hilderbrand bellowed and shuffled backward. Blood spurted onto his pants. His hands flew to the knife. Stiff-fingered, he grasped it. Pulled it out. It dropped to the floor, spattering crimson. He flailed for footing. The wound pulsed, pulsed, his slacks staining wet.

I scooted forward, toward the knife. Couldn't let him get it . . .

"Bill!" Patti scurried to his side.

Curses sprayed from his mouth. "Help me!" He pressed both hands against his leg. Red oozed through his fingers. "Get something. For . . . tourniquet."

Patti ran toward the kitchen.

I scrambled to the knife. Picked it up. The handle was sticky.

Hilderbrand listed sideways and slammed to the floor. The blood came hard and fast. On his pants. The hardwood.

Patti appeared with a dishtowel. She fell to her knees in the pud-
dling red beside him, furiously tying it above the wound.

I tried to get up. My legs wouldn't work. Tried again. Nothing.
The third time I made it. I shuffled toward the kitchen, still clutch-
ing the knife, seeking a phone. It took me forever to get there.
Behind me, Hilderbrand grunted and cursed in the same breaths.

There—on the counter. A phone. I dropped the knife into the
stainless steel sink. It clattered like the end of the world. My coated
hand yanked up the receiver and punched in three digits.

"911, what is your emergency?"

"He's . . . bleeding . . . to death. Hurry."

"Who?"

No time for stupid questions. They could see the address. "He'll
die, do you hear? Come *now!*"

I threw down the phone. My legs felt like water, and my heart
quivered. On borrowed time I listed into the hallway. Patti had tied
the tourniquet and was pressing both hands against Hilderbrand's
leg. His eyes were closed, his face pale.

"Has the bleeding slowed down?" The words barely came out. I
leaned against the wall.

Patti threw me a look of rancid hatred. "If he dies, I'm coming
after you. I swear it."

Great. Now two people wanted me dead.

I pushed off the wall. Dragged myself in an unending journey to
the front door. When I finally arrived I opened it wide—and found
myself face to face with two policemen, preparing to knock.

I gasped. They stared at me. I could guess how I looked: dishev-
eled and head-bandaged, like walking death.

"We're looking for Lisa Newberry." One officer stepped forward. "We got a call there might be some kind of disturbance."

My mind wavered. Sherry. She'd called the police to protect me
from myself.

I raised my bloody palms. The officer's hands reflexed toward their guns.

"Need . . . ambulance." I staggered backward. "In there."

My legs gave out. One of the policemen caught me on the way down. The other one shoved past us into the hallway.

Darkness and nausea swept through me. The policeman lowered me to the floor.

"Call Officer . . . Bremer. Redwood City." My pleading fingers plucked at the man's wrist. "Tell him . . . I'm not. Crazy."

The room crumbled to black.

Chapter 39

FOR THE SECOND TIME I AWOKE IN HILDERBRAND'S HOUSE. Sound and movement curled as a policeman helped me up and into the TV room. He was tall and muscular, and practically had to carry me. My body felt like lead. I sagged onto the couch and stared at the blank TV. Hilderbrand must have switched off the murder DVD when I fainted the first time. Was it still in the player?

Officers' voices mixed with Patti's, then Hilderbrand's. Police radios squawked.

"She stabbed him." Patti's voice pulsed with panic. "You have to arrest her!"

The chip.

I eased myself to lie down on the couch, eyes fixed on nothing. Vaguely I registered Patti's accusations. Realized I may be going to jail. If Hilderbrand died . . . I couldn't even grasp the concept. My brain would barely function.

An ambulance shrilled up the street, the shattering noise dying to a strangled wail. More footsteps and voices, the clank of equipment.

"All right, get back now, let us look at him."

An efficient exchange of medical findings followed. Blood pressure, heart rate.

"Will he be okay?" Patti sounded like she was crying.

"You may have saved his life, ma'am. But we've got to get him to a hospital right away."

I heard the metallic sound of a gurney.

"Where is she? Lisa Newberry?" Patti's voice rose. "You arrest her, you hear?"

"We'll look into it."

"Can you get my statement at the hospital? I'm going with him in the ambulance."

"We'll catch up to you."

Lies. She'd feed them lies. There was only one thing that could prove my story. Even the murder DVD wouldn't do that on its own. I needed the chip they'd taken out of me.

Footsteps approached the back of the couch. I looked up to see the policeman who'd caught me when I fainted.

He walked around the sofa and faced me, hands on his hips. "How are you feeling?"

Marvelous. "D-did you call Officer Bremer?"

"Not yet."

"He'll tell you. At least the first half of the story."

The officer regarded me. "What's the second half?"

I pushed up the sleeves on my shirt. "Look." Dark bruises covered my upper arms. You could almost see the outline of Hilderbrand's fingers.

"How did that happen?"

"Hilderbrand. He was going to kill me. I grabbed the knife to defend myself."

"Miss Stolsinger said you broke into the house and had that knife in your hand."

"Didn't break in." How to explain all this? "Walked in."

"And the knife?"

"He was going to kill her. Patti. I had to stop him."

"What made you think he was going to kill her?"

I closed my eyes. What chance did I have here?

The gurney clinked and rolled. The EMT's voices faded through the door. The second policeman came and stood behind the couch.

I swallowed. My throat was so dry. "See the TV?" I pointed. "Play the DVD."

The officer in front of the couch glanced over his shoulder. "What's on it?"

"Patti Stolsinger's murder."

He exchanged a look with his partner. "Wasn't that her here just a minute ago?"

"Yeah." My stitches throbbed. Gingerly, I touched my bandage. Amazing that it was still there.

"Before you h-haul me away." I shifted on the couch and winced. "Get a search warrant for this house. And Cognoscenti. Hilderbrand's company. You need . . . to find the brain chip they took out of me before he destroys it."

"*Brain* chip?" The cop behind the couch spoke up.

His partner pushed out his lower lip. Clearly his afternoon was getting weirder by the minute. "And what are we supposed to find on that?"

"Everything on the DVD." I raised a shaking arm and pointed to my brain. "And they put that chip in *me.*"

Disbelief flicked across both their faces. "Why?" they asked in unison.

I drew the longest sigh of my life. Would I ever know the full answer to that question?

"Because they wanted me to see the murder. Believe it happened."

The first cop spread his hands. "Because . . . ?"

They'd just have to ask Hilderbrand, wouldn't they.

Dizziness swooped over me. I was going to faint again. I managed one more answer before I went under.

"Best I can figure . . . I was . . . the lab rat."

TUESDAY, MARCH 20—
SATURDAY, APRIL 21

Chapter 40

TUESDAY MORNING I AWOKE IN THE HOSPITAL—AGAIN.
The police had brought me in Monday after driving me away
from Hilderbrand's house, concerned about my throbbing head and
weakness. A doctor examined me and suggested I stay overnight for
observation. Nurses put in an I.V., which made me feel much better.
I was badly dehydrated.

But I didn't exactly get to rest. That evening police questioned
me for hours in my private room. The two Atherton cops were
joined by Officer Bremer, who could verify at least what he knew
of the events leading up to the stabbing at Hilderbrand's house.
Apparently Patti and Hilderbrand were still demanding my arrest,
claiming I'd sneaked into the home with a knife, threatening to kill
them both. Hilderbrand was also in the hospital. I heard he required
more than a few stitches in his leg. I'd nicked the femoral artery,
which could have killed him if Patti hadn't acted so fast.

By the time the cops left my room, they'd pieced together
enough evidence to know there was far more to the story. The DVD
of Patti's "murder" had told a tale of its own. Didn't look like my

arrest was going to happen. In fact they posted a guard outside my door Monday night. Patti was in the same hospital, watching over Hilderbrand. I was terrified she'd slip into my room while I slept.

If I slept at all.

Somehow in all the firestorm Monday evening, I managed to call Sherry. She was nearly hysterical with fear. Once she'd called the police, she hadn't heard what happened. After our call, Sherry turned around and phoned my mother. By the time I was ready to check out of the hospital early Tuesday afternoon, Mom was back at my side.

"What about your meetings at work?" I asked her.

She waved her hand in the air. "They can manage without me."

"And I can't?"

My mother gave me a look to end all looks. "You nearly got yourself killed."

Yeah. There was that.

By the time I arrived home Tuesday, the police, armed with warrants, had conducted searches of Hilderbrand's home and Cognoscenti. At his house they found the dragon's head ring and black suitcase. At the Cognoscenti lab they discovered the main prize—a small plastic container labeled "Memory EC." Inside—a tiny brain chip.

For the remainder of that week I rested when I could—between more interrogations with law enforcement. Police forces from three towns—Redwood City and Atherton, plus Palo Alto, where Cognoscenti was located—were involved in the major investigation. One of the craziest they'd ever encountered. Interviews with all involved parties would last for days. They took Mom's and Sherry's statements. Agnes Brighton's—who finally learned the woman in her drawing wasn't dead. The two salesmen at the jewelry store. The doctors who'd operated on me, and the nurses. Employees at Cognoscenti, including Jerry Sterne and Clair Saxton.

And of course, they tried to interrogate Hilderbrand. Didn't happen. By Monday night at the hospital he had an attorney and was refusing to talk. No surprise there.

It didn't take long for the story to break to the media. I found myself hounded by the press. National TV shows offered me large sums of money to talk to them. I wanted no part of it. Had refused to talk to *any* reporter. Besides, if I had, it could have hurt the investigation.

I just wanted to get on with my life. Whatever that was.

The police had to call in specialists to examine the so-called "Memory Chip." The technology was so far advanced few experts could decipher its contents. In the end two technicians from Cognoscenti itself looked at the evidence. Their findings yielded my ultimate vindication. It *was* the first chip that had been implanted in my brain. The device was an actual Empowerment Chip, capable of sending out electrical impulses to cure depression. Of course Hilderbrand had needed to use a real EC for his cruel experiment. If I'd remained depressed, I wouldn't have had the strength to do anything about the murder scenes in my head. I'd have just gone off the deep end.

Which I almost did anyway.

The chip also contained the brain's encoded version of Patti's murder scenes from the DVD. Hilderbrand had placed the filmed scenes in order on the chip, ensuring that each would, one by one, jump the synapses of my brain and into my memory. Apparently that technology was light-years ahead of any other researchers'. Some of the scenes Hilderbrand had placed repeatedly on the chip, so they'd play again and again. Others he'd purposely skewed—the dragon ring disappearing, day turning to night. The date on his watch. Apparently he wanted to see if every detail would come through.

Even when confronted with the Memory EC, Hilderbrand still refused to talk. So the police went after Patti. And they had the tools to do it.

California has a torture law, Penal Code 206. I heard about it so often in those days, I could practically quote it. Anyone who intended to cause another person "cruel or extreme pain and suffering for the purpose of revenge, extortion, or for any sadistic purpose" was guilty of torture. The "bodily injury" had to be physical. Therein would lie the arguments for future defense lawyers.

Was my mental torture physical?

But the prosecutor was gunning after Hilderbrand with everything he had. And his argument would be backed by science—the very information I'd learned online. The chip's data had jumped the synapses in my brain. Had neurologically altered my memory forever. *That* was physical.

The sentence for conviction under California's torture law: life in prison. The police threatened to charge Patti with the crime as well.

That's when she started to talk.

Later I would hear bits and pieces of her interrogation from the police and prosecutor. Since I was the victim they were doing their best to keep me informed. I wouldn't learn the entire picture until the case went to court.

The Empowerment Chip was Hilderbrand's invention, Patti told police. It stood to make him millions of dollars, but he wanted more. He wanted to make the ultimate brain chip, the kind that existed only in books and movies. The kind that could be used in the most top secret of missions, that certain agencies and organizations would pay brilliantly for.

"I do love a good spy novel," Hilderbrand had told me. To this day I can see his chilling smile as he spoke those words.

The Memory Chip could alter a person's brain. Drive that person to do things he would never do. Or perhaps create a whole new life for that person through altered memories. The possibilities were wild and endless. And absolutely captivating to a man who lived for power.

Hilderbrand chose me out of all the EC trial candidates to receive his first Memory Chip. He'd been working on the technology for years. Had done all the experiments he could on animals. Now he needed a human.

So why Lisa Newberry? Patti shrugged as she gave the answer: I was widowed and alone. No family nearby to help. Most important, I'd been attacked and nearly choked to death. If the murder scenes of strangling and stabbing a female would terrify anyone, it would be me.

However, things didn't happen quite as planned. Hilderbrand expected me to believe I was going crazy. And he expected the Memory Chip's final scene with the date of March 19 to "play" sooner than it did. He'd convinced himself once I saw an actual date—one that was soon approaching—I would contact Cognoscenti in a panic, if I hadn't done so sooner. If Cognoscenti never heard from me, Hilderbrand would have cooked up a reason to call me and rope me in. He needed to know how well the chip had worked. And he planned to offer me his deal—a sum of money and removal of the chip. He'd have the results of his experiment, and he'd have my silence. No one would have believed me anyway. And I'd have never known the identity of the people in my "memories." In time those memories would have faded. I would have forgotten Patti's face.

But Hilderbrand hadn't counted on my mother coming along to help. Or the way we'd found his house, his identity, and Patti. How I'd found the dragon's head ring.

Ironic, isn't it. In my brain, Hilderbrand's Empowerment Chip had overpowered his own memory experiment.

After Patti gave her statement and with all the evidence collected, the D.A. charged Hilderbrand with a long list of crimes, including torture. Patti had even told the police he'd broken into my apartment himself, and threatened me through the phone call and note. The burglary charge might stick after all, even without "foreign fingerprints." Police had found Agnes's composite drawing and the handwritten note in Hilderbrand's house.

Hilderbrand was currently out on bail. A good reason for me to leave town. I had other reasons as well. I'd return to testify when they needed me.

"I don't know about the case," I told Mom. Three weeks had passed, and I was visiting her in Denver. "He'll have the best lawyers money can buy."

"Wait till a jury hears what he did to you." She firmed her mouth. "He's going *down*."

I spent a lot of time praying during that visit. About what God wanted me to do, where I should go. I wasn't about to make a decision this time around without His guidance. He'd gotten me through this far.

I also looked up old friends. And got to know my mother more. As the days passed God helped me realize she'd been right all along about my returning to my hometown. Now I no longer felt I had to fight the idea. I no longer had something to prove.

Saturday, April 21 was my moving day. I was more than set to leave town. Mom flew down the day before to help me pack. By Saturday morning boxes were stacked everywhere. Nothing was left unboxed except the furniture. And the coffeemaker. It was 8:00 in the morning. Mom and I had been at it since 5:00. The moving truck was scheduled to arrive any minute.

A knock sounded on the door, already ajar. Sherry poked her head in. "Hi!"

"Come on in." I smiled at her over the counter. "You have Jay set to babysit?"

"Yup." She closed the door and threaded her way between boxes. "I'm all yours."

Her voice sounded chipper, but I knew she was sad to see me go.

"Want some coffee?" Mom pointed to my brewer. "It's the last thing to get packed."

"Sure, thanks." Sherry sidled up to the other side of the counter and set down her purse. I poured some coffee into a Styrofoam cup.

Sherry took a sip. "Where are you two staying tonight?"

My mother and I exchanged a glance. "At the same hotel we stayed at the night this place got broken into," I said. "You know— for old time's sake."

Sherry laughed.

Tomorrow morning Mom and I would get up early and start the drive in my car to Denver. An apartment awaited me, about ten minutes from her house. But I wouldn't be there for long. I'd already begun looking at houses. In Denver I could afford one. A little house like Ryan and I had wanted, with a yard where I could plant my flowers and bushes. Where I could see them grow and revel in their colors. Thanks to Mom, an exciting job awaited me too—working for an organization that helped victims of crime. I knew a few things about the subject.

Sherry set down her cup, her mood changing. "Did you see the *Newsweek* article?"

Oh, no. "Is it out already?"

She rummaged in her purse and pulled out some folded pages. "Here."

I stared at them. "Does it have my picture in it?"

"Afraid so."

Of course it did. My eyes closed. My picture in a national magazine. I *hated* this. I didn't want to be forever defined by what had happened to me. I wanted to be defined by what *I* did. By my future.

I took the pages from Sherry and set them on the counter. "I'm not sure I can look at it right now."

"Yeah. I understand."

My mother picked up the article and started reading.

Sherry gestured toward the paper. "Patti blames Hilderbrand for everything."

"I'll bet."

"Says he made her go along with his plan. She was afraid he'd hurt her if she didn't."

"Could be partly true." I'd certainly seen how uncomfortable she was when she visited me in the hospital. Of course, even that visit was staged. Hilderbrand wanted to know if I'd ever "seen" the watch date sequence before my surgery. If not, he'd have to figure out why.

Mom looked up. "Lisa. You know that older man we saw at Hilderbrand's house that day? It was his father. Here's the guy's picture."

I moved to her side to look. "Yeah, that's him. Did he know what was going on?"

"He claims he didn't. He just happened to be visiting his son that day. Some female reporter hunted him down and got his story. The father told her he saw us on Hilderbrand's street. Claims we were stalking his son."

Oh, great. The whole nation now thought I was a stalker. Everywhere I went, people would look at me. "Is this going to hurt my job, Mom?"

She shook her head. "They know the truth."

The creak of a large truck's brakes filtered through the open kitchen window. I hurried over to gaze down at the street. "It's the moving van."

About time. I wanted out of there.

A truck door opened and closed. Followed by a second. Men's voices drifted up.

Mom finished the article and looked to Sherry. "May we keep this?"

"All yours."

Tiredness trickled through me. I leaned against the wall and sighed.

Mom placed her hands on my shoulders. "Lisa. You'll be fine."

Would I?

"I know it seems like a lot. The move, all this media attention. And later, the trial. But you can handle it. And I'll be right there beside you."

I looked at her, mouth twisting. My thoughts at that moment weren't exactly brave. I didn't *want* to handle it. I just wanted to hide.

"I didn't choose this, Mom." I sounded like a little kid.

"Honey, most of life we don't choose. The question is—when it chooses us, what are we going to do?"

I nodded. *God, I know You're here to help me through this, too.* Man, would I need it.

Footsteps sounded in the hall. The movers knocked loudly.

"I'll get it." Sherry turned from the counter.

Mom cupped my chin. "So, come on now. Ready to move on?"

I took a deep breath. "I am so ready."

Together we walked to the door.

Discussion Questions

1. To what things or concepts in the story does the title *Double Blind* refer?

2. *Desperate people make desperate choices.* Why do you think the book starts with this line? Does it refer to characters other than just Lisa?

3. Some might criticize brain technology like the Empowerment Chip, saying that enduring difficult times makes a person stronger. Therefore no one should be able to "turn off their pain" so easily. Would you agree with any part of this argument?

4. If such technology existed, should it be available for people suffering from extreme trauma, such as patients of Post Traumatic Stress Syndrome?

5. If the Empowerment Chip existed, do you know anyone whom you would urge to have such an implant? Why?

6. Have you ever lived through depression? If so, how would you describe it?

7. How would you characterize Lisa's voice in this story? Does her voice add to her characterization and the tension of the book? Would the book have been as effective if told in third person?

8. To what extent was Lisa Newberry right in blaming her mother for her own lack of self-esteem? To what extent was she wrong?

9. Did you end up empathizing with Lisa's mother at all when you heard her side of things?

10. Lisa was caught between her mother and best friend, who didn't like each other. Have you ever been caught between two people you love? How did you handle it?

11. Based on Lisa's knowledge at the time, was she right to accept money from Hilderbrand?

12. In time Lisa realizes she's based the ultimate truth of God's nearness and love on her own emotions. Have you ever done that? What is the problem with doing that?

13. At one point Lisa asks herself, "Can any other person really make you feel whole?" How would you answer that question?

14. Beneath the surface plot of a desperate woman and a brain chip, what is this story really about?

15. Did this book give you any insights into your own life or a loved one's struggles?

BRANDILYN COLLINS

SEATBELT SUSPENSE®

SeatbeltSuspense.com

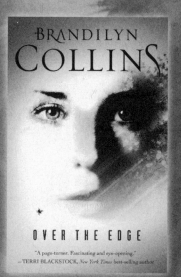
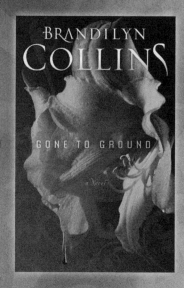

Sometimes

the truth hides where **no one** expects to find it.

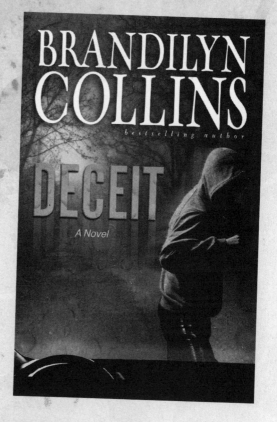

BRANDILYN COLLINS

bestselling author

DECEIT

A Novel

Joanne Weeks knows Baxter Jackson killed Linda—his second wife and Joanne's best friend—six years ago. But Baxter, a church elder and beloved member of the town, walks the streets a free man. The police tell Joanne to leave well enough alone, but she is determined to bring him down. Using her skills as a professional skip tracer, she sets out to locate the only person who may be able to put Baxter behind bars. Melissa Harkoff was a traumatized sixteen-year-old foster child in the Jackson household when Linda disappeared. At the time Melissa claimed to know nothing of Linda's whereabouts—but was she lying?

In relentless style, Deceit careens between Joanne's pursuit of the truth—which puts her own life in danger—and the events of six years' past, when Melissa came to live with the Jacksons. What really happened in that household? Beneath the veneer of perfection lies a story of shakeable faith, choices, and the lure of deceit.

Read the first chapter at: http://brandilyncollins.com/books/excerpts/deceit.html

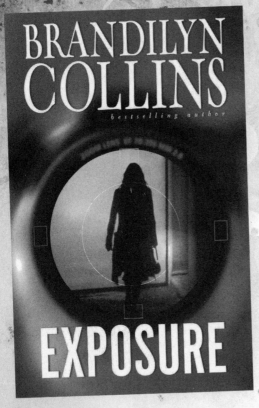

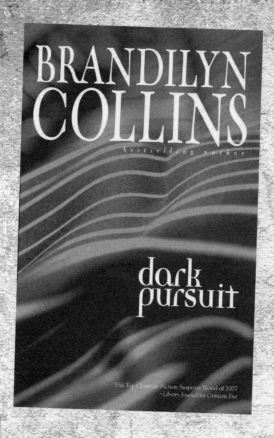

The Top Christian Fiction Suspense Novel of 2007
~Library Journal for Crimson Eve

Novelist Darell Brooke lived for his title as King of Suspense—until an auto accident left him unable to concentrate. Two years later, recluse and bitter, he wants one thing: to plot a new novel and regain his reputation.

Kaitlan Sering, his twenty-two-year-old granddaughter, once lived for drugs. After she stole from Darell, he cut her off. Now she's rebuilding her life.

But in Kaitlan's town two women have been murdered, and she's about to discover a third. She's even more shocked to realize the culprit—her boyfriend, Craig, the police chief's son.

Desperate, Kaitlan flees to her estranged grandfather. For over forty years, Darell Brooke has lived suspense. Surely he'll devise a plan to trap the cunning Craig.

But can Darell's muddled mind do it? And—if he tries—with what motivation? For Kaitlan's plight may be the stunning answer to the elusive plot he seeks...

Read an excerpt at: http://brandilyncollins.com/books/excerpts/dp.html

Kanner Lake series

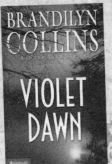

Paige Williams slips into her hot tub in the blackness of night—and finds herself face to face with death. Alone, terrified, fleeing a dark past, Paige must make an unthinkable choice.

In *Violet Dawn*, hurtling events and richly drawn characters collide in a breathless story of murder, revenge and the need to belong. One woman's secrets unleash an entire town's pursuit, and the truth proves as elusive as the killer in their midst.

Leslie Brymes hurries out to her car on a typical work day morning—and discovers a dead body inside.

Why was the corpse left for her to find? And what is the meaning of the message pinned to its chest?

In *Coral Moon*, the senseless murder of a beloved Kanner Lake citizen spirals the small Idaho town into a terrifying glimpse of spiritual forces beyond our world. What appears true seems impossible.

Or is it?

Realtor Carla Radling shows an "English gentleman" a lakeside estate—and finds herself facing a gun. Who has hired this assassin to kill her, and why?

Forced on the run, Carla must uncover the scathing secrets of her past. Secrets that could destroy some very powerful people. Perhaps even change the face of a nation...

On a beautiful Saturday morning the nationally read "Scenes and Beans" bloggers gather at Java Joint for a special celebration. Chaos erupts when three gunmen burst in and take them all hostage. One person is shot and dumped outside.

Police Chief Vince Edwards must negotiate with the desperate trio. The gunmen insist on communicating through the "comments" section of the blog—so all the world can hear their story. What they demand, Vince can't possibly provide. But if he doesn't, over a dozen beloved Kanner Lake citizens will die...

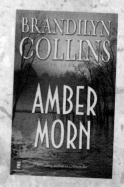

Read the first chapters at: http://brandilyncollins.com/books

Hidden Faces series

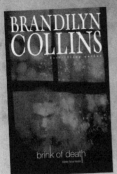

When a neighbor is killed, desperate detectives ask courtroom artist Annie Kingston to question the victim's traumatized daughter, Erin, and draw a composite of the suspect. But what if Annie's lack of experience leads Erin astray? The detectives could end up searching for a face that doesn't exist. Leaving the real killer free to stalk the neighborhood...

For twenty years, a killer has eluded capture for a brutal double murder. Now, forensic artist Annie Kingston has agreed to draw the updated face of Bill Bland for the popular television show *American Fugitive*.

To do so, Annie must intimately learn Bland's traits and personality. But as she descends into his criminal mind and world, someone is determined to stop her.

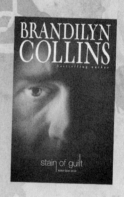

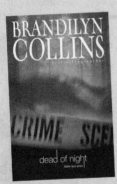

A string of murders terrorizes citizens in the Redding, California area. Forensic artist Annie Kingston must draw the unknown victims for identification. Dread mounts. Who will be taken next? Under a crushing oppression, Annie and other Christians are driven to pray for God's intervention as they've never prayed before.

After witnessing a shooting at a convenience store, forensic artist Annie Kingston must draw a composite of the suspect. She and friend Chelsea Adams soon find themselves snared in a terrifying battle against time, greed, and a deadly opponent. If they tell the police, will their story be believed?

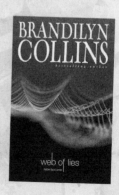

Read the first chapters at: http://brandilyncollins.com/books